FATAL

A CURVY GIRL ROMANTIC SUSPENSE

F-BOMB: CURVY VIGILANTES
BOOK 5

MARY E THOMPSON

Fatal

F-BOMB: Curvy Vigilantes, book five

Copyright © 2023 Mary E Thompson

Cover Copyright © 2022 Mary E Thompson

Cover Photo from depositphotos, Copyright © curaphotography

Break (Mask) from depositphotos, Copyright © K3star

Published by BluEyed Press, All Rights Reserved

No part of this book may be reproduced in any form or by any electronic or mechanical means, including information storage and retrieval systems, without written permission from the author, except for the use of brief quotations in a book review.

This is a work of fiction. All characters, businesses, locations, and events are either products of the author's creative imagination or are used in a fictitious sense. Any resemblance to real persons, living or dead, is purely coincidental.

Ebook ISBN: 978-1-953879-38-7

Print ISBN: 978-1-953879-39-4

Audiobook ISBN: 978-1-953879-40-0

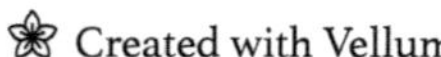 Created with Vellum

F-BOMB: CURVY VIGILANTES

Say hello to the Curvy Vigilantes, a group of plus-size women who protect their city. They have no training, but they don't need it. All they need is the desire to right wrongs and to protect the ones they love... and maybe some help from the men strong (and smart) enough to fall for these kick-ass curvy women.

F-BOMB: CURVY VIGILANTES
Forsaken (subscriber exclusive)
Fury
Framed
Feign
Fierce
Fatal
Fear
Flee
Fracture
Faith

SUBSCRIBE NOW AT MARYETHOMPSON.COM

To whoever needs to hear this today...
YOU ARE STRONG.
YOU ARE AMAZING.
IT'S OKAY TO FALL APART SOMETIMES.

1

Tears rolled down Raina London's face as she walked back into the safe house she'd called home for six weeks. Blood stained the floor, and splintered wood littered the hallway. She turned into the room that was hers and tried not to let the fear rolling through her overwhelm her. She had to be strong. She had to pack her things and get the hell out of there.

It had only been one night. One night since the man she once thought she loved broke into what was supposed to be a safe house and tried to kill her. Would have, too, if not for the heroics of the people helping Raina. She was willing to die for them, and if she thought the terror would end, she would. But she knew Damon Street. He would never give up. Once she was dead, he'd set his sights on someone else. There was no such thing as safe if he was alive.

Lorelei Sloane, one of Raina's protectors, stood in the hallway outside the bedroom. Raina could feel the other woman's presence and was grateful for it as much as she hated it. Damon stole Raina's freedom, her sanity, her life as she knew it. And he wasn't done.

Raina stuffed the clothes she'd brought with her into a suitcase and ignored the carnage left behind. Being there again was too soon. And Damon knowing where it was meant she couldn't stay there. They were moving to another safe house. One no one would be allowed in or out of. One that would restrict Raina's already restricted world to a pinpoint.

She hated Damon. She'd never thought she could hate someone the way she hated him, but she did. If he died, she wouldn't feel an ounce of sadness. But the man was invincible. She almost wondered if he was immortal. He definitely had more than his fair share of lives.

"Are you ready?" Lorelei asked quietly.

Raina nodded, zipping up the suitcase and turning back to her one and only remaining protector. Lorelei's partner, Adam Johnson, was in the hospital. He would join them when he was out, but for the moment, it was just the two of them.

No match for Damon, if he tried again.

And he would. Raina knew he would. He hadn't stopped trying to get her back since she left him almost a year ago. After he nearly killed her. She'd never go back to him willingly. But she knew she'd never be free of him, either.

Lorelei wasn't back to full strength, but she understood Raina's need for someone she knew to be there. Adam's cousin waited in the SUV outside for them. Their driver for the day since Lorelei suffered a minor concussion. Liam was staying with Lorelei and Raina until Adam was released from the hospital. Adam's concussion was more serious, but he would be out soon.

It was a mess. A mess that could have been avoided if Raina hadn't fallen for a man who was more evil than human.

She kicked herself for the mistakes she made. For letting Damon suck her into his life. For being so weak she believed his lies when he claimed to love her and wanted to only protect her. All the therapy she had helped, until she looked into Damon's eyes again.

How did she not see him before? How did she miss the way he looked at her?

She knew the answer even as the questions rolled around in her head. She didn't want to.

Sure, he hid his true self from her for a long time. A man like him didn't show how evil he was on day one. But there were little signs. Moments, snippets, clues. Raina ignored them. She thought she was crazy for thinking Damon was anything less than the perfect man he presented himself as.

And people died because of her error in judgement.

Raina followed Lorelei out to the waiting SUV and sat in the backseat. She struggled to breathe or think or function. Her mind was numb, like the rest of her.

Damon is free.

Marcus's words from the night before rattled around in her mind. After months of hunting him, he was out within hours. All the hell he put her through, the people he killed, the lives he ruined, all wiped clean by one lawyer in an expensive suit.

Raina was going to be sick.

Liam slowed and turned into the driveway of a small house. The garage door opened in front of them, and he rolled the SUV right into the garage. He turned off the vehicle, and they all waited until the garage doors slid closed behind them.

"Home sweet home," Liam said.

Raina reached for a smile, but it was hard to find one. Liam seemed nice enough, friendly and kind and smart as hell, but he wasn't Adam. She'd gotten used to Adam and Lorelei. The three of them got along easily. She fit with them. But Liam...

Raina just wanted it all to be over. Liam was fine. Lorelei was fine. Adam was fine. Raina just wanted to go home. Sleep in a bed she picked out. Take an endless hot shower and forget all about Damon Street.

Too bad that wasn't going to happen anytime soon.

ADAM JOHNSON CLOSED his eyes and groaned. He hated being stuck in the hospital. He knew it was where he needed to be, but he still hated it.

When Raina walked in that morning with Lorelei, and they told Adam that Damon Street was free, Adam shook with rage. He started yanking off the pads stuck to his body. He was not going to leave his partner and their witness alone. He couldn't. He had to be there to help them.

Of course, Lorelei and Raina both forced him back into bed, and a nurse came in and reattached all the leads, annoying Adam to no end. He'd never been a fan of hospitals, and knowing he was leaving two women who meant a lot to him without additional protection infuriated him.

Street surprised Adam when he broke into the safe house and knocked Adam out before he had a chance to warn the others. He later learned Street also got to Lorelei. Raina and Edie were vulnerable, and Street would have killed all four of them if Mackenzie hadn't shown up when she did.

Adam's stomach rolled at the thought.

He knew the important thing was that they were all alive. But he still felt like a failure to have gone down first.

He didn't even put up a fight and slow the bastard down. Street surprised Adam and cold-cocked him as soon as Adam saw him.

Failure was common. It was expected. It was something all agents experienced. He'd lost witnesses before. Lost coworkers. Lost leads. But none of them were as important to him as Raina.

Not that he was willing to admit to anyone else that he'd developed feelings for her. That was between Adam and the shower wall.

His phone buzzed with a text alert. Adam snatched his phone from the table next to his bed and swiped to open Liam's text.

All set. Moved in. No one will get close.

Adam let go of a breath he hadn't been aware he was holding. He knew Liam would protect Lorelei and Raina, but it still grated on Adam that he wasn't there to do it himself.

Thanks. Hopefully I'm free tomorrow and can relieve you.

No worries. Caitlyn's staying with Taylor and Dex. We're all used to this. Rest and recover so you're 100.

Copy.

Adam set the phone on the table again and tried to focus his mind. The goal hadn't changed. Take down Damon Street. The problem now was that the man was free and knew who they all were. They had to not only find him again, but make sure the arrest warrant meant a judge wouldn't grant bail. At any level.

Adam thought they'd done that, but they were all wrong. And Street was out.

A nurse came in a little later and asked Adam how he was doing. The guy was a sports fan and liked to talk, so Adam passed the time hearing stories from him about local teams. It meant Adam didn't feel so completely abandoned and alone.

Fucking hospital.

The nurse left, and Adam stared at the walls again. He thought living in a safe house was boring. He would never complain again. About a safe house, a stakeout, anything.

Afternoon turned to night, and Adam fell asleep. His dreams were a jumbled mess of Street, Raina being hurt, and purple fucking pansies. That last one Adam couldn't explain. Weird shit happened in his mind.

Morning came again, and the doctor finally said Adam could leave the hospital. It was the best damn news ever.

He let Liam know, and Liam arranged transportation to take Adam to the new safe house.

Only another hour or so and he'd be back with Raina and Lorelei.

"ARE WE BEING FOLLOWED?" Adam asked Dunn, Liam's boss. They'd met once before, but Adam didn't know Dunn well.

"No," Dunn answered. He checked all his mirrors again. "I've been changing direction and going in weird routes to watch. I haven't seen anyone following us."

"We can't risk exposing the safe house again."

"I know," Dunn growled.

Adam didn't know why Dunn was annoyed by that. It wasn't like Dunn was the one who was knocked out with a gun to the back of his head.

"We have security on this place twenty-four-seven. No one will get anywhere close without us knowing."

"What kind of security?"

"Motion and heat, signal blockers, and personal surveillance."

"You're going to have someone watching us?"

"Yes," Dunn said. "Outside the house, at least. We have the ability to add cameras inside, but we haven't done that yet. Is that something you want?"

Adam shook his head and winced. His brain was still scrambled, and sudden movements made him nauseous. "No, outside should be fine. Especially in this cold. You'll be able to pick up on heat signatures."

"Yep." Dunn turned into a driveway and pulled straight into a garage, parking beside an identical SUV. He closed the garage door, then got out.

Adam followed Dunn inside, wanting to see with his own eyes that Lorelei and Raina were okay. And Liam. He should worry about his cousin, too, but Liam hadn't been attacked.

Liam met them at the garage door, his hand on the weapon in his holster. He looked at them both, then past them to make sure there wasn't a third person sending them in at gunpoint. Liam relaxed and nodded to his boss, then hugged Adam gently.

"Glad you're alive."

"Same," Adam said. "How're Lorelei and Raina?"

"Resting. It's been a long few days," Liam said.

"Yeah, it has. How's this place?"

Liam shrugged, but Adam knew his cousin outfitted the

house with every toy he could find. It was an F-BOMB safe house, one they were borrowing since the FBI safe house was clearly not as safe as they'd all expected.

"Windows and doors are tagged. Including the egress. Cameras at all the entrances. Heat and motion around the whole perimeter. No one will get within a mile of this place without us knowing."

"What if they pull into the driveway and just start shooting?"

"Windows and walls are all bulletproof. Won't stop them forever, but should slow down whoever shows up long enough for you to get out."

"And how would we do that?"

"Secondary exit out the back. Garage opens both ways so you can drive out the back and disappear into the woods, then get back on the road half-a-mile south of here."

"Jesus, you really thought of everything."

"Not our first rodeo," Dunn said with meaning. They lost someone. No more chances. Adam respected that.

"What do I need to know?" Adam asked the other two.

Dunn and Liam exchanged a glance.

"Tell me."

"Street's in the wind. As expected. The lawyer who bailed him out is not talking. Says his client will appear in court if there are charges that are substantiated. He's calling foul on everything. The way evidence was collected, the circumstantial nature of it all, everything. He's saying Street isn't guilty and that he's been framed for everything we have him on."

"What about beating the shit out of his girlfriend? Doesn't that count for anything around here?" Adam barked. He'd seen the police report from the night Raina left Street. The bruises on her face and body. The X-rays showing the broken bones. The fear in her eyes. If nothing else, they should have been able to hold him for that.

"He has a court date. But the rest? We know it's all him, but our proof isn't good enough." Liam's voice was soothing but did nothing to calm Adam's frustration.

"Are you fucking kidding me? He knocked me out cold, same with Lorelei. Doesn't that count for anything? We're FBI agents. Attacking us and holding Raina and Edie at gunpoint should be something worth holding the fucker on." Adam was baffled. What the hell kind of lawyer wanted a man like Damon Street out in the world? The only answer was a crooked one.

"The judge agreed with the lawyer," Dunn told Adam. "We believe they're both involved in Street's organization."

"Fucking hell. Makes sense, though. So, now what?"

"We play their game and we nail him. We can't stop now when we're this close," Dunn said.

"I agree. It sounds like we need to take out the judge and the lawyer, too, though. Otherwise, Street will keep going free."

Dunn and Liam nodded.

The three men talked a little longer, then Liam and Dunn left. Adam insisted he was okay and could handle things, but once they left, he sat on the couch with his eyes closed, willing the throbbing in his brain to subside.

Ten minutes later, the squeak of a door down the hall had Adam lifting his head and pretending to be fine again.

Raina stepped out of the room and looked both directions. When she saw him on the couch, her lips lifted in a ghost of a smile. "Hey."

"Hey." Adam was striving for casual, but seeing her made his entire body ache. He wanted to wrap her in his arms and protect her from all the evil in the world. He wanted to kiss her senseless and make sure she never knew hate again. He wanted to erase the bruises and scrapes from her body and keep any harm from ever coming to her again.

But he couldn't do any of that. Because he was her protector, not her boyfriend. She was recovering from an abusive asshole of an ex, and the last thing she needed was an overprotective asshole trying to convince her to be his woman.

Nope. He had to keep his feelings to himself and treat her like any other witness.

"How are you feeling?" he asked when she got closer.

Raina sat next to him on the couch and tucked her feet under her. She shrugged. She propped her elbow on the back of the couch and put her head in her hand, then cringed and changed positions.

Street dragged her around by her hair. She was lucky he didn't rip chunks out from what Lorelei told Adam. One more thing Adam wanted the sick piece-of-shit to pay for.

"I'm tired," Raina finally said. "I feel like I could sleep for a week, but when I close my eyes, I see him." Her words went soft at the end. She drew in a breath. "I never should have left him."

"Why would you say that?"

"He would have killed me by now if I'd stayed there. Then all the people I care about wouldn't be in danger, and I wouldn't be living in fear. I know he's going to kill me. He's not going to stop until he does. All I'm doing right now is delaying the inevitable. And the fear is getting to me. He's thriving on it, feeding on it. He knows I'm scared, and he's enjoying playing with me. With all of us. And I hate it."

"I know. But we'll get him. We'll take him down, and he'll never hurt you again."

Raina breathed a mirthless laugh. "I thought that before.

I don't think I can believe that. Not now. Not after the last few days. The only way Damon will ever stop is if he's dead."

Adam saw the determination in her gaze. She knew Street better than anyone else. She was right. Adam knew in his soul she was.

Which meant there was only one answer. Damon Street had to die.

2

———————

RAINA STEPPED OUT OF THE SHOWER AND GRABBED FOR HER towel. Another bland white towel in a bland, boring bathroom. Safe houses were essential, but damn, it was depressing. She would have loved to have something to hold her interest. Bright towels, fancy soaps, a plant. Something.

But that wasn't the point. She wasn't staying there long term. No one was. Best-case scenario, the safe house wasn't ever used. But she knew it was. She knew they all were. Because Damon wasn't the only evil in the world.

Raina wrapped her hair in the towel and picked up her panties from where she'd set them on the toilet. More white. More plain. More bland.

Raina groaned and slipped them on, yanking on the gray sweats over the top, then adding her black tank. She was done wearing a bra. She was done trying. She was just fucking done.

She untwisted her hair from the towel and stared at her reflection in the mirror. The woman who looked back was one she barely recognized. Vacant eyes, frizzy hair, empty.

Raina turned away before her brown eyes filled with

tears. She hated the person she'd become. The person Damon turned her into.

"You okay?" Lorelei asked from the other side of the bathroom door.

Raina opened the door and looked at the woman who'd become a friend over the last few months. "No."

Lorelei gave her a smile that was just as empty as the promise she was going to utter. "It'll be over soon."

Raina snorted. "No, it won't. This is my life now. I know eventually you two will have to go back to your jobs and lives and I'll be on my own. We're just delaying the inevitable right now."

"Don't say that," Adam growled.

The roughness of his voice sent a shiver up Raina's needy spine. If her situation wasn't so fucking sad, she might let herself be attracted to Adam, but she was the worst kind of bad bet. And he had too much to offer the world. She couldn't drag him down with her.

Raina shook her head and turned toward her room. She couldn't face either of them. Not when she was so full of anger. She would blow up at them, and they didn't deserve it. Neither of them had done anything wrong. They were just as stuck as she was, but Damon wasn't after them. Damon would leave them alone as soon as they weren't protecting her. She was his goal.

"Raina," Adam said gently.

Raina held up her hand without turning around. "I need a minute." She closed the door to her room, leaving them on the other side while she struggled to pull herself together.

She threw her dirty clothes toward the laundry basket in the corner, not caring when they fell far short. Raina flopped facedown on the bed. More fucking white. She growled and pushed herself up again, yanking at the sheets, pulling them all off the bed and dumping them in a heap in the middle of the room.

She sat down again and let the tears come. They'd been in the new safe house for a week. One more week of hiding. Hoping Damon didn't find her and kill her. If she could go back to the night she met him, she'd slap herself for even considering getting involved with him.

A sob slipped out. She slapped her hand over her mouth, but there was a knock on the door.

"Can I come in?" Lorelei asked.

"Fine." Raina swiped at her tears. She was sure Lorelei and Adam both knew when she cried or got angry or lost her shit, but she tried to keep it behind closed doors.

Lorelei looked at the sheets on the floor and stepped around them, joining Raina on the bed. "Is there anything we can do to make this easier?"

"Kill Damon." Raina had finally accepted that was the only solution. She had never been a violent person, or a person who believed in deadly force, but that was before Damon Street dragged her across the room by her hair and made it clear he was going to make her his again, no matter what she had to say.

Lorelei sighed. As an FBI Agent, she couldn't plan something like that. She'd lose her job and go to jail. But Raina knew Lorelei didn't disagree.

"I'll be fine. The white made me mad."

Lorelei nodded as if she understood what that meant. "We're going to get groceries tomorrow. Is there anything you want?"

Raina sighed. She loved to cook. It was something that made her feel good. To feed her body and soul and that of whoever she was cooking for was a joy. Damon had stolen even that from her. He preferred to order in when Raina lived with him. At first, she thought it was sweet that he didn't want her to have to fuss over him. Nope. That wasn't it. He didn't want to risk her putting something in his food.

The bastard was smart.

"Whatever you guys want is fine," Raina finally said.

"Adam's going to pick junk food and meat if we let him make the list."

"Hey! I resemble that remark," Adam said from right outside the door.

Raina looked up and found his blue-green eyes focused on her. Again, it sent a shiver through her. One she could not let take hold.

"You okay?" Adam asked.

Raina shook her head. No use lying.

Adam smiled sadly. "There are a lot of people looking for Damon."

"Which only proves how dangerous he is. We finally had him. He was in custody. And he got out. How in the hell did he get bail?" Raina's throat tightened with the emotion that bubbled right at the surface constantly. She sucked in a ragged breath and tried to push it down. "It's just not fair."

"He has to report to court. If he doesn't show up, his lawyer will be charged the million dollar bail he posted. And he'll be on the hook for Street. He'll be back in custody."

Raina shook her head. "You have no idea what he's capable of."

"I have some idea," Adam said, rubbing the back of his head where Damon hit him and knocked him out.

Violence was Damon's first answer. It didn't matter what the question was, he turned to violence. Raina learned that time and again before she left him. And she learned even more about what he was capable of after. When she found out who he was and the depths of his darkness.

"What do you guys want to make for dinner?" Lorelei asked.

Adam glanced at Raina and held her gaze. She let herself sink in for just a minute. One minute of feeling a little safer than she'd felt for months.

Raina opened her mouth to answer when one of the many alarms went off.

Lorelei jumped up from the bed and put herself between Raina and the door as Adam turned and hurried down the hallway.

Raina froze. She hated herself for it, but she froze. Bile rose up in her throat as she imagined walking into the living room and finding Adam in a heap once more. Watching Lorelei get hurt. Staring down Damon as he approached her with that gleam in his eyes that said he was going to make her pay.

"Come with me," Lorelei said, looking back at Raina.

Raina forced herself off the bed as the alarm stopped screeching. Her feet barely carried her forward, her entire body shaking in fear.

Lorelei walked down the short hallway to the living room, where Adam was on the phone.

"Yeah. Okay. Yeah. Hang on." Adam turned the phone from his ear and looked at Lorelei and Raina. "Liam said something tripped the motion detectors outside, but he doesn't see anything on the cameras or the heat sensors. We need to check it out."

"I'll go," Lorelei said.

Adam nodded sharply. "Lorelei's going to look. Watch for her to make sure everything is working."

Raina sucked in a gasp. She never considered the

cameras and security and high-tech everything in the house not working. That someone could have messed with them and gotten close.

Lorelei stuffed her feet into the boots she had near the door. She opened the door a crack and looked out, both directions, before she stepped out into the cold evening air, pulling the door closed behind her.

Raina stared at the door and wrapped her arms around herself. Adam was still on the phone, but Raina was lost in her fear. Her gaze was locked on the door, her fear bouncing around inside her as she waited for the door to open.

Lorelei or Damon. Who would walk through when it did?

Raina's hands hurt from squeezing them into fists. Her breathing was shallow and panicked.

The door opened, and Lorelei stepped in. She closed the door behind her, locking it before she returned her gun to the holster she wore around her waist. "I didn't see anything out there. No footprints, nothing."

"Hear that?" Adam asked. "Yeah. Thanks. Okay." Adam hung up the phone and shrugged. "Liam was watching you. Said he saw you the entire time so everything is working. It might have been an animal that tripped the sensors."

Lorelei shrugged. "Maybe."

They both turned to look at Raina. She wasn't sure what they saw, but their faces changed instantly and they rushed to her.

"Come sit, Raina. It's okay. You're safe." Lorelei's voice was soft and soothing and did nothing to take away the fear that was making Raina shake.

"She needs to snap out of this," Adam said. "She's not okay."

"Would you be?" Lorelei asked.

"I'm fine," Raina choked out. "I... I'm okay."

Lorelei rubbed her hand up and down Raina's arm. The sensation brought back a little more of reality.

"Three things," Adam said, his voice low and strained.

Raina knew what he was asking her. He'd been doing his best to help her with the anxiety she was sure was permanent in her life now. "Fireplace, coffee table, boring white walls."

"Good," Adam said. "Three scents."

Raina closed her eyes and inhaled deep. "Crappy shampoo, bananas, you."

Adam cleared his throat.

Raina realized what she said. Her cheeks flushed hot. "Sorry."

"No need to be sorry," Adam said. "How are you feeling?"

"Angry."

"Good. That means the fear is moving to the back again," Lorelei said.

"Yay," Raina said sarcastically.

"Let's see what we can fix for dinner," Lorelei said. She patted Raina's thigh and stood, reaching for Raina to follow her.

Totally normal. For someone in protective custody. Lucky Raina.

ADAM SAT on the armchair he'd claimed and reviewed the footage from earlier. No matter how many times he slowed it down, he couldn't see anyone around the property where the alarm went off.

But he didn't trust it.

Every time he talked to his cousin or checked in with his boss, he heard about another threat. Someone was sitting outside Shelter in the Storm, a shelter for abused women and children run by the police chief and his wife, two nights ago. They drove off when Marcus went outside, but the threat was clear. Mackenzie, a nine-one-one operator who helped put Damon behind bars, was followed after her shift more than once.

Damon was in hiding, and everyone believed he would stay that way, even though he was supposed to report to court in five days. If he didn't show up, no one knew where he was.

Which meant Raina would still be in danger.

Adam hated the look in her eyes when she walked out of the bathroom. They'd all been living together for close to two months. Two months of constant vigilance and fear. Not that Adam was afraid. Protecting someone was part of his job. It wasn't every day he came face-to-face with a criminal as adept as Damon Street, but Adam would give his life for Raina. Or Lorelei.

But he'd rather eliminate the threat instead of go down again.

Adam wanted to kick his own ass for letting Damon get his hands on Raina. When Lorelei told him what Damon did, Adam wanted to rip the man to shreds with his bare hands. He wanted to see the life drain from Street's eyes. To know he'd never hurt Raina, or anyone, ever again.

The overwhelming hatred and fury that rose up inside Adam was something he knew he shouldn't keep inside. He should ask for a reassignment. He should tell his boss, or at least his partner, how he was feeling. But Adam wasn't going to do either. He was going to use those emotions to make sure Street never got the jump on him again, and ended up on the floor if they ever came face-to-face again.

Lorelei laughed at something Raina said, and Adam realized he was clenching his hands into fists and gritting his teeth so hard his jaw hurt.

He slowly released the tension in his body, knowing he needed to do something physical to get rid of his stress. If he were home, he'd head to the gym and beat the fuck out of a speed bag, but the safe house didn't come with a gym, and Adam couldn't leave.

The solitude was getting to him, too. Lorelei didn't have an issue with having to stay put, but she was frustrated to not be out there looking for Street. Adam was restless. He wanted Street found. He wanted Raina safe. And he wanted to get the hell away from her before he broke down and admitted how many times he'd pictured her smile when he was stroking his cock in the shower.

Rule number one was don't fuck the witness. Don't get involved. Keep it professional. Adam had never broken that rule. He'd never wanted to until he met Raina. He'd crossed a few lines in his past, and he planned to cross another one when he came face-to-face with Street again, but Adam couldn't afford to break rule number one. Not now, not ever.

"You hungry?" Lorelei asked, interrupting his thoughts.

Adam looked up and saw her standing in front of him with a bowl. "Thanks. Sorry. Lost in thought."

"Anything good?" Raina asked as she sat on the couch opposite his chair.

Adam shook his head, but Lorelei answered first. "Trust me, you do not want to know what goes on inside of that head."

Raina chuckled at Lorelei's joke, and Lorelei winked at Adam before she turned away.

They were good partners. Adam was grateful for Lorelei, both for the way she'd handled this assignment and for the number of times she'd saved his ass. She was a damn good agent, smart as hell, and easy to be around. Her cousin was tied up in the whole disaster of a case they were in Niagara Falls working on, so it was good for both of them to be in the area.

Lorelei and Raina talked while they ate. Adam didn't join in their conversation, though. He ran through everything they knew so far, which was admittedly not much. Damon Street had a network of more people than they knew. It was believed he was near the top of the organization, but no one knew if he was actually in charge or not. He'd been an enforcer for decades, something they only learned recently, and had either worked his way up or killed his way up. Both were equally possible.

The number of bodies the organization had dropped grew by the day, and at times, it seemed to be near infinite.

Shortly after dinner, Raina said goodnight and went to her room. Long days of little to do but worry was exhausting, and Raina slept more than Adam suspected was normal for her.

Lorelei checked Raina's room and talked to her for a few minutes before she joined Adam in the living room again.

"Are you good out here tonight?" Lorelei asked.

Adam nodded. "Definitely. All good." He jerked his chin toward Raina's closed door. "She okay?"

Lorelei shook her head once, her dark brown afro jolting with the sharp movement. "She's fucking done. She's scared of her own shadow and has herself damn near convinced Street's going to show up at any minute. She's not the same woman we met two months ago."

Adam had been thinking the same thing, but he wasn't

going to say any of that. There were things a woman could say about another woman without sounding callous, but if a man said them, he'd get torn apart. "Do we have anything on the judge that granted bail?"

Lorelei snorted. "Please. He's an overworked weekend judge who rubber stamped something without paying much attention to it."

"That or he's in Street's pocket."

"Always a possibility, too. Unfortunately."

"I wish we could get the fuck out of here. I know it's cold as balls out there, but even some fresh air would make this all a little easier."

"There is one option." Lorelei met Adam's gaze with an open one of her own.

"You look way too relaxed for whatever this option is. What the hell could we possibly do differently?"

Lorelei leaned forward. She clasped her hands together, her dark brown fingers crossing as she rested her forearms on her thighs. She glanced at the hallway, as though she didn't want Raina to overhear her suggestion.

Which only made Adam even more curious.

"You could go on the run."

"What?" Adam barked.

Lorelei shrugged. "If you two posed as a couple and took off..."

"You're fucking nuts. No. Why would we do that?"

"Because it would get all of us out of this house. I hate sitting here every day knowing the man who ordered a hit on my cousin is still out there. You, and everyone else, can tell me a hundred times a day that he's not likely to go after Karli again, but I can't shake it. We should be out there. We should be helping find him. Keeping tabs on him."

"No one knows where he is," Adam said, hating the words as he spat them out.

"Exactly. But we could find him. He has to be somewhere."

"Raina is safer here. With both of us. Two people protecting her, no one in and no one out. No one knows where we are. If we left and Street found us—"

"You'd protect her."

"Like I did last time he found us?" Adam knew Lorelei couldn't argue with him on that point. He'd hate himself forever for letting Raina, Lorelei, and Edie get hurt. For not putting up a fight at all. Street cold-cocked Adam before he knew what was happening, but he was a fucking FBI Agent! He should have known someone was in the house. He should—

"Stop beating yourself up," Lorelei snapped. "That's not going to make any of this any better. You have to let it go. Shit happens. We are all alive. That's the important part. We will get Street again. Every single one of his victims will get justice."

Adam held Lorelei's gaze for a long minute before he nodded. "I hope you're right."

3

———

Adam paced the living room like a caged animal. He hated waiting for updates. He checked his phone, growling when the clock on the front hadn't changed.

"Sit down," Lorelei admonished.

"I can't. They should have called by now."

"You're making her more nervous," Lorelei hissed.

Adam glanced back to where Raina was sitting at the kitchen table, watching him with wide eyes full of fear and ringed with tears waiting to fall.

"Dammit," Adam breathed. He forced his ass to the armchair and flipped the phone over to stare at the useless fucking thing. Why hadn't anyone called yet?

The safe house had been quiet for days. Their grocery delivery was simple the previous weekend, but aside from that, they'd had no contact with the world outside the four bulletproof walls that kept them separated.

Stir-crazy didn't even begin to describe how Adam felt. He'd convinced himself they would be getting out of there today. That Street would be hauled off to jail and not allowed to walk free with the rest of the world while he waited for the trial that would put him away for life.

It would mean Raina was safe. It would mean she could go back to a normal life.

But it would also mean Adam wouldn't see her again. The selfish dick he was hated the idea of not having to live with her. As much as he was sick of being stuck in the house, he was not regretting the assignment and the hypnotizing woman it brought into his world for a little while.

Adam looked over at Raina and found her gaze locked on him. She chewed her bottom lip, the flesh white next to her teeth and bright pink around that, like she'd been worrying it the whole time he paced the living room.

He needed to reassure her that everything was fine, even though he didn't believe it.

"I'm sorry," Adam said, holding Raina's gaze. "I didn't mean to upset you."

She shook her head, her light brown locks teasing the tops of her breasts with the move. She hadn't worn a bra in days, and it was testing his resolve even more than her presence had the entire time. "It's not you. I'm just anxious. I know today matters a lot."

Adam opened his mouth to tell her it was just one step when his phone rang. The old-school ringtone he chose because it reminded him of the phone mounted on the wall in his parents' kitchen was too loud and grated all his nerves.

Adam stood and tapped the screen to answer the call before the phone could ring again. "Johnson."

"You alone?" Liam's voice was guarded, cautious. Something wasn't right.

"I can be."

"Do it," Liam said.

Adam glanced at Lorelei, telling her without words that something was not okay. Lorelei's eyes widened. She stood and moved toward Raina, talking to her as Adam moved down the hallway toward the bedroom.

Adam closed the door as a sob broke from Raina. It gutted him, like it did every time he heard her cry, which was far too damn often.

"Okay," Adam said, letting Liam know he was alone.

"Street didn't show."

"What the fuck? He's required. Is there a warrant out for his arrest?"

"No."

"You better spit out a few more words, or I'm going to have a few for you."

Liam sighed loudly, not any happier with the situation than Adam, but Liam's woman was safe and not being threatened by the psycho who was currently not in prison.

"His lawyer showed up and said Street was not there because the charges against him were all fabricated and he felt as though Street was being targeted by the police and FBI and us, and showing up in an open court was more of a risk than they were willing to take."

"Are you fucking...?" Adam released a frustrated breath and tried to wrap his head around what Liam said. "And the judge let it stand?"

"The chances of the judge not working for Street have dropped to zero. No judge would ever let this go."

"This is a fucking joke. This judge needs to be put in jail, and all of this needs to go in front of someone else."

"I agree, and we're working on that, but for now, there are no pending charges."

"How in the ever-loving fuck did that happen?" Adam slammed his fist against the wall, wincing when the drywall cracked. Guess the interior walls weren't bulletproof.

"The lawyer said you and Lorelei weren't reliable witnesses since you both had head trauma. Raina and Edie weren't reliable because Raina is a disgruntled ex-girlfriend, and Edie is a drug addict. The fact that none of you were there made the judge agree—"

"We couldn't take the chance! He would have followed us back here to kill Raina!"

"I know," Liam said, his tone softer, soothing.

All it did was piss Adam off even more. "Don't fucking handle me. Not you, Liam."

Liam exhaled loudly. "I'm not trying to. I'm just as angry about all of this as you are. We all are. Captain Patrick went off on the judge and almost got thrown in jail for contempt. It was bad. The whole thing was bad. But the lawyer sat there and smiled like he expected everything we did. He had an answer for every charge, and he had an excuse for everything."

"What about abusing Raina?"

"The lawyer said he never touched her. That she was mugged and didn't want to admit it. She left Street after that because she was ashamed that she blamed him."

"Fuck!" Adam put his head against the wall and closed his eyes. "I'm starting to see why he's never been locked up."

"This is next level. I've never seen a lawyer like this. We've gone against some pretty ugly criminals, but none have had this orchestrated of a setup. The judge just sat there, looking annoyed whenever we tried to say something to change his mind."

Adam let out a long breath and pushed off the wall. He

walked over to the bed and sat on the edge. He rested his elbows on his knees and wished he could go out for a punishing run until he couldn't stand upright any longer. Something that would give him rest.

"I know none of this is what you wanted to hear today. We were all hoping you and Lorelei could help us with the case and Raina could go back to her life, but now we don't know when any of that will happen."

"Yeah."

"Do you need a break? Need one of us to stay there and you can take a few days off? Or Lorelei can?"

Adam shook his head before Liam even finished the question. "No. I'm not leaving Raina. We've been with her the whole time. We're not going anywhere."

"Okay, okay," Liam said defensively, making Adam wonder how harsh his tone was.

"Sorry. I didn't mean to get nasty."

"All good. I know this isn't easy on any of you. Have you talked to your parents lately?"

"No. I touch base every few weeks, but I'm not even sure they know I'm in this area." Liam's dad and Adam's dad were brothers. Their parents all still lived in the town where they grew up in northern Vermont. Liam got out of there as soon as he graduated high school, and a year later, Adam did the same. Neither of them had ever looked back, even though Adam had two brothers and a sister who stayed in the area.

"What about Holly?" Holly was Adam's sister and the only member of his immediate family he stayed in touch with on a more regular basis.

Adam drew a breath and let it out slowly. He knew what Liam was doing, and it was working. Adam adored his little sister. She was a doctor, and Adam was so damn proud of her his chest swelled with pride and emotion just thinking about her. "She's doing well. She and Mallory are thinking about a summer wedding."

"Yeah? That's great news. I didn't realize they'd gotten engaged."

"Mallory surprised Holly one night. I didn't ask for details, but Holly said it was romantic and sweet. And she had an engagement ring for Mallory, too. But Mallory asked first."

"Good for them. I know it hasn't been easy for them, but I'm happy they found each other."

"Yeah, me, too." Adam breathed a little easier. "Thanks."

"I know how this goes. You know I do. When Caitlyn was the one in danger, I felt just like you do now."

"Raina and I aren't together. Nothing is going on."

Liam snorted. "Just because you aren't together doesn't mean there isn't something going on. I saw the look on your face when Lorelei told you what Street did to Raina."

"How could I not be pissed off? Weren't you?"

"Of course, but I was pissed because he's a horrible human who manipulated her and hurt her over and over. You were pissed because you have a thing for her."

"That's not..."

"Adam, I'm not judging you. At all. I was supposed to be protecting Caitlyn when I fell for her. You and Raina have been stuck under the same roof a lot longer than Caitlyn and I were. You don't get to choose when you meet the person who flips you inside out."

Adam breathed a laugh and shook his head. "She really fucking does."

Liam chuckled softly. "Feels better to admit that, doesn't it?"

"Yeah, but I would never tell anyone else. Lorelei would have me tossed off the case for violating the rules and getting emotionally involved. And Raina—"

"I'd never say a thing," Liam said. "I'm just letting you know I understand what you're going through and that it's that much harder when it's a woman you care about."

Adam sighed. "Yeah. Yeah, it is."

"Listen, I gotta go. We're working on next steps. I'll be in touch once we have a plan."

"Sounds good. Thanks."

Adam hung up the phone and stared at it until the screen went dark. He did not want to go out there and tell Raina that not only was Street free, but all the charges against him were dropped for lack of evidence. Lies. All fucking lies. But it meant he was out there and no one was going to put him away. And she wasn't safe.

A knock on the door raised Adam's head. Time to face the music. "I'm coming."

Lorelei was on the other side of the door when Adam opened it. She raised her eyebrows, asking for the update.

"All charges were dropped. He's free."

"You're fucking kidding me."

Adam shook his head. "Said he was targeted by the police, FBI, and Liam's group. Didn't even show up today because of it. Liam said the judge was in on it and the lawyer knew everything they were going to say."

"How is that possible?"

"When you're a criminal, it's easy. But whatever the reason, he's free."

"Shit."

Adam nodded. "Yeah. Nothing changes, just means we have to stay here longer."

"You should seriously think about getting out of town. Like I said before—"

"No. Not an option."

Lorelei sighed. "Fine. I'm going to take a shower. Raina's laying down. She knew it was bad when you locked us out of the call. I think she crashed."

Adam glanced at the door that separated Raina from where they stood in the hallway. "Probably good she's getting some sleep."

"I agree. You think you can start dinner?" Lorelei asked with a smirk.

Adam snorted. "Might not be the best idea for us, but sure, I can give it a shot."

Lorelei clapped him on the shoulder and pushed past him into the bedroom they shared. One of them stayed alert at night while the other slept in the bedroom. They gave Raina her own room so she had a sense of stability in a shaky world.

"What did you want tonight?"

"Raina and I were thinking spaghetti and meatballs. Meatballs are in the freezer. Put them on a cookie sheet and stick them in the oven. Start the water to boil the pasta. Should be easy enough for you."

"You give me far too much credit."

Lorelei grabbed her clothes from the dresser she was using and followed him out of the room again. The house only had one bathroom, but they were making the most of the situation.

"Thanks for trying," Lorelei said.

Adam nodded. He needed to step things up. He was letting Lorelei do too much of the heavy lifting between being available for Raina when she needed someone to talk to and doing almost all the cooking. He was staying in touch with Liam since they were cousins, but other than that, he hadn't been much of a help so far.

The bathroom door closed, and Adam went to the kitchen. He read the directions on the meatballs and set the package on the counter. He started the oven and set a cookie sheet on the counter while the oven heated. The package was small, and leftover were always good, so he dumped all of them onto the tray. Lorelei was a stickler for the rules and insisted on waiting for the oven to pre-heat, but Adam didn't want to wait that long. He slid the cookie sheet into the cold oven.

"I saw that," Raina said from not far behind him.

Adam spun and smiled at her smirk. "I don't know what you're talking about."

She shook her head. "Your secret is safe with me."

"Thanks. Lorelei would have me skewered."

Raina chuckled.

"I thought you were resting."

She shook her head. "I couldn't sleep." She turned on the water and washed her hands while Adam waited to answer whatever questions she had. She knew Street was going to court earlier, and she knew it wasn't good. But she didn't know the details yet.

"Raina, I—"

"Can I help with dinner?" she asked.

Adam leaned back, surprised she wasn't jumping in and asking about court. He closed his mouth and nodded. "Of course."

Raina bent at the waist to get the stockpot from one of the lower cabinets, and Adam nearly groaned at the sight of her hips tipped up for him. Her perfectly round ass was covered in hot pink sweats and all he could think about was the other pink he wanted to bury himself in.

"Do you think this is big enough?" Raina asked, holding out a large pot.

It's definitely big enough. Adam shook his head at himself, trying to dismiss the dirty thought, but Raina saw him.

"No?" She bent at the waist to retrieve another pot.

"No! It's fine. Sorry. All good." Adam reached for the pot, hoping she didn't notice the way his sweats tented around his full erection. Maybe he should take Liam up on the offer to get out of there for a little while. Take the edge off his desire for Raina. A little distance before he grabbed her hips and lined himself up at her entrance and lost his fucking mind inside her.

"Are you okay?" Raina asked, looking at him like he was losing his mind. "Oh, God, was it that bad?"

"Was what that bad?"

"Damon. I didn't really want to know because I figured it's bad news, but you look like you're going to be sick. What happened?"

Adam cleared his throat and forced himself to focus on Raina. He was lusting after her, and she was fearing for her life. He was such an asshole.

"Sorry. I'm fine. I promise."

"But Damon's still free, isn't he?"

Adam nodded.

Raina let out a breath. She straightened her shoulders. "Okay. It's not a surprise. We just have to wait a little longer until his trial. I can do that. I can handle this."

She forced a smile that turned Adam's stomach. She thought there was going to be a trial.

"We need some water in this pan. Then we can start the pasta."

"Raina…"

She looked at him, then shook her head. "No. Don't tell me right now. Let me believe it's all going to be okay. For just a few minutes. Please."

Adam didn't like it, but he nodded. He could give her that.

She flashed him a grateful smile and set the pot in the sink. She turned on the water and asked, "What was your favorite dinner growing up?"

"Growing up? Um, I don't know. Maybe burgers? We didn't get to grill often living in Vermont, so it was a treat when the weather was nice enough for my dad to grill. What about you?"

She nodded. "I get that. It makes sense. My favorite was always spaghetti and meatballs. My grandma would make it whenever we'd go to her house, and it was so good."

Adam held up the jar of sauce he found in the pantry. "Was it as good as jarred sauce?"

Raina laughed and shook her head. "Of course not. Nothing could compare to jarred sauce."

Adam laughed with her, enjoying the smile on her beautiful face. Her hazel eyes looked brighter than they had the last two weeks.

"My best memories as a kid were spending time with my grandma. She lived next door to us, and when I'd get off the bus, I'd go to her house."

"You had spaghetti and meatballs every day?" Adam teased her.

Raina laughed and slapped his arm. "No. She'd only make it when all of us were there for dinner. When I'd go after school, she'd have cookies for me."

"What were your favorites?"

Raina tipped her head back, a faint smile on her face as the memories of the past washed over her.

Adam wanted to keep her right there in that moment. She was at peace. Happy. Fear couldn't touch her right then. It was the most relaxed Adam had ever seen her.

"Butterscotch, definitely. They were like chocolate chip cookies, but with butterscotch chips instead. Her chocolate chip were good, too. And molasses."

Raina groaned, the sound going right to Adam's dick. He swallowed an answering groan and cleared his throat. "I don't think I've ever had butterscotch cookies."

"You're missing out. When all of this is over, I'll make some for you." Just that quickly, the joy in her face faded. "If I'm still alive."

"I'm not going to let anything happen to you," Adam growled, knowing the words were lies as they slid from his mouth.

Raina flashed him a smile that said she knew the same. Street had already gotten to her when she was under his protection. He'd already proven he was more capable and dangerous than any of them realized. That he would stop at nothing to reclaim Raina as his, no matter what she or anyone else said about the matter.

"I never apologized for not protecting you when he—"

Raina shook her head. "No. Stop. You can't blame yourself for that."

"It was my fault. He got the drop on me. I was the first line of defense, and he knocked me out without me even putting up a fight."

"There was nothing you could have done to stop him. We're all alive. That's the important part."

"Thanks to Mackenzie, not me."

Raina shook her head. "It doesn't matter who stopped

Damon. He was stopped. And he's going to pay for what he did."

Adam winced. He tried not to, but he did. And Raina caught it.

"Oh, God," she breathed. "He's not going to jail, is he?"

Adam shook his head. "All charges were dropped."

"Oh, my God, I'm going to die."

4

———

Darkness filled the edges of Raina's vision. A clatter barely reached her ears. Her legs gave out, and she sank to the floor, the jolt of landing shocking her out of her trance.

"All charges?" she whispered.

Adam was right there, his face filling her vision. "Three things, Raina?"

"Fuck three things," she snapped. Tears poured freely from her eyes. "He's going to kill me. If I'm lucky, that's all he'll do. He wants to punish me."

Adam sighed heavily. Irritated.

Well, fuck him, too. Raina didn't have time to worry about his emotions. The man half of Niagara County was looking for was only looking for her. He didn't care who he had to kill to get to her, he was going to find her. And take what he wanted from her.

A pound of flesh would be easy. Nothing was easy with Damon. He was going to take it all. And he was going to leave his mark on her.

Raina struggled to draw a breath, wishing death would come for her instead of waiting for Damon to deliver it. The things he whispered in her ear two weeks ago when he found her said it all.

You're mine.

I'll make you pay.

You will bleed.

The memory of his hot breath on her cheek and his fist in her hair made the room spin. If she wasn't already on the floor, she would have fallen.

They all thought she was brave for wanting to go back to him. For wanting to sacrifice herself. Her secret shame was she just wanted it to be over. She wanted the people she cared about to be safe, but she wanted death to come. To know Damon couldn't hurt her again.

"He can't get close here."

"You said that before," Raina snarled. She wasn't being fair to Adam. Damon was smarter than any of them knew. He had been evading police and murdering people for decades. And he had connections deeper than the Niagara Gorge. He would get away with anything. He had.

"I'm sorry," Adam whispered.

The pain and regret in his voice finally sank in. He didn't say anything else, just sat there with her on the floor while the water boiled on the stove above their heads. The oven was warm behind her back, a reminder they were in the middle of cooking dinner when the latest bomb was dropped on her.

Raina angrily swiped the tears from her cheeks and let out a frustrated breath. She had two choices. Give in or fight. When she walked out on Damon for good, she chose to fight. To live her life and to stay away from him.

At that time, she had no idea how dangerous he was. She didn't know the things he'd done or what he was capable of. Raina knew he would try to get her back, but she'd never imagined he would go to the lengths he had to reclaim her as his.

But it didn't change. She still refused to be his. She refused to be with anyone who saw her as property. Who thought a woman only had one place. Who thought he could punish her for not following his orders.

Raina was terrified. That fear dragged her deep at times. The moments of hope were few and far between anymore, but she had to be stronger. She had to pick herself up and stop letting fear rule her life. That was what Damon wanted. He knew fear was powerful. He used it.

No more.

Raina pushed herself off the floor and grabbed the box of pasta on the counter. She tore it open and dumped it into the rapidly boiling water, giving it a stir before tossing the box into the recycling bin.

Adam rose to his feet smoothly, as though it didn't take any effort. He stepped back just enough to put space between them, but he didn't go far.

They didn't speak for several long moments. Raina let the rhythmic process of cooking soothe her until tears no longer welled in her eyes. She focused on the task, refusing to admit even to herself that the focus helped. She wouldn't tell Adam.

He stayed right there. His solid presence comforting her as much as it bugged her. She hated that she couldn't be on her own. That she was still in protective custody. That all charges against Damon had been dropped, but she wasn't free.

She wouldn't ever be free. Not as long as he was alive.

"I hate him. I wish he was dead," she admitted softly.

Adam stepped closer. He rested his hand on the counter

next to her. "Me, too," he said so softly she wasn't sure she actually heard him.

Raina looked up at him. Adam was so close she could see the dark blue ring around the inner circle of his eyes. If she lifted onto her toes, she could press her lips to his and have Damon no longer be the last man she kissed.

"I hate that he ever touched you. That he ever caused you pain," Adam continued. "I want to kill him for it. To let you feel safe again."

"You can't say that," Raina whispered. She'd gotten a crash course from Francesca and Stacey when she escaped Damon and stayed at Shelter in the Storm. If Raina said she wanted to kill Damon, and he ended up dead, she'd be the primary suspect. She learned to only admit that truth in private, when there were no witnesses.

"I don't care. I'd happily go to jail if it meant you never had to feel this way again."

Raina licked her suddenly parched lips.

Adam's gaze dropped to her mouth. He moved just barely closer to her.

Raina sucked in a breath. In the weeks they'd lived together, Adam had never given her the impression he thought of her as anything other than a nuisance. But the heat in his gaze said he was feeling a whole lot of other things that Raina never expected.

"Adam?"

His hand lifted slowly, giving her plenty of time to pull back if she wanted, but she didn't want to move. She wanted his touch. To have a man who wasn't looking to hurt her put his hands on her.

He cupped her jaw, and Raina released a shaky breath. His other hand came up, the two capturing her head.

Damon held her like that more than once. But his touch

never made Raina feel safe and protected. Cared for and desired.

"Raina," he breathed. He lowered his head toward her, his gaze locked on her, silently asking for permission she was more than happy to grant.

A door opened down the hall, movement that reminded them they weren't alone.

Raina froze, unsure what Adam was going to do. Unsure what she wanted him to do.

Adam closed his eyes and took a step back. His fingertips trailed along her jaw, his touch fading with each second until Raina wanted to cry at the loss.

His Adam's apple bobbed with his audible swallow, then he turned away from her, cutting off the connection Raina ached to feel again.

She focused on dinner and making it good. She drained the pasta, then twisted the lid off the jar of sauce and emptied it into a microwave-safe bowl to heat it up. When the sauce was hot, she took the meatballs out of the oven and tossed all of it together in a large serving bowl she found in an upper cabinet.

"Did you make her do all the work?" Lorelei asked in a mocking tone.

Raina looked over her shoulder at Lorelei and smiled. "I needed the distraction."

Lorelei's gaze flickered to Adam, and he nodded. His eyes drifted to Raina, but she turned away before she could get caught in his orbit again.

She was toxic. Marked for death. Getting involved with any man was the worst idea on the planet, but getting involved with the man who was tasked with keeping her safe was just plain stupid. He wasn't going to sleep with his partner, so Raina was the only option. That's why he looked like he was going to kiss her. Not because he wanted her, but because she was there.

Raina set the bowl on the counter and put three bowls and forks next to it. She excused herself to use the bathroom, needing a minute away from Adam.

She locked herself in the bathroom and added one more thing to the list of reasons she hated Damon Street.

Raina was going to die without knowing what it felt like to be with a man who was truly, honestly good. And it was all Damon's fault.

"WHAT THE HELL is wrong with you?" Lorelei hissed. "I told you to make dinner, and you made her do it?"

Adam shook his head as he stared after Raina. He wanted to go after her, but he knew that was the wrong choice. He should have kept his hands to his fucking self instead of touching her. He knew better.

"Adam," Lorelei snapped.

He looked at his partner and knew she saw more than he wanted her to see.

Her head tilted to the side, and her eyes went soft. "I care about her, too. She's been dealt a shit hand, and she doesn't deserve all of this."

Adam shook his head. "No, she doesn't. It's not fair, and it's not right."

"I agree, but we're doing our best. I'm guessing you told her about all the charges being dropped against Street?"

Adam nodded. "She said something about everything would be fine once he went to jail, and she must have seen it in my face."

Lorelei snorted. "For an experienced agent, your poker face sucks."

Adam rolled his eyes. He'd never had an issue keeping his expressions neutral before he met Raina. For some reason, she changed everything.

"It's better she knows, though. We were going to have to tell her. Having it out in the open is good."

"Nothing about this situation is good," Adam growled.

Lorelei sighed. "All too true." She picked at her nail, a sure sign there was something else she wanted to say.

Adam waited patiently for his partner to look up at him.

Lorelei chuckled. "I hate when you do that."

"And I hate when you don't just spit it out."

Lorelei scowled at him playfully, like a sibling. Adam was pretty sure his sister, Holly, had given him the same look the last time they were together. "Do you think we're going to be able to stay with Raina?"

"What do you mean? Why wouldn't we?"

Lorelei glanced toward the bathroom to make sure Raina wasn't there, and Adam's heart skipped. Lorelei was serious.

"If there's no case, no charges, nothing we can bring Street in for, Raina is no longer a witness," Lorelei whispered.

Adam leaned back against the edge of the counter, letting it hold him up as his world was swept out from under him.

Lorelei was right. Adam hadn't thought about it, but it was true. Even though they all knew there was a case and that Raina needed protection, their bosses might deny it and Raina could end up on her own.

"We can't let that happen," Adam snapped. "We have to protect her."

Lorelei nodded. "I agree, but I'm not sure how we're going to do that. I have about a month of vacation I can use, but I'm not sure if it'll be enough. We might need to get your cousin involved with this and have F-BOMB watch her."

"Fuck."

Lorelei was quiet while Adam worked through the problem in his mind. Liam and his team would definitely help, but they had cases they were working on. Plus, Raina would likely fight it. She already said she felt like a burden. She would never risk her friends or living with one of them again, so she would end up on her own if F-BOMB didn't take her in.

Adam didn't know if that was a real option. They were helping out, and they said they were willing to do whatever they needed to do, but they also had a business to run.

"We might have to wait and see, but you could get out ahead of it and take her—"

"No," Adam growled. "I already told you that's not an option. She's safer here. We all are. Together."

"Yeah, but—"

"No, Lore. I... I already let her down once. I already fucked up once. I need to know Raina is safe. Being here with F-BOMB watching the house and you and I in here together is the best option."

Lorelei nodded slowly. "Okay. I won't ask you again."

"Thank you."

The bathroom door opened, and Adam's gaze was drawn to Raina as she approached. His gut twisted at the thought of anything else happening to her. He would not take that chance. Her safety was the most important thing.

THERE WAS one thing Damon Street hated, and currently, that one thing was barking orders at him as if Damon was Trevor's pet.

"You fucked up. You are staying here. You are not to go after Raina or anyone else. You're going to let all of this blow over."

Damon palmed his cock through his pants. "I'll give you something to blow."

"Do you think this is a fucking joke?" Trevor asked. He got up in Damon's face.

Damon shoved Trevor, sending Trevor stumbling backward.

Trevor nearly lost his balance and landed on his ass, but he caught himself on the edge of a chair and snarled at Damon once more.

Damon barely held back his smirk. "Why the fuck am I talking to you instead of the boss?"

"Because the boss is fucking pissed! Do you know the risk you took? Not to mention the threats you made against the Company. Did you really think you'd be welcomed back with open arms?"

"I was promised a job."

"You were promised freedom. I still think that was too generous."

"Yeah, well, lucky for me you don't call the fucking shots."

"I do where you're concerned. You answer to me. I'm your go-between. You don't get to talk to the boss. Not anytime soon."

"What?" Damon bellowed. That was not what he signed on for. He'd done everything that had been asked of him. For decades. He was a loyal soldier. Moving anything and everything the Company needed him to move and eliminating any threats against them.

And he was repaid by putting a punk-ass bitch between him and the boss? Fuck no. That was not the agreement he made when he called from fucking jail.

Trevor smirked. "You need to prove your value. To prove that you can follow orders."

"I've been proving that since you were in fucking diapers."

"And you fucked up. Did you think all would be forgiven? You were given chances. You were told to leave that bitch alone. Instead, you forgot that there's plenty more pussy. You got stuck on that one and refused to pull your head out of your dick. Now, you're starting over."

"The boss can tell me that to my face."

Trevor laughed loudly. He shook his head and clutched his gut.

Damon waited patiently. If he timed it right, he could deliver a blow that knocked Trevor on his ass for good.

Damon leaned back, readying himself, but Trevor saw it coming and sucker-punched Damon, catching him square in the nose.

Damon howled as blood trickled down his face.

"I said you don't get to see the boss. You need to do as you're fucking told." Trevor got up in Damon's face, ignoring the blood to hold them nose-to-nose. "You're fucking basic. You're nothing. You don't get a goddamn say in any-fucking-thing that goes on around here. You're going to do what you're told and keep your fucking head down. And if you don't, I'll happily cut it the fuck off for you."

"Fuck you," Damon snarled, the insult losing effectiveness when Damon choked on the blood pooling in his throat.

Trevor chuckled and tossed Damon away. Damon tripped and fell, sprawling across the floor.

"Stay away from your whore. Stay away from everyone involved in the shitstorm you created. The boss doesn't have time to clean up anymore of your fucking messes. Neither do I."

"You're going to be the next mess."

Trevor clocked Damon as he started to get up. The blow sent Damon back to the floor. His head spun and vomit rose in his throat. He choked it back, but he was too dizzy to get up again.

"Clean up this fucking mess. You're fucking pathetic. One day, I'm going to kill you. Until then, fuck off, old man."

Damon watched Trevor go, carefully avoiding the blood staining the floor.

Damon was not going to be the one dead. Trevor would never see him coming. Until it was too late.

5

———

RAINA SLAMMED HER BOOK CLOSED AND HUFFED OUT A breath. She growled and tossed it to the coffee table.

"You okay?" Lorelei asked from the kitchen.

"No. I'm not okay. I'm bored. I know I shouldn't complain about that, but I'm bored. Can I go outside?"

Lorelei laughed. "You know there's five feet of snow outside, right?"

Raina glanced at the covered windows that blocked the outside world from her view and shrugged. "I'll be able to breathe. That'll be to my shoulders, maybe a little higher." She twisted her hair up, letting it fall when she couldn't come up with a tie for it.

"You'll freeze."

"You're making excuses." Raina faced off with her protector. The reasonable one, not the one who made her insides quiver and her body ache. Nope. That protector had been hiding for three days, since he almost kissed her in the kitchen. Three days of pent up orgasms that Raina couldn't exactly take care of when she was being watched twenty-four-seven. It was bad enough she couldn't lock the door when she took a shower, but to have one of them burst in on her mid-orgasm was horrifying enough for Raina to keep the desire inside.

But she was failing to keep the frustration it was causing from building up and boiling over.

"It's not safe," Lorelei said. Her dark brown eyes were kind and sympathetic, but she didn't really know what Raina was feeling. Lorelei wasn't being hunted. And she was tough as fuck and not scared of anything.

"Argh! I just want to get the hell out of here. Go for a walk. Get some fresh air. Do something normal. I hate this!"

Lorelei joined Raina in the living room and went straight to the bookshelf next to the TV. She picked up a deck of cards. "Want to play a game?"

"Fifty-two pickup? Because all I want to do right now is destroy something."

"Let's see what we can find in the basement."

Raina shivered. She knew it was irrational, but since Damon snuck into the last safe house through the basement, she'd been afraid of the basement in this house. "Are you sure that's a good idea?"

Lorelei turned at the tremble in Raina's voice and moved back to her side. "He's not down there. There are sensors on the windows. And cameras everywhere. This place is a fortress."

Raina wanted to be brave. Hell, five seconds ago she was demanding to be let into the backyard. But the truth was, she was so bored and horny and scared that she wasn't sure if she wanted to cry or scream or run out into traffic and end it all.

No. That last one... She didn't want to die. Not really. She wanted this to be over, which manifested as a lack of shits to give if Damon found her or not, but Raina wanted to live.

She wanted Damon to face the music and be brought to justice. She wanted a life.

"Okay," Raina finally whispered. She followed Lorelei to the basement door, jumping when the damn thing squeaked. Raina's heart pounded, the pulse of blood the only thing she could hear.

Lorelei took a step toward the basement, flicking the switch to turn the light on.

Raina looked down the wooden staircase to a painted concrete floor. It was a happy blue color that made her smile for the first time in days.

"It doesn't look so bad."

Raina shook her head and followed Lorelei down the stairs. It was not a huge space, but it was decent. There was a couch and two more stuffed chairs. A folding table sat on the one side with four chairs around it. There was a computer setup on the other side of the basement with more tech equipment than Raina had ever seen.

"Wow," Lorelei gasped. "They weren't kidding about the surveillance. I didn't know this was down here."

"Did Adam?" Raina asked.

Lorelei nodded. "Probably. He's been down here almost every day. When he stays up at night, he spends time down here."

"Do you think we're bothering him being down here?"

Lorelei shook her head as Raina talked. "He won't care. And he likely won't hear us. One thing we've learned on the job is to sleep when we can and to only be alert when necessary. He's probably pretty solidly asleep right now."

Raina nodded and tried not to wonder what Adam wore when he slept. Boxers? Sweats? Nothing? Her cheeks heated at the thought. She pressed her thighs together to stop the throbbing there and walked across the room, past the folding table, to a small exercise area. "I didn't know this was here."

Lorelei looked at what Raina was doing and moved toward her. "Adam mentioned he was working out, but I didn't know where. I should be on the treadmill more often, but it's not my strong suit."

Raina snorted. "Mine either."

They shared a grin and moved to the punching bag in the corner.

"That could help get out some of that anger you have inside."

"Can I tape a picture of Damon to it?" Raina asked.

Lorelei smiled. "I'm not going to tell you no."

Raina chuckled and tapped the speed bag. She'd never learned the right way to throw a punch, and at the moment, she wasn't sure it mattered. She just wanted to hit the damn thing.

If only it actually was Damon.

She punched the bag, letting it swing and bounce. It hurt a little, but Raina didn't really care. It felt good. Raina punched it again. And again. And again.

She punched until tears streamed down her face and the fight inside her swung wildly on the bracket. She sank to a heap in the middle of the floor and let it all out, not caring that she was breaking down. It had been a long few months. Between the time she spent at Shelter in the Storm after leaving Damon for good to living with Karli, then going into hiding when she thought Karli was killed and finding out Damon was behind it all because of Raina.

She was so far past okay she wasn't sure she ever could be okay again. She was hiding from a man she once told herself she loved. He would kill anyone and everyone who got between them.

Raina never thought she'd wish harm on another person, but Damon wasn't human. He was evil, pure and simple. He was willing to kill to get to her, and he would kill her when he had the chance. There was no way for them both to survive. Kill or be killed.

Lorelei stood there, not distant, but not supportive either. That wasn't her job. Her job was to keep Raina safe, not to make her feel better. Karli shared once that Lorelei was the closest Karli ever had to a sister, but Lorelei was not affectionate or emotional. It made her a great agent, but not a great person to cry to.

"What's going on?" Adam snarled. "What happened?"

Raina hated the way her body leapt at the sound of his voice, at the protective, angry growl that she told herself was only because she woke him up.

"We came down here for a change of scenery. Raina was using the punching bag as a substitute for Street's face and got emotional."

"And you just left her there?" Adam's footsteps thudded across the floor until he reached her. He didn't hesitate or even ask. He just scooped her up like she weighed nothing and carried her back to the couch.

Raina, God help her, couldn't resist burrowing into the man who smelled like sleep and soap and sexy man. Sobs continued to rip through her, but Adam shushed her and held her tight to his body, rubbing his hand up and down her spine.

Raina was vaguely aware of Lorelei tiptoeing up the stairs and leaving the two of them alone in the basement, but Raina was too worn out to care at the moment.

Her breath hitched, and her body twitched. She tried to slow the tears, but everything was pouring out of her and the flood kept coming.

Eventually, her hiccups slowed, and exhaustion wrapped her up tight and pulled her down to sleep. Safe. Warm. Adam.

ADAM FELT the moment Raina fell asleep. She went from crying and shaking to snoring and still. It surprised him how quickly she fell asleep, but he guessed she was sleeping even worse than he was.

And he wasn't sleeping for shit.

When he heard Lorelei and Raina open the basement door, his entire body went on alert. When they first got to the safe house and he heard the squeak the basement door made, he wanted to fix it, but the reminder of how Street snuck up on him in the last house had Adam ignoring every instinct to silence the door.

Now, he was grateful for it for another reason. He heard them go downstairs, and he heard their muffled voices as they explored the basement.

The first swing of the speed bag had Adam reaching for his clothes, but once he realized what the noise was, he took his time getting dressed. He was going to get himself a cup of coffee before checking in with Liam, but then he heard Raina sob and his entire body seized up with fear.

Walking downstairs and finding her crumpled into a pile on the floor was not what he expected, but it was better than the alternatives his paranoid mind came up with in the few seconds it took him to get down the stairs and lay his eyes on her.

He knew touching her was a bad idea. It was part of their training to stay neutral. Don't get involved. Don't comfort witnesses when they get upset. That's not your job.

Lorelei was stronger than he was. She stood there and let Raina cry, but Adam couldn't do it.

When Lorelei walked up the stairs and left them alone, Adam knew he should have extricated Raina from his lap and followed Lorelei upstairs, but he couldn't let go. Holding Raina, even when she was upset, was like waking up and finding out his dream was actually happening.

And after the fucked up dreams he had, a good one coming true was more than a blessing.

He pressed his nose to her hair and inhaled the scent that was different on his body. Sharing shower products and personal space meant he was hard whenever he stepped into the shower and smelled the scent he'd come to identify with Raina, but holding her and being able to breathe it in off her skin was a whole different kind of torture.

He shifted on the couch, trying to ease the pulsing in his dick. She was curled against him, her thigh pressed to his crotch, and his dick had wasted no time with the meet and greet.

Resisting her had become an exercise in avoidance, and all that work was shattered with one sob and a slumber in the basement. Adam was right back to where he started and hard as fuck with a sleeping woman in his arms that he had no right to want in his bed.

He leaned his head back on the back of the couch and pulled her closer to him, loving the way she snuggled against him and let him hold her. She was exhausted, but the fact that she fell asleep with him and stayed that way made him feel like he was doing something right. She trusted him. And if she trusted him, he hadn't completely fucked up.

The light outside the basement windows faded as the afternoon turned to evening. Sunset was early in mid-

January and darkness fell before it was close to time for dinner.

Raina stirred a few times, but she stayed asleep, her body limp and warm against Adam's. He told himself he should ease out from under her and let her sleep, or carry her to her room, or something, but he couldn't bring himself to do it.

He was a selfish prick, keeping her all to himself and pretending it was not only okay but that she was actually his. That she wanted him as much as he craved her.

Raina groaned and shifted, rubbing her thigh against his erection. She stilled, her entire body changing just as quickly as when she fell asleep.

"It's Adam," he whispered, hoping his voice and the reminder of where she was would help her relax.

She sighed, a shaky exhale that told him just how scared she was. She pushed herself up and avoided his gaze. "Sorry. I didn't mean to fall asleep on you."

"You needed it. Have you been sleeping at all?"

She shook her head and stood. She walked a few feet away from him, keeping her head down. "I see him when I close my eyes."

"I didn't know it was so bad you never slept. We could have gotten you sleeping pills or something." Adam rose from his seat but didn't move toward her.

"No," she blurted. "I need to be alert. If I'm on something when he shows up, I won't be able to fight him off." She laughed mirthlessly. "Not that being wide awake ever helped in the past."

"We're not going to let him get to you again. There are people watching this house at all times."

"Inside?" She glanced back at the couch where they were curled up together just a minute ago.

Adam shook his head. "I told them no, but they can if you'd feel better."

"No. That's... No."

Adam nodded, not sure what he should say to her. They hadn't spoken much, even though they'd been living together for months. It made him an ass, but it was self-preservation.

Until he blew it all up and held her.

Now, it was all he could do to resist reaching out to her again.

"What time is it?" Raina asked.

Adam pulled his phone from his pocket and showed her the screen.

"No wonder I'm hungry." She flashed a weak smile and turned toward the stairs.

Adam followed behind her, absolutely not staring at the way her sweats pulled tight across her plump bottom or the way her hips shifted with each step she took. He was definitely not thinking about how good she felt in his lap and how badly he wanted to drag her back downstairs and show her how hungry he was for her.

Lorelei was in the kitchen when they made it upstairs. She shot Adam a look of disapproval but pasted on a kind smile for Raina.

"Dinner is almost ready."

Raina nodded. "Thanks. Sorry I didn't help. And that I fell apart."

"Happens to everyone," Lorelei said with a kind smile.

"I'm going to use the bathroom and wash my hands before we eat, then I can help you with anything else that needs to be done."

"Sounds great. Thanks, Raina." Lorelei kept her focus on Raina while she walked out of the room, but as soon as the bathroom door closed, Lorelei turned all her focus onto Adam. "What the fuck were you thinking?"

"I couldn't let her sit there," Adam confessed.

"It was hard for me, too, but—"

Adam looked at his partner and saw realization spread across her face. "Oh, Adam. No. Really?"

Adam shook his head. "It's nothing."

"I thought maybe you thought she was pretty, but I didn't know it was like that. Are you sleeping with her?"

"No. I know where the line is. She just... She's strong and brave and I know she's off-limits."

"Uh, yeah."

"Nothing is going to happen."

Lorelei eyed him carefully, her gaze narrowing before she turned back to whatever she was cooking for dinner. "If the situation were different, I wouldn't be against it."

Adam stumbled backward, nearly falling over the edge of the couch.

Lorelei turned and saw him and chuckled. "Don't look so surprised."

"You're as much of a robot as I am."

She scowled. "We have to be in this job. Getting involved means opening someone else up to being threatened. But she's already being threatened. I know it's against every protocol out there, but when you aren't being an ass and avoiding talking to her... I'm so stupid. That's why, isn't it? You don't hang out with her because you're in love with her."

"I'm not in love with her," Adam protested.

"Well, it seems as though—" Lorelei stopped. Her gaze went to the front door. "What was that?"

Adam shook his head. "I didn't hear anything."

Lorelei moved closer to the door, pulling her ever-present gun from her waistband. "Check the alarm. It sounded like someone's outside."

Adam pulled his phone from his pocket, but before he could open the app to see the cameras, a text came in from F-BOMB.

Intruder.

Get out.

Now.

6

———

Cold sweat broke out on Adam's back. He'd never been afraid before, not once, but it was different now. Everything was different now. Because of Raina. Because he cared. Because if something happened to her, he wouldn't be able to face himself in the mirror ever again.

He signaled to Lorelei, letting her know without words that she was right and they needed to go. Lorelei nodded toward the back of the house where Raina was still in the bathroom.

Adam swallowed the lump in his throat. It had been a while since Raina made any noise. Did that mean she'd already been taken? Did that mean—

She stepped out of the bathroom, and Adam nearly dropped to his knees with relief. She saw his face, and her eyes went wide.

Adam put a finger to his lips. Raina shook as she nodded, swallowing roughly.

Adam pointed to the kitchen. There were go-bags in the vehicle, but leaving meant abandoning everything else they had. Not that any of them had much, but it was hard to walk away knowing you'd never return.

Again.

Raina stayed down, crouching as she hurried through the living room. Adam opened the garage door, scanning the cavernous space with his eyes and his gun before he led Raina down the steps and to the SUV.

Adam pressed the button on the SUV to start it up, thankful F-BOMB had thought to give them an electric vehicle so whoever was prowling around outside wasn't alerted to their impending departure before they were gone.

Five seconds went by before Lorelei appeared at the doorway to the house. She looked behind herself once more, then slowly closed the door that led to the house. Adam knew it meant whoever was outside hadn't made it inside yet. Their escape was unknown to whoever it was trying to get to them.

Who was he kidding? They were trying to get to Raina. Not him. Not Lorelei. Raina was the one in danger.

Lorelei climbed into the backseat of the SUV with Raina, leaning over her to keep her head down and her body covered. Adam hit the button to open the door at the back of the garage. It was the first signal to anyone around that there was movement inside the house. And it wouldn't go unnoticed.

The door opened quickly, and as soon as it was up high enough, Adam hit the gas. He saw a figure, dressed in all white to blend in with the snowy landscape, coming around the corner of the house as he took off down what he hoped was the dirt path that headed straight for a gap in the trees.

Raina gasped, clearly seeing the same thing Adam did. Adam hit the button to close the garage, knowing it might not stop the person, but it was likely they would chase after the vehicle instead of trying to get access to the house.

A ping hit the back of the SUV. A bullet. Absorbed by the bulletproof vehicle. But no less deadly if it hit the right spot. Like a tire.

Adam swerved as Raina sucked in a breath. "He's shooting at us."

"Adam is going to get us out of here," Lorelei said. "Keep your head down."

Adam prayed the path through the woods was clear and visible as he turned onto it. If they got stuck, they'd be sitting ducks for the hell that was after them. He knew F-BOMB was on the way, likely along with the police and FBI, but until backup arrived, it was all up to him to get them the hell out of there.

Another bullet hit the vehicle, and a tree splintered and snow sprayed over the windshield with the next shot that missed them entirely. Adam didn't look back, just drove. Eyes focused on the snow-covered path that he could only hope would open onto the road and not lead them deeper into the darkening woods.

Branches scraped the sides of the vehicle, causing Raina to jump with each screech. Adam's nerves were shot, his knuckles as white as the snow that floated around them with each bump he hit in the rough road he flew down far too quickly.

Snow parted ahead. Darkness revealed a clearing.

The road.

Adam slowed his speed to make the turn back onto the main road. The packed snow and wet dirt beneath the tires sat lower than the pavement. They bounced wildly as the SUV climbed the few inches difference and slid, snow-caked tires spinning on the wet road before the treads cleared and caught.

Adam hit the gas again, glancing in his mirror for approaching headlights. When he didn't see any, he grabbed his phone from his pocket and handed it back to Lorelei. "Get in touch with them."

"Already on it," Lorelei said. She had the same contacts he did, and was alternating between texting and watching their six.

The speakers in the car rang loudly, making all three of them jump. Adam sucked in a breath and hit the button to connect the call. "Yeah."

"We're watching you. Take your next right."

"Copy." The voice belonged to Liam's boss, Daniel Dunn. As pissed as Adam was that someone got that close to them, he was grateful for the backup that was not only watching them but would be flooding the house in search of whoever was there.

"One-point-three miles, take a left," Dunn relayed.

"Any idea who that was?" Adam asked as he watched the odometer.

"Not yet."

"It was Damon," Raina whispered from the back.

Adam looked in the rearview mirror at her ghostly white face and fearful hazel eyes.

"Did you see him?" Lorelei asked.

Raina shook her head. "No, I mean, I couldn't see his face, but who else would it be?"

"It could have been someone looking for one of the people in our organization. Or it could have been random," Dunn said.

Adam snorted. "What are the chances of either of those?"

"Slim," Dunn admitted.

"Do you have someone going out there?"

"Ten-four," Dunn said. "Next left."

Adam slowed to make the turn and found himself in a neighborhood. "You sure this is right?"

"Yes. End of the street on the right."

Adam creeped forward, looking at the houses around him and wondering why in the hell there was a safe house in the middle of a neighborhood until he pulled in the driveway. The garage door was up and his cousin was standing at the edge of it.

"His request. We'll be in touch." Dunn hung up the phone as Adam parked the SUV in the garage.

Liam hit another button, and the garage closed behind them. He came around to the driver's door and opened it once the garage was closed. "You okay?"

"We're not injured, but I'm not sure okay is the right word," Adam answered honestly.

Liam nodded. He pulled Adam out of the vehicle and into a hug. He slapped Adam's back roughly, holding on a little longer.

The adrenaline faded from Adam and the realization of how close they came to death hit him. He shook for a minute before nodding and letting go of his cousin.

"Caite's got food and more is on the way," Liam said. He pointed to the door at the back of the garage, where a closed door sat.

Adam looked over at Lorelei and Raina. Raina looked like the only reason she was standing was because Lorelei was holding her upright. Adam went to them.

Lorelei nodded at him and went into the house with Liam, leaving Adam and Raina to follow them.

"Are you okay?"

She breathed a mirthless laugh. "Really?"

He shook his head and pulled her into his arms. Just for a minute, he told himself. Because she was scared. He was being a good person.

Raina held on. She trembled against him. A wet spot formed on his shirt from her tears.

He couldn't let go. The longer he held her, the more he wanted to. He knew it was a bad idea. Getting attached was dangerous. The proof of that was right there. He'd almost hesitated earlier when he got the text. Because he thought something might have happened to her.

But he still couldn't let go.

She finally drew a shuddering breath and pulled back slightly. "I'm sorry."

Adam brushed her hair back from her face and cupped her jaw. He wiped the tears lingering on her cheeks and tilted her face so he could look into her eyes. "You never have to apologize to me."

"But—"

"Never. I am here to keep you safe, and I know I already failed you once, but I will not let it happen again. I promise you."

Her breath hitched, but she nodded. She swallowed roughly, then glanced at the door where the others went. "We should go in. I'm sorry I kept you out here."

"You needed a minute. Everyone understands that."

She smiled weakly at him, then led the way into the house.

Adam hadn't been to Liam's house before, but he'd seen pictures. It was a simple house, neat and clean and definitely decorated by Caitlyn, Liam's girlfriend. They walked into a small mudroom where Adam kicked off the shoes he'd shoved his feet into before they ran for their lives. Raina didn't have shoes on.

The mudroom opened to a bright and welcoming kitchen with sky blue cabinets and black countertops and appliances. A wooden table sat on the far side of the kitchen with Lorelei, Liam, and Caitlyn around it.

Caitlyn jumped up when she saw them and came over. She winked at Adam and wrapped Raina in her arms. "I'm Caitlyn, and I am so sorry for what you're going through. I know a little, but this is just too much."

"Thanks," Raina whispered.

"Come sit. Do you want coffee? Tea? Food? Lorelei said she was making dinner when she heard the noises. Lily is coming with food and dessert, because she loves to bake. I think most of the team is coming." Caitlyn went into the kitchen to start a tea kettle, talking over her shoulder as she moved around the space.

Raina followed Caitlyn, smiling just enough for Adam to think she was okay.

Adam joined Lorelei and Liam at the table.

"Any word?" Adam asked.

Liam shook his head. "No one was there. There were tracks, so there's no question if someone was there, but they were long gone. Footprints led to tire tracks. They're going to see if they can get an idea of what kind of vehicle they might have been on, but for now, we just know someone tried to get in."

"What about the cameras? Did you get a look at him?"

Liam shook his head again and glanced at Lorelei. She winced, clearly knowing what was coming. "He was smart. Likely was there before or spent time looking at the place. Wore white to blend in and avoid cameras for a lot longer than we thought possible. We're guessing he might have been hiding in the woods for a little while, covered so the exterior of his snowsuit was cold and hid his heat signature longer."

"Then what the fuck are all your fancy toys for?" Adam growled.

"Trust me, I'm just as pissed as you."

"Really? Someone was shooting at you tonight?"

Liam pressed his lips together and shook his head.

"This whole thing is fucked up."

"Yeah, it is. But you guys are here. We have space to put you up for the night, and we'll work on a plan tomorrow."

"I told him they should go on the run," Lorelei said.

Adam shot her a glare that would have made most men cower in fear, but Lorelei was far stronger than any man Adam had ever known, and all she did was stare back at him.

"On the run?" Liam asked.

Lorelei shrugged. "A couple traveling would draw less attention than three people in a safe house. We're sitting ducks. And without knowing how long this is going to take, we're only going to draw more attention to ourselves over time. People notice things. They'll notice when no one leaves or when something is delivered. We don't go outside. The driveway is cleared, but you never see anyone. It's almost crazy it took as long as it did for someone to show up."

Liam looked between the two of them. "She's not wrong. I think you should consider it."

"Consider what?" Raina asked.

"The two of you pretending to be a couple and leaving town," Lorelei said.

Raina looked at Adam. Her eyes widened. She opened

her mouth to say something, but before she could, the door-bell rang.

"WHO'S THAT?" Raina blurted. All the fear she was working on pushing down rushed right back to the surface. Logically, she knew Damon wasn't going to show up and ring the doorbell. He wouldn't let anyone know he was there until he was already inside and had a knife to her throat.

But she was still scared. Terrified.

"That's Lily. She said she was going to bring food." Caitlyn squeezed Raina's shoulder on her way by and went to the front door.

Raina heard happy voices and a baby's gurgle before the door closed and locked and the two women and a little girl came back into the kitchen.

"This is Lily," Caitlyn said, carrying the bag of food that smelled like heaven to Raina's suddenly starving stomach.

Lily smiled at everyone. Her blue eyes were kind. She was curvy and instantly put Raina at ease with her friendly attitude and concern. "How are you?"

Raina shrugged, knowing no one would believe her if she said she was fine.

Lily nodded. "I get that. Want to hold the baby? She seems to make everything better."

Raina chuckled and accepted the little girl. She reached up and grabbed Raina's hair, holding on tight and tugging.

"Tessa," Lily scolded softly. She reached over and extricated Raina's hair from Tessa's grip. "Sorry. I'm developing a bald spot from her doing that. I think she's afraid someone's going to drop her."

"How old is she?" Raina asked.

"Seven months. She's trying to start crawling, but she's not quite there yet. I don't think I'm ready for that."

Raina chuckled. She always thought she'd have kids. She'd hoped for them when she was younger. But tomorrow wasn't certain for her at the moment, so there was a small part of her that was grateful she hadn't brought a child into the disaster her life had turned out to be.

Especially one with Damon. She'd thought she was pregnant once. It was the driving force behind her leaving him for good. She was wrong about the pregnancy, but she knew she couldn't stay any longer. That she couldn't risk herself and a baby.

"Do you have kids?" Lily asked.

Raina shook her head, staring into the blue eyes of the little girl.

"Are you hungry?" Caitlyn asked Raina, pulling her focus from the baby.

Raina's stomach answered for her with a loud rumble that made all of them chuckle.

"I agree," Lily said. "Archer was watching the house where you were tonight, so I was keeping myself busy by cooking. It's busywork for me. Distracting enough to make the time pass quicker."

"Don't let Lily fool you. She's an amazing cook," Caitlyn said.

Raina followed the women to the food lined up on the counter. Lily took Tessa back while Raina filled a plate with food. Some kind of pasta casserole loaded with meat and cheese, an entire tray of broccoli, and the softest bread Raina had ever had in her life.

Caitlyn and Lily followed right behind her and led her to the dining room where a bigger table allowed all of them to sit together. Lorelei, Liam, and Adam came in a minute later with their own food, and Raina remembered what Lorelei said before Lily showed up.

"Why do you think we should pretend to be a couple?" Raina asked Lorelei.

Lorelei glanced at Adam. He scowled in her direction, but he smoothed out his expression when Raina caught him. Lorelei turned her gaze to Liam, who looked far more approving of the idea.

When Lorelei met Raina's gaze, Raina braced for whatever Lorelei was going to say, but she was not prepared for the truth.

"A couple is irrelevant. No one notices or cares. The three of us together draws attention. Especially when we're in the house and no one leaves or comes in. Hiding draws attention."

"And you think being out in the open won't?"

"I think if your story is good, no one will think twice about it. Maybe change your appearance so you look a little different, but nothing major. We believe Street has a network he's using to track you. If you leave town, his reach won't be as comprehensive."

"We'll be safer."

Lorelei nodded. "I believe so, yes."

"I think she's right," Liam said. "We can maintain surveillance on you. Track your vehicle and phones, monitor your locations, but leaving the area will make it harder for Street to have eyes on you."

Raina looked at Adam. "You don't agree."

Adam held her gaze for a long moment. "It would leave us without anyone else if something happens. We'd be on our own without backup."

"But you promised you wouldn't let anything happen to me again."

"Yeah, I..." Adam nodded. "I did, and I meant that, but if Street—"

"If he finds us, I know you'll do everything you can to protect me."

"I would, yes."

"Then I think we should do it. Clearly, staying here isn't working. He's already found us twice. And leaving means getting out. Fresh air and sunshine and living for however long I have left."

"Raina..."

"No," she said sharply. "I don't want to die in a safe house. I don't want to die at all, but I sure as fuck don't want to die hiding from him where he's going to find me in just a few weeks. I want to live. See things. Enjoy my life. I'm going to be scared no matter what. I'm going to be looking over my shoulder until he's six feet under, and maybe after that, too. But I'm sick of being stuck in a safe house."

Adam looked like he was going to throw up. His face went pale, his lips twisted into a grimace.

Raina looked at Lorelei and Liam. "Is there someone else who can go with me?"

"What?" Adam barked.

Raina leveled him with a look that relayed exactly how she felt about his refusal. "You don't want to go, I do. They agree with me. You're outvoted. This is happening, and if you won't do it, I'll find someone else who will."

Adam scowled at her.

Everyone else in the room stayed silent, even baby Tessa. The tension in the room was thick. But Raina refused to back down.

"Fine," Adam said. "I'll do it."

Raina forced a sneer into a smile. "Gee, thanks."

Adam scowled again, looking like he'd rather do anything else.

That was just fine with Raina. She'd keep her distance from now on. She needed him to protect her. She didn't need him for anything else.

7

———

Adam didn't say much after he agreed to go on the run with Raina. It was a horrible idea. Being alone with her? The only thing that would do was wear down his resolve to keep his distance from her.

But he was out-voted. And fuck if he was going to let anyone else pretend to be the other half of a couple with her.

"We should all get some sleep," Lorelei said after too many hours of planning and talking and absolutely zero information about whoever had tried to get into the safe house. "We'll touch base with our bosses in the morning and finalize the plan from there."

Adam grunted his response, more than a little annoyed with his partner. Maybe if he was able to think clearly, he would have agreed with her about this plan, but clear went out the window when Raina walked in the door. Adam hadn't been able to focus on anything else. And now he was going to be the only one standing between Raina and the man who thought she was his and intended to kill her once he proved she was.

What the fuck was he thinking?

The others got up and moved toward the stairs that led to the second floor, where the bedrooms were. Adam knew there were three bedrooms upstairs, which meant two people would have to share if he followed the crowd.

"Are you coming?" Lorelei asked.

Adam shook his head. "There are only three bedrooms. I'll sleep on the couch."

Lorelei looked at Liam for confirmation. At his nod, she turned back to Adam. "I'll take the couch. You didn't get much rest today."

"I've been on nights. I'm good. I'm not tired enough to go to sleep yet, anyway." The lie slipped out easily. Adam choked back the yawn that tried to disprove it.

Lorelei looked closely at him, likely seeing through his deception, but she didn't call him on it. "Okay. Good night."

"Night," Adam said, waving to the others. He forced a smile as they all headed up the stairs.

Raina never looked back.

Adam listened to the sounds of the house, water running, toilets flushing, doors opening and closing before everything upstairs fell silent. He turned on the TV and lowered the volume, needing something to distract him before he got too wrapped up in what tomorrow would bring.

A pretend vacation with Raina pretending to be in love with him. He was so fucked.

The TV flickered and played a movie. One movie turned into another one, and Adam finally drifted to sleep. When the early morning light streamed through the gauzy curtains and shined on him, he woke up just as slowly as he fell asleep.

Until he remembered what his plan was for the day.

Adam used the downstairs bathroom and started the coffee. He didn't hear anyone up at night, but that didn't mean the others slept well. Adam rubbed his neck, trying to work out the kink caused by sleeping upright on the couch, and searched for coffee mugs.

"Creamer's in the fridge," Caitlyn said from the entrance to the kitchen.

Adam almost dropped his mug. He hadn't heard her come down the stairs. "Good morning."

She flashed him a smile. "I didn't mean to scare you. Years of neighbors who would complain about the sound of me walking taught me to be light on my feet."

"All good. Want a cup?" Adam offered her the mug he poured but hadn't drunk from yet.

"I'll get mine. Thanks for starting this. It's usually my first task of the day."

"Are you usually up earlier than Liam?"

She chuckled and shook her head. "No. Definitely not. But I didn't sleep well."

"I'm sorry we brought all this to your house. I didn't know where we were going until I pulled into the driveway."

Caitlyn shook her head. "I wouldn't have had it any other way. You and Lorelei are always welcome here, no matter who you're bringing with you."

Her gaze was a little too pointed for Adam's liking, so he just nodded and let it go.

Caitlyn didn't have the same idea. "So, you and Raina?"

Adam shook his head. "No. It's a job."

"So was Liam protecting me."

"It's not the same. There are rules."

"Love doesn't follow rules," Caitlyn said softly.

"FBI Agents do."

Caitlyn grinned widely at that. "Are you ready to pretend to be in love?"

Adam choked on the sip of coffee he just took. He set the mug down with a splash as he coughed up the liquid in his lungs. When he could breathe again, he cleaned the counter and the edges of his mug and turned back to a smug-looking Caitlyn. "You're cruel."

She laughed. "Just asking a question."

Adam chuckled with her, not admitting a thing.

They both turned when they heard footsteps on the stairs. Liam looked between the two of them, then made a beeline for Caitlyn. "You two good?"

"Yep," Caitlyn said. "Just talking about today. Adam's going to have an easy time pretending to be in love with Raina."

"Oh yeah? Why's that?" Liam asked. Even though he called Adam on his feelings for Raina, he was oblivious to the depth of those feelings.

"He's a really good agent," Caitlyn said smoothly. She lifted on her toes to kiss Liam. His hands dropped low on her waist and held her close while the two of them said good morning in a way that made Adam insanely jealous.

Not of either of them, but of what they had. He'd lost hope of finding love years ago. One failed relationship after another convinced him women couldn't handle the rigors of his job. The demands on his time and attention and the long hours or days where he wasn't available.

Liam had been through the same, but he not only found Caitlyn, but was making it work. They'd only been together a few months, but looking at them, it seemed as though they'd been in a relationship much longer.

Lorelei was next down the stairs, with Raina last to join the crowd. Caitlyn and Liam made breakfast for everyone, and a second pot of coffee. Lorelei waved Adam to the other room so they could check in with their boss.

"Morning." Assistant Special Agent in Charge Wellington Mooney wasn't a man who wasted a lot of words. The fact that they got a greeting at all was enough for them to exchange a glance.

"Morning, sir," Lorelei said. "We wanted to check in and give you an update on our situation."

"Are you on your way back to Boston?"

Lorelei gave Adam a questioning look. He shook his head. He didn't know what their boss was talking about, either.

"Boston? No, sir. We're still on the case."

"The case that's been dismissed by the judge? There is no case. I need you both back here."

"But sir—"

"Has there been a change in the situation? Has Damon Street been charged with anything new? Is there new evidence that has made a judge change their mind about the charges that were presented before?"

"Well, no, but—"

"Then there's no case. You're both needed back here. We have other things happening, and I need you."

Lorelei looked at Adam wildly. She wasn't ready to go anymore than he was.

Adam took the phone from her. "With all due respect, sir, we don't think we should be leaving right now. Someone tried to break into the safe house where we were staying yesterday. We believe it was Street and that the threat is still very much active."

"Did you see him?" Mooney asked.

Adam and Lorelei exchanged a glance, silently debating

lying to their boss. They both shook their heads before Adam said, "No, sir. But—"

"There's no case. I don't know how I can be more clear than that. If there are no charges brought against this guy, and no new evidence, then we have nothing. Look, I feel for the woman who was abused. I know how these things go, but I can't afford to loan my people to them indefinitely."

"I'd like to use my vacation time," Lorelei blurted. "Sir. I have enough to take the next month off."

Mooney sighed heavily through the phone.

"I'd like to do the same, sir," Adam heard himself say. Going back to work was the perfect excuse to get out of going on the run with Raina, but even as the thought passed through his mind, he knew he wouldn't let anyone else stay with her.

"Are you fucking kidding me? You two are willing to use all your vacation time to work on this case?"

Lorelei met Adam's gaze and shrugged. She was in. He nodded. He was, too.

"Yes, sir. We owe it to the woman we've been protecting. This man ordered a hit on my cousin. I can't walk away from this one. I have to see it through. We believe the judge who dismissed the case is working for Street's organization. The local PD and Adam's cousin's company are working hard on making the charges stick. I can't leave. Not yet." Lorelei's voice bordered on begging, but Adam knew it was genuine. She would take her vacation and not think twice, but if she could get permission to stay, it would be even better.

"You feel the same, Johnson?" Mooney barked.

"Yes, sir."

Mooney sighed heavily, a sound that came across as a groan. Papers shuffled, but neither Lorelei nor Adam dared say another word until their boss did.

"Fine. I'll approve another two weeks. After that, you'll have to use your vacation time if things aren't wrapped up, or unless there are charges that stick."

"Thank you, sir," they said together.

"I'll—"

"There's one more thing, sir," Lorelei said before he could dismiss them. She grabbed the phone from Adam and brought it closer so she could speak into it.

"What?"

"After the attempted break-in last night, we would like permission for Adam to go into hiding with our witness."

"Excuse me?" Mooney growled.

"This area is relatively small and very connected. We've learned Street has been operating here for decades. His reach is beyond what we imagined. We think he's been able to find us twice now because he has people everywhere. He can tell when a house is occupied but no one is leaving or entering. He can find ownership records. He has people helping him. If Adam and Raina go on the run, pretending to be a couple that's on a vacation, we think it'll be harder for Street to find them and they'll be safer."

Silence was the only answer they got back. The silence lasted so long, Adam started to wonder if their boss had hung up on them, but the phone was still counting the seconds of their call.

Adam looked at Lorelei, but she just shrugged. They waited, hoping Mooney would say something soon.

"Fine," Mooney finally snarled. "Two weeks for that, too. Then we need to have another conversation."

"Yes, sir. Thank you, sir," Lorelei gushed.

"Don't make me regret this."

"You won't, sir," Adam said, knowing that comment was for him.

"I better not. I'll be in touch." Mooney hung up before they could say anything else.

Lorelei let out a heavy breath, like she'd been holding it the entire conversation. "I thought he was going to refuse."

Adam nodded. "I'm a little surprised he didn't."

"He knows this is huge. Career-making huge. If he's being supportive of it, his name will be tied to it, even if he's not here."

"Probably true. But now we're on a clock."

"We've always been on a clock," Lorelei argued.

Her point was dead-on. They'd been racing Street since they arrived. And the clock never stopped ticking.

"We need to make a plan for you guys to go. And for you to get clothes," Lorelei said.

Adam nodded, knowing the only way the whole thing was going to work was if there was no plan. "Let's all talk for a few minutes."

They joined Liam, Caitlyn, and Raina in the kitchen. Adam nodded at Liam, letting him know all was good.

"Our boss approved Adam going with Raina, but he's only giving us two weeks to get things done. After that, he expects us to either have charges that stick or we have to use vacation time to stay here. We're both willing, but we all want this to be over," Lorelei said.

"Agreed." Liam met Adam's gaze. "You can't tell anyone where you're going."

"What?" Lorelei blurted.

"I was thinking that, too," Adam said.

"Why?" Raina asked.

"If anyone knows where we are or where we plan to go, Street could get it out of them," Adam said.

"No one would tell him anything," Raina argued.

"They might not have a choice," Liam said softly, looking

at Caitlyn. "If he tortures Caitlyn, she'll tell him everything. Hell, if he threatened me with her life, I'd tell him. People are human. When their lives are on the line, or the life of someone they love, they choose the threat right in front of them instead of the potential threat down the road. We're taught in the military to withstand that, but when I was in, the people I was fighting didn't have a gun to the head of the woman I loved. It's different."

Caitlyn went to him and wrapped her arms around his side. He kissed the top of her head and held her close.

Adam swallowed roughly. He agreed with Liam. If Street wanted information from Adam and was torturing Raina to get it, he'd sing like a canary.

"You're right, but I don't like it," Lorelei said. "We need a way to contact you."

"We have phones that are protected. They're linked to our network. The only way someone could find you or call you is if they were a part of our network," Liam said.

"That works," Adam said.

"What if I need to get in touch with him?" Lorelei asked.

"I assumed you'd be staying in the area with either Karli or one of us. We can give you a phone to stay in touch, or we can link you to our network," Liam said.

"I'm good with either. I haven't spoken to Karli, though. All of this has happened quickly. She doesn't even know we came here last night," Lorelei said.

"Let's get these two some stuff packed up so they can get on the road, then we'll get you to Karli's or to wherever you want to go," Liam said.

Lorelei agreed, and the focus of the room turned to Adam and Raina. F-BOMB had collected their things from the safe house and delivered everything overnight, so they had their clothes and suitcases. Everything was thoroughly searched to make sure no tracking devices were left in their stuff and all of it was clean.

The biggest problem was the clothes they had wouldn't last them for two weeks. Not without finding a place to do laundry. Adam was a little shorter and skinnier than Adam, but his clothes fit well enough for Adam to make it work. Caitlyn was shorter and a few sizes bigger than Raina, but the two of them found things Raina could pack for the trip. Caitlyn packed another bag for Raina of extra bathroom products, and Lorelei added a few things she had in her bag.

"What about the SUV?" Liam asked as they carried the suitcases into the garage.

Adam looked at it, remembering the shots it took the night before. "It's good, but the dings might draw attention."

The two of them circled the vehicle, examining the indents left behind by the bullets. Only two, but enough that it could be something noticeable.

"Let's go to the office and swap vehicles. We can drive this one around. We'll give you another one. Gas? In case you end up somewhere that doesn't have a charging port?"

Adam nodded. "Good idea. We need cards. I'd rather not have to go into every gas station up and down the East Coast to pay cash for gas."

"We have all that stuff at the office. Let's load up and we'll all go together."

Adam put his and Raina's suitcases into the trunk while Liam went inside to tell the women they were all leaving. Adam sat in front with Liam driving. The women talked in the backseat, carrying the conversation and giving Adam a break from having to engage.

At the F-BOMB office, Liam created IDs for them, including fake driver's licenses and credit cards that would charge back to F-BOMB for their transactions. The cards would go through multiple channels and were not easy to trace, but Liam also gave Adam a few thousand dollars in cash to avoid using the card everywhere.

"We will be able to follow you with the card purchases, but they'll be buried in our company purchases and not something anyone else can get into. It's the safest we can make things."

Adam nodded. "Thanks for your help with all of this. I thought the FBI had all the resources out there, but what you guys do here is next level."

Liam grinned. "The benefits of the private sector."

Adam chuckled. He tucked everything Liam gave him into the borrowed wallet he was going to use. All his and Raina's real identification would stay locked up in F-BOMB until they returned. No one wanted to risk someone seeing it and reporting back to Street.

"One last thing," Lorelei said, joining them in the office. "We need to change your look."

Adam groaned at the brown hair dye in her hand until he saw Raina right behind her, sporting rich auburn locks.

His feet carried him forward without his brain processing what he was doing. Liam cleared his throat before Adam made a fool of himself and dragged Raina down the hall and had his way with her.

This trip was a horrible idea.

But it was too late to do anything but buckle up and drive. And pray they came out of it alive.

8

———

Raina glanced sideways at Adam. The chestnut brown hair looked weird on him, but not bad. Just not what she'd gotten used to. Lorelei assured her the dye she used on them would stay for a few weeks but would eventually fade.

Raina picked up the ends of her red hair and looked at them. She'd always loved the natural highlights in her hair, but the rich red color was a bold statement she couldn't deny she liked. A lot. Maybe she'd do something more permanent next time.

If there was a next time.

Adam cleared his throat, drawing Raina's attention.

"I was thinking we could start in Pennsylvania. There are lots of places in the Poconos where we could lie low for a few days."

"Okay," Raina said. She didn't think she actually got a vote, and even if she did, it wasn't like it mattered. It wasn't a fun trip. It was anything but fun.

"Is there anywhere you want to go?" Adam asked.

Raina shrugged. "I'm not sure I really want to go somewhere I've been thinking of going."

"Street would know?"

Raina shook her head. "Bad mojo or whatever. If it's a place I have a desire to see, do I really want to go there under these circumstances?"

"Well, yeah, but—" Adam cut himself off mid-sentence, letting his *but* hang in the air between them.

"But what?" Raina prompted. She wanted to know what he was going to say.

"Nothing." Adam flashed her a strained smile.

"Not nothing. What were you going to say?"

He looked over at her. His face was pale, and it wasn't just a trick of the dark hair. He looked ghostly white.

"What?" she breathed, looking out the window behind her. She didn't see anyone or anything that would put that look on his face.

"Nothing."

"For fuck's sake, Adam, we have to pretend we're in love. We can't do that if you can't even finish a damn sentence. What were you going to say?"

He sighed heavily. He looked at her again, wincing when his gaze snagged on hers. "What if this is your only chance to see something you've always wanted to see?"

"Why... Oh." She knew what they were doing. She knew why they were there. She knew she might not make it through this alive. Hell, she just had the same thought. But hearing his doubts piled onto hers made her want to curl up on her side and give up entirely.

Her stomach twisted with the knowledge that she could be on her way out of New York State for the last time. She might never see Lorelei or Karli or Stacey, Francesca, or Jessica again.

Raina had always had a healthy sense of how limited a person's time on earth could be. Car accidents, health issues, random violence all took people every day. She knew they could get into an accident on their way to the first place Adam wanted to stop.

But none of that prepared her for being stalked by another human being. If Damon could be called human.

Raina fell silent, staring out the window as the landscape rushed past. Tears stung her eyes and rolled soundlessly down her cheeks. She felt Adam's gaze on her every so often, but he didn't say anything.

Miles passed and hours faded by. Adam stopped for gas and went through a drive-thru for lunch. He stayed behind the wheel, not speaking to her as he carried her away from the only place she'd ever wanted to call home.

Growing up in Milwaukee, Raina loved being near the water and had a good childhood. When she went to college in Dayton, Ohio, she saw the beautiful variety the world had to offer and craved more of it. Moving to an international city like Niagara Falls gave her everything she wanted and more. She loved the excitement of the city, the people she met, and the circle of friends she'd found, especially when she reconnected with Karli.

Damon took so much of that away. He poisoned Raina and the city she'd grown to love. But she broke free from him and the hold he had on her. She was starting to live her life again. She was starting to believe she could have one.

But Damon wasn't done with her. And he was making it clear he never would be.

Raina hated him with a burning fire she never knew she could possess. She ached to see him dead. To know he could never hurt her or anyone else ever again. And even as she knew that was the answer, she craved another choice. Hatred was what made Damon. Hatred was born from fear, something Raina saw over and over again with her clients.

It had been more than a year since she'd worked as a massage therapist, but she still remembered the feel of a person's fear, hatred, and pain dissipating beneath her fingertips. She'd trained in Reiki and would incorporate some of those techniques with clients she felt were in need of more than a simple manipulation. It always ended with them in tears and confessing they were dealing with something major. Something they hadn't been able to deal with until Raina put her hands on them.

She loved helping people through their healing process. Walking away from the career she loved was an easy choice at the time. Damon convinced her to rely on him exclusively. He told her he wanted to spend more time together, and he promised to take care of her. She thought they were heading toward marriage at the time, and agreed.

It wasn't long before things changed and she realized just how wrong she'd been about him.

Through all of it, Raina still thought of Niagara Falls as home. She still wanted a life there, a future. But before she could have that, she had to survive.

"We're here," Adam said softly.

Raina looked up and realized they were parked in front of a large house with a sign above the porch that welcomed them to Cooke's Bed and Breakfast.

"It's cute," she said, forcing down the dread that had become her constant companion on the drive.

"We can go somewhere else. If you're used to—"

"It's fine," she said quickly. She avoided looking at him by getting out of the SUV and walking to the back to get her suitcase.

Adam grabbed for his own suitcase and the bathroom bag, setting the smaller one on top, then closing the trunk. He held out a hand for Raina to walk ahead of him.

She opted for the ramp instead of lifting their suit-cases up the stairs in the front. The place was charming, with its wide front porch and cheery colors. The sunny yellow trim was a unique touch, but worked perfectly with the dark blue color of the house. The front door was the same bright yellow color. Wind chimes hung on each corner of the porch, a light breeze making them tinkle with a subtle, joyful sound that lifted the edges of Raina's lips.

She opened the front door and was immediately hit with the warmth of the inside and the powerful scent of choco-late chip cookies. It smelled like a home and felt welcoming and safe. Her shoulders sank in instant relief.

Adam followed her through the door, thanking her for holding it for him. He led the way to the small desk to the right, reaching it just as the swinging door behind the desk opened and revealed a woman with a gray bun and sharp brown eyes. A dark-skinned man with kind brown eyes and a bulk to him that added to the safe feeling Raina had upon entering.

"Welcome to Cooke B&B," the woman said brightly. "I'm Norma, and this is my husband, Tom. We're the owners, and we're so happy you stopped by our little slice of heaven. How can we help you?"

Adam smiled at them both, then launched into their cover story. "I'm Mark, and this is Lisa. We were hoping you might have a room for a few nights."

"Of course we do. This time of year, people go to the big ski resorts and forget all about little places like this. Are you two not skiers?"

Adam glanced at Raina, silently asking the question.

Raina stepped forward and plastered on a smile. "We're actually honeymooners. We eloped over the weekend and decided to just drive around and make our own adventure of the trip."

"Honeymooners?" Norma said, her smile slipping. "I never would have guessed. Usually honeymooners are all over each other and can barely get a word out for all the kissing."

"Norma," Tom warned in a low voice.

Norma waved him off and didn't even glance his way. Tom flashed Raina and Adam an apologetic smile before Norma jumped right back in.

"All I'm saying is you two look more like siblings than lovers. I was going to ask if you needed one room or two, but I guess if you're lovers, you only need one. We have a very nice room with a king bed and a hot tub for two. All our rooms have private bathrooms, of course. Will that room suit you?"

"Sounds lovely," Raina said. "We'll take it."

Adam merely grunted.

Raina glared subtly at him, but not subtly enough. Norma caught the look as she slid the reservation form across the desk. Adam grabbed it and ignored the look from Raina.

"You two had a fight, didn't you? That's why I didn't catch the sexual energy between you. Oh, now, sit in the hot tub and remember why you got married. Tom and I have been married for forty-three years. When we first got together, it wasn't easy. None of it had been easy, but communication is the key. We have six kids, and we have had more than our fair share of fights, but the makeup sex is always worth the temporary inconvenience of a spat, isn't it?" Norma waggled her brows, and Adam coughed loudly.

"Of course," Raina said, feeling her cheeks heat. Just the thought of sex with her had Adam ready to run if his grunt was a hint. They needed to get to their room and stay there for a while so Norma and Tom didn't get suspicious.

"Give them the keys, darlin'," Tom said softly.

"Oh, right. So, the room is on the top floor. You two look young and healthy enough to be able to handle some stairs. Tom will take your luggage up for you, if you'd like. You've missed dinner, but there are a few places open not far from here if you'd like a recommendation, or if you'd like us to order food in for you so you can focus on making up."

Adam let out another strangled cough, but Raina refused to look back at him.

"We can go get something. Thanks, though."

"Okay, if you're sure. Breakfast is in the room across the way from seven to eleven every morning. We know some people like to stay in bed a little later in the morning, so we're ready when you are. The breakfast menu is on every table. Everything is unlimited and included with your stay, but is cooked to order. If you're in a hurry, we have some grab and go options, but as you two are here for your honeymoon, I imagine you'll just be heading back to your very private room after you refuel."

"Norma," Tom groaned.

"There are a ton of adorable shops in the area, and we have some great activities if you come up for air long enough to join us. When you decide how long you'll be staying, let me know. Check out is noon, and if you don't check out, we'll assume you're staying another night." Norma paused long enough to look at Tom. "Is there anything I've forgotten?"

"God, no. I think you've embarrassed these two enough for one night."

Raina chuckled with Tom and liked his kindness and

care for his wife. One day, Raina hoped she'd find a man like that.

"They're not embarrassed. No need for that. Once they make up and find their footing, they'll be all over each other and no one will question their story."

Raina sucked in a breath but plastered on her best smile. Adam was deathly silent.

"Keys, Norma," Tom warned.

"Oh! That's right. When you two come back down to go to dinner, I'll give you a few suggestions. Some places close on Monday night, but I'll call ahead and make sure you can get a table so you don't have to wait."

"Thank you. You're very kind," Raina said. She grabbed the handle of her suitcase and turned toward the stairs.

Adam took the key and waved off Tom's offer to help carry things upstairs.

Raina led the way, puffing by the time she got to the second floor. Being stuck in a safe house and before that being in a shelter didn't do much for her physical endurance.

Adam was barely breathing harder than normal. When Raina stopped in front of the door to their room, he looked like he rode an elevator instead of carrying two bags up two flights of stairs to the third floor.

Adam unlocked the door and held it open for Raina to go in first. She flipped the first light switch she saw. The entire room lit up.

"Holy cow," she breathed.

They were in the honeymoon suite. No doubt about it with the sensual look and feel to the room. A dark wood, four-poster bed was on an elevated platform against one wall. Gauzy white fabric hung between the posts. The bed was covered in crisp, white sheets and a comforter that sported red stitching around the edges in a decorative pattern.

The other furniture in the room was the same dark wood as the bed and subtle in the way it was arranged around the room so as not to intrude on the primary focus of the room.

Sex. The room was all about sex. Sex Raina and Adam would not be having. Not in the bed, and definitely not in the hot tub.

The hot tub was positioned under the window, empty but inviting nonetheless with the deck full of unlit candles and a basket that held bubble bath and bath salts and condoms. Lots and lots of condoms.

The door slammed behind her, snapping Raina back to the present. If they actually were on their honeymoon, it would have been an amazing place to stay. A table with two club chairs sat in one corner of the room next to a mini-fridge and microwave. Perfect for late night energy replenishment sessions. That they weren't going to have.

Raina needed to stop thinking about sex and Adam. He was protecting her. Nothing more.

She wheeled her suitcase across the room to set it near the hot tub, then turned to look at him.

His gaze was locked on the bed. Shocked, like he expected there to be more than one of them in the room they were sharing under the guise of being married.

Raina opened her mouth to tell him she would sleep on the floor when Adam's gaze slid to hers. She stopped at the raw hunger she saw there.

"Adam?" she whispered.

He continued to stare at her, his gaze lingering over her body like he was using his hands instead of his eyes.

Raina's nipples perked up, and her thighs clenched. She

couldn't remember the last time a man looked at her the way he was. Damon had wanted to possess her, but Adam's gaze said he wanted to worship her. To strip her bare and love her all night.

Adam sucked in a breath, his chest rising sharply like he hadn't been breathing and was at risk of collapsing if he didn't let the air into his lungs at that moment. The move snapped their eye contact. He blinked rapidly. Shutters fell over his eyes, and he once again looked at her with that same distant, vacant look he usually gave her.

Then he turned and walked into the bathroom, locking the door without a word.

Well, then. Yet again, Raina was learning exactly where she stood with him. On the other side of the door and not in that warm look he'd let her see for just a minute.

It was better that way. She wasn't a good bet. And getting involved was a bad idea.

When Damon was dead and Raina was free, then she could think about dating again. Until then, her protector was off-limits. All men were off-limits.

She needed to remember that when she was pretending to be in love with him or Damon wouldn't be the only threat she faced.

9

———

Dinner out of the room built for sex was the reprieve Adam needed from the ache that settled in his gut. All he could think when he saw that bed was how many ways he could get Raina to come for him. But he wasn't allowed to touch her.

Except for when he was pretending to be in love with her.

Fuck him. This was why he refused this ridiculous idea when Lorelei suggested it. And she knew! He told her he was attracted to Raina, practically admitted he was halfway in love with her, and Lorelei still told Liam and Raina about her half-cocked idea and trapped him into following through with it.

Because there was no fucking way he was going to let someone else pretend to be Raina's new husband. Fuck that.

So, he held her hand when they walked down the stairs and past their suspicious hosts and out the door to the SUV. He opened Raina's door and smiled at her when she met his gaze with her unsure one. And he put his hand on her back to lead her into the restaurant.

He thought it would be safe when they sat down and picked up their menus. It should have been safe. Fucking small towns.

"You must be Mark and Lisa. Norma called and said to be on the lookout for you. Newlyweds? Congratulations! I'm Wendy."

"Hi, Wendy," Raina said with a bright smile. "Everyone is so nice here."

Wendy chuckled, her plump figure shaking with her laughter. She had gray hair tucked back into a neat ponytail. Her blue plaid dress was covered with a white apron that made her look like she belonged in a set from the 1950s. "It's part of the charm of the town. We like to make sure visitors know we're happy they're here. Our little town couldn't support itself if people didn't come here to visit."

"Well, we're happy to be here. What do you recommend for dinner?" Raina glanced back down at her menu, ignoring Adam entirely.

It didn't bother him. Not at all.

"The pork chop dinner is a real favorite. Spaghetti parm is another one people love. If you're a steak fan, we have a fabulous ribeye, too. Our sides are the best. Real comfort food here." Wendy tapped Raina's menu with the end of her pencil. "I can give you two a few minutes to check everything out while I grab some drinks. We don't have champagne or anything that fancy, but we have sparkling wine."

Raina looked over at Adam, a question in her eyes. Was she asking permission?

"I'll just take a water," Adam said, his strained voice barely kinder than a grumble.

"I'll take sparkling wine, please," Raina said, sliding a glare toward Adam before she focused on Wendy again.

Wendy clucked. "You two. Some good food will get you

back to right. Norma said you seemed like you were fighting. Still at it, I see. But you won't be able to stay mad about anything after we feed you. I'll be right back with those drinks."

Wendy walked away, stopping to talk to half the restaurant on her way.

Adam turned his focus back to his menu but caught Raina staring at him. "What?"

"You need to get over whatever this is," Raina hissed. "I know I'm the last person you want to be here with, but you agreed."

Adam held her glare for a long moment, warring with himself. If he told her the reason he didn't want to be there, it would mean crossing a line he couldn't uncross. He couldn't do it. "Fine."

She sucked in a sharp breath. Shock? Definitely not what she expected him to say. She lowered her gaze to her menu and lifted the edge, blocking her face from his view.

Adam sighed and lifted his menu. He needed food. And sleep. That was it. Everything would be better after they had both.

Wendy came back with drinks and took their orders. She gave Raina an extra look, but Raina shook her head subtly. Enough for Wendy to not ask anything else before she glared hard at Adam.

Fuck.

Adam's mood plummeted even further as Raina sat across from him and avoided his gaze. She smiled at Wendy and spoke to her as though they were old friends, but when she wasn't there, Raina was silent. Angry. Hurt.

Adam wanted to say something that would fix it, but he knew anything he said would not fix things. It would make it worse.

They ate their dinner, and he paid the bill with cash, leaving Wendy a large tip and thanking her for the hospitality. Raina repeated the same thanks and promised they'd come back.

The ride back to the B&B was silent. Adam kept his distance from her on the walk up to their room. Before the door even slammed shut, Raina was on her way to the bathroom, leaving Adam alone in the room with his frustration and anger.

He blew out a steadying breath and tried to calm his racing heart. He didn't want to hurt Raina, but getting involved with her wouldn't be good for either of them. Aside from not knowing if she was even interested in him, Adam knew he could get fired for sleeping with her. And he could be putting them both at risk.

Raina stayed in the bathroom for ten minutes. Adam thought about knocking on the door, but he decided to set up the room while she was on the other side of the door. He opened the closet and found an extra blanket and pillow. His options were limited, but the floor seemed to be the best one.

He laid out the blanket and pillow near the table in the corner, figuring it would give Raina plenty of room to walk around and not worry about tripping over him. He opened his suitcase and was just grabbing shorts and a tee to sleep in when the bathroom door opened.

Adam spun to face her, his gut clenching when he saw her puffy eyes and splotchy face.

"Are you okay?"

She scoffed and glared at him, not answering.

"Raina?"

"What? What do you want me to say, Adam? I'm on the run because my psycho ex is trying to kill me, and I'm stuck with a man who can't even have a conversation with me, let alone pretend he likes me. This is never going to work. We haven't fooled anyone. They think we're fighting because you can't stand being here. I should have just gone with Lorelei. At least it wouldn't be hard to pretend we like each other."

Adam growled.

"See? That's what I'm talking about. You grunt and growl and snarl at me. No actual words."

"I'm..." Adam inhaled slowly and let it out even slower. "I'm sorry. I promise, my behavior is not because I don't like you."

"Could have fooled me," she mumbled. "I'm tired. I need sleep. Are you sleeping on the floor?"

Adam looked at the blanket he laid out and nodded. "Yeah. I figured that was for the best."

Raina stared at his blanket for a long moment, then shook her head. "Whatever." She grabbed clothes from her suitcase and the bag full of toiletries, then returned to the bathroom.

Adam debated waiting for her, but after how long she took last time, he figured he could change right there and it wouldn't be a big deal. He shoved his jeans down and stepped out of them, quickly stepping into his shorts. He stripped off his shirt and bent to reach for the new one when he heard the bathroom door open and Raina gasp.

Her gaze was locked on his chest, trailing lower. The hunger in her eyes was enough to send a jolt to his dick. She licked her lips.

Adam growled, his hunger ramping up fast to match hers.

She looked up at him, raw need in her gaze. Her nipples hardened beneath the thin tank top she'd changed into.

Adam took a step toward her, but Raina sucked in a breath and braced herself. She didn't want him. She was surprised, not turned on.

Adam walked past her to the bathroom and closed the door softly, resisting the urge to slam the door and let out his anger. He was not thinking clearly. And he was taking it out on her. It wasn't fair.

He used the bathroom and brushed his teeth. He wasn't ready to face Raina, but he had no choice.

Turned out he didn't need to worry. She was in the bed with the covers pulled up to her chin, eyes closed. One light was still on near his side of the room, but everything else was dark.

Adam turned off the light and settled on his too thin blanket on the too hard floor for too little sleep. But at least Raina was comfortable.

Raina's nightmares didn't stop just because she was in the same room as someone else. She hoped they would, but when she woke up with her heart pounding and sweat beading all over her body, she knew that hope was useless.

In her dream, Damon found her and Adam and tortured Adam while he forced Raina to watch. Then he killed Adam and was coming toward Raina when she woke up.

It took her a minute to figure out where she was when she woke up. Adam's soft snores told her she didn't wake him, which was good, but it also meant she was dealing with the nightmares on her own.

When she had a nightmare in the safe house, she would leave her room and talk to Lorelei, if she was up. But trapped in the B&B with Adam meant she was even more alone than she'd been before.

"What's wrong?" Adam's voice came through the darkness.

Raina gasped and jumped. "I thought you were asleep."

"You made a noise. I thought you were having a dream."

"I was."

"What was it about?" Adam asked.

Talking to him in the darkness felt different. Safer. Easier. And Raina found herself replying. "Damon found us. He tortured and killed you and was coming after me."

Adam was silent for a long moment, long enough that Raina wondered if he fell back to sleep. Then he spoke. "I'm sorry. Have you had a lot of nightmares?"

"Almost every night," Raina admitted softly.

"Shit. Why didn't you tell me?"

"Lorelei knew."

Adam sucked in a breath. "Because you're friends."

Raina laughed mirthlessly. "No. Because she talks to me. She asked how I was doing."

He was quiet again. "I'm sorry you're stuck with me."

Now it was her turn to be silent.

"I know you didn't want this."

"I don't want any of this. I wanted Damon to stay behind bars. To not be free ever again."

"I know," he whispered.

"Why did you agree to go with me when you clearly don't want to be here?"

He sighed heavily, and Raina held her breath. She wanted the answer, but she wasn't sure it was something she was ready to hear.

"Under normal conditions, we would keep a witness in custody and take turns protecting them. Your situation is different. After last time Street found us..." Adam broke off and was silent for a minute. "I would never forgive myself if anything happened to you."

"Damon is clever and far more capable than any of us ever imagined. He knows things it shouldn't be possible for him to know. I don't blame you for him getting into the safe house before."

"I do," Adam snapped. "Maybe not for him getting in, but definitely for him getting his hands on you. He never should have touched you."

The fiery passion Adam spoke with made Raina's body flash with heat. "I chose to be with him."

"And you chose to walk away. No one has the right to force another person into a relationship. Into anything."

"Damon doesn't see it that way."

"He's fucking wrong. You don't owe him anything. And he is never going to touch you again if I have anything to say about it."

Raina chuckled softly. "Thank you."

"I mean it," he said, shifting and drawing her gaze. "I will die before I let him touch you ever again."

Raina's heart clenched at both the fear that swept through her and the passion in his voice. "I'm sorry you got roped into this assignment."

"I'm not. I wouldn't trust anyone else to keep you safe. Or be able to stand knowing some other agent was allowed to touch you and pretend they were in love with you."

"Clearly it doesn't require a lot to do that. You've barely touched me."

"And I'm sorry for that," he whispered. "I don't want to make you feel uncomfortable. We should have talked about it."

"About what?"

"About boundaries and limits. Where and how you are comfortable with me touching you."

Raina swallowed roughly. Even without seeing Adam, the conversation left the air thick with tension and lust. Or maybe that was just for her. He seemed to be perfectly fine.

"I... I don't know. I guess I never thought about any of it."

"We might have to kiss," he said, his voice dropping lower.

She inhaled sharply. "Okay."

"I should hold your hand when we're out. And touch you. Liam and Caitlyn are always touching each other."

Raina chuckled. "So are Karli and Cade."

"I don't want people to get suspicious. We need to convince them we're in love so we're invisible."

"I agree," she whispered. Her heart was in her throat. Pretending to be in love with Adam was becoming less and less of a challenge, even with him being distant.

"Should we practice?" he asked.

"Now?" she squeaked.

He chuckled softly. "It doesn't have to be now. Maybe after you get a little more sleep."

Raina looked toward the window. No light shined around the edges of the curtains. It was still the middle of the night. "Probably a good idea."

"Okay."

"Okay," she said. She smiled to herself and turned over. She was going to kiss Adam when she got up. It was going to be a good day.

WHY DID he think it was a good idea to practice kissing Raina? God, he was stupid. Kissing her would only make everything worse.

He blamed his lack of sleep and even greater lack of blood to his brain when he suggested it. Thinking with his dick when he was tired always led to bad decisions. But this was one of his worst.

Raina walked out of the bathroom after her shower, a billow of steam following her. She was wrapped in a white towel that barely came together at the ends.

He was going to fucking die if those ends separated and gave him a flash of even more skin than he saw from her long, curvy legs and bare shoulders. The towel was tucked around her full breasts.

Adam was sure he stopped breathing. He definitely stopped thinking. All his blood headed south. Again.

"Sorry," she said with a blush. "There's no fan in there and I couldn't seem to dry my body off. There's also only two towels. I'll go back in and finish getting dressed in a minute."

"No—" Adam cleared his throat so the rest of his words didn't sound like he was being strangled. "No problem. Take your time."

She smiled at him again. It was the first time she'd smiled at him. In weeks of living together. They'd spent more time together than Adam had spent with anyone else besides Lorelei in years, and Raina barely smiled at him the entire time.

He knew she was scared, but after their talk last night, he knew there was a lot more to it. It was him. It was the way he'd chosen to keep his distance from her that made her think he didn't like her.

He had to make sure she knew that wasn't the case.

Raina swung the bathroom door open and closed a few times, puffing the overheated air out of the bathroom until she ducked back in and closed the door.

Adam scrubbed a hand over his face and told himself they were just pretending. It wasn't real. She didn't want him. But he had to put on a show.

When Raina left the bathroom dressed for the day, Adam took his turn in the shower, letting his body enjoy the look of Raina in her towel for a few minutes while he stroked himself to a silent orgasm.

He finished his shower quickly and groaned when the bathroom was full of steam again. He opened the door, stepping out like she did with a towel tucked around his waist.

"They really need a fan in there," he said with a sheepish grin.

Her gaze went to his bare chest. She nodded absently.

"Then again, they probably think most of the people who stay in this room are either showering together or not bothering to close the door."

Raina's gaze snapped to his with his words. The blush on her cheeks darkened. "You're probably right. I never thought of that."

Adam thickened behind the towel with her gaze locked on his. If he wasn't careful, his dick was going to be making an appearance between the edges of his towel.

Adam cleared his throat and went back to the bathroom, waving the door like Raina had, then changing into jeans and a long sleeve tee for the day. When he walked out of the bathroom, Raina was sitting on the edge of the bed. His blanket and pillow were folded up and back in the closet so housekeeping didn't see them on the floor.

"Are you ready for breakfast?" Adam asked.

Raina nodded and stood. "Before we go, should we...?"

Adam inhaled quickly. He knew what she was asking, even without the way she was staring at his lips.

Adam nodded and moved toward her. "Are you sure about this?"

Raina shrugged. "It's not like we really have a choice. We're pretending to be newlyweds. We could have said siblings."

"This is much more believable."

Raina nodded and licked her lips. The slickness was a temptation Adam couldn't resist. He stepped in front of her, close enough that she had to tilt her head back to meet his gaze.

He cupped her neck, his fingers diving into her damp, silky hair. His heart pounded, tension filling the moment. His cock lifted, checking out the situation as desire swamped Adam.

Then he leaned forward and pressed his lips to Raina's and everything changed.

She sucked in a breath at the first contact of their lips. The sharp intake parted her lips, giving Adam access to slip his tongue into her mouth. Raina's hands slid up his chest, grabbing hold of his shirt and pulling him closer.

Her tongue tangled tentatively with his, both of them cautious as teenagers for their first kiss, with the knowledge of adults running underneath the experience.

Adam's other arm snaked around Raina's waist and hauled her closer. Their heads tilted together, like they planned the move ahead of time.

Adam swept his tongue through her mouth, loving when she moaned softly and gave it right back to him, teasing him and tasting him the same way. Her body was warm and lush, cradling his as they both got lost in a pretend kiss that felt far from fake.

A noise outside the room made them jump apart, both panting and staring at each other. Adam's hand stayed on her waist, and one of her hands was still on his chest.

"Ready for breakfast?" he asked, his voice rough and strained.

She nodded, looking brighter and lighter than she had in days.

He opened the door for her, resting his hand on her back as she walked out the door ahead of him. She looked up at him. It was different. Everything was different.

But at the moment, different was good. Damn good.

10

———

Raina looked back at Adam as she walked down the stairs in front of him. She didn't expect the connection she felt with him when they kissed. She thought it would be good, but good didn't even come close to that kiss.

That kiss was electric, magnetic, powerful. It was like sticking her finger in a socket and keeping it there after the jolt that should have sent her flying across the room.

"There they are!" a woman's voice bellowed from below.

Raina lost her footing, swinging around to see who was speaking. Before she tumbled down the steps, Adam caught her around her waist and hauled her against him.

And his very hard body.

"You okay?" he whispered.

She nodded, righting her feet under her as she tried to stop her cheeks from burning under his far-too-close appraisal.

"We were starting to wonder if you two were going to stay in your room all day long. Figured you'd need to refuel at some point." Norma. Their gracious, and nosy, host.

"We were just enjoying the morning," Adam said

without missing a beat. "You said breakfast was until eleven. We didn't realize we were late."

"Breakfast is until eleven," Tom said, stepping forward and gently nudging Norma out of the way. "You're welcome to sit wherever you like. Coffee and water are on the sidebar with pastries. We'll give you a minute to get settled. Hot breakfast is made to order, and I'll be happy to cook up anything you like."

"Thank you," Adam said, gently steering Raina toward the coffee and away from Norma.

He poured coffee for both of them and fixed Raina's while she looked at the pastries and grabbed them both ice water. They met at a table and sat, picking up the menu of breakfast options.

Raina's stomach growled as she read over the list. She wanted all of it. Tossing and turning and trying not to think about sex with her protector burned a lot of calories.

"Hungry?" Adam asked with a smirk.

Raina rolled her eyes at him. "More than I should be."

"Eat up. We're going to burn some more calories later."

Raina gasped at his blatant comment and wondered where in the hell it came from. They kissed, and it was good, but—

"Now that's more like what I'd expect from newlyweds," Norma said from right behind Raina. "I see you two made up."

Adam lifted Raina's hand and kissed her palm, then trailed his lips down to her wrist. He nodded, his gaze locked on Raina's.

Raina's entire body heated under his approving smile. He was good. So good she almost forgot they were pretending.

"I have never been able to stay mad at Lisa for long,"

Adam said smoothly, dropping her fake name into the conversation.

And dropping her back into reality.

Raina pasted on a smile as fake as her name and flashed it toward Norma. "Mark is a charmer. Always has been."

Norma grinned and clapped her hands. "Oh, you two. I knew that room would force you to get back to the reason you came on this trip. I tell you, when you walked in the door, I was sure you were going to need two rooms. And I sure as heck didn't think you were lovers. But this is better. You look like you like each other now."

"We definitely like each other," Adam said easily.

"Norma," Tom growled as he came out of the kitchen. "Are you harassing these two again?"

"I was just telling them it's good they made up. I'd hate to imagine them not taking advantage of that huge bed. Oh, and the hot tub. You have to try that out. Rumor has it lots of babies have been conceived in that tub. We have it cleaned thoroughly between guests. Don't worry about that. Everything here has the best level of cleanliness. When we're talking about swapping fluids—"

"Norma!" Tom barked.

Raina almost choked on her coffee.

Adam looked like he wanted to crawl under the table.

Norma rolled her eyes. "Bunch of prudes. They're on their honeymoon, my love. They need to know that room is safe for them. That they can use every single surface in the room and do not have to worry about anything."

"Dear Lord, woman, stop embarrassing them. Poor girl's cheeks are so red she looks sick. Let me cook them breakfast so they can go on about their day." Tom focused on them and smiled. "Would you like me to cook something? Or has my wife run you off already?"

Adam looked at Raina for her to order first. She cleared her throat. "Pancakes," Raina choked out.

"Chocolate chip, banana, blueberry? Or plain, of course."

"Chocolate chip please."

"Got it. Bacon, sausage? Side of scrambled eggs?"

"Sure," Raina said.

Tom grinned, his dark brown eyes sparkling with delight. "You got it. And for you, Mark?"

Adam looked taken aback for a second, but he recovered quickly and ordered a strawberry banana waffle with bacon, sausage, and scrambled eggs.

Tom dragged Norma to the kitchen with him. Raina smiled at them, catching Tom pulling Norma into his arms as the door swung. "They're sweet."

"They're dangerous," Adam whispered.

"What do you mean?"

"They pay too much attention."

"That's what it's like at places like this. Part of the appeal."

"I wasn't expecting him to remember my name."

"Have you never stayed at a place like this?"

Adam shook his head. He took a sip of his coffee and reached for Raina's hand. He wound their fingers together. "We need to keep up appearances, even when we think they aren't watching."

Raina nodded and tried not to let the ruse get to her. She knew what she was getting into. Just because she had a crush on her protector, and felt like she'd been lit on fire when she kissed him, didn't mean anything.

Tom brought their breakfast back out after a little while, and they ate while talking about pretend plans for the day. The only thing they really had to do was get in touch with the team and make sure there was no chatter about their location.

Raina groaned at her first bite of her pancake. It was perfectly fluffy and loaded with chocolate chips. The buttery flavor and sprinkle of powdered sugar on top were delicious.

"Good?" Adam asked, his voice strangled and strained.

Raina looked up at him. His gaze was on her lips. She licked, catching a smear of chocolate.

He shifted in his seat and swore under his breath.

"You okay?"

"Not even a little bit. How's your food?"

"Amazing. How's yours?"

He cut off a piece of his waffle and popped it into his mouth. He nodded, then groaned the same way she had.

It was her turn to stare. His tongue darted out to lick a droplet of butter trying to race down his chin. He chewed and nodded, then swallowed and met her gaze.

They locked eyes. Raina wondered how in the hell breakfast was sexy, but at that moment, it was.

"How is everything?" Tom asked, breaking into their private moment.

"Excellent," Adam said without looking up from Raina.

"Great to hear. Enjoy." Tom walked away. Whispers from the kitchen were answered by Tom's sharp reply that Raina couldn't hear but understood clearly.

Don't interrupt.

Raina stabbed another bite of her pancake and lifted it over the center of the table, silently offering it to Adam.

He looked from the fork to Raina, then leaned in and claimed the bite she offered. He groaned again, then offered her a bite of his waffle.

Raina leaned forward, her gaze locked on Adam's as she

closed her lips over her fork. His gaze dropped to mouth, then slid back to her eyes.

The bright blue of his eyes was navy, dilated with desire.

Raina shifted in her seat, feeling that desire between her thighs.

They ate silently, sharing their food and devouring it quickly. As one, they rose from the table and hurried toward the stairs, anxious to disappear.

"Are you doing any exploring today?" Norma asked before they were able to escape to the room she gave them. The room designed for sex. The room she was currently keeping them from.

"Later," Adam growled.

"There's a lot to do around here. If you want some ideas, feel free to ask us. We'd be happy to point you in the right direction of whatever suits your fancy."

Adam stopped, his foot hovering over the bottom step. Raina jerked to a halt next to him, her hand locked in his.

His eyes were closed. His body was rigid. Tension filled the lines of his face.

"Thank you," Adam said softly. "We should probably take advantage of that now. See the area while it's nice out. It's supposed to snow later, right?"

Norma nodded when they turned to her. "It is. We're expecting a storm later that'll likely shut down some of the roads in the area. But they'll be back open by morning. It's only about two feet of snow."

"Thank you," Adam said, releasing the grip he had on Raina's hand. "What would you suggest we do today?"

Raina gawked at her fake husband and wondered why in the hell he was talking about craft fairs and lunch spots when he could have been giving them both orgasms.

ADAM WAS IN A SHITTY MOOD. He was seconds away from burying himself in Raina and forgetting about the outside world. Then Norma said *suits your fancy*. Adam's mom used the phrase. She would have been horrified he was going to take advantage of Raina when she was scared and vulnerable and counting on him to be there for her.

He was ashamed of himself. And that shame put him in a shitty mood.

Which meant Raina was in a shitty mood, too. Because he was back to being an asshole to her.

They wandered through the craft fair Norma mentioned, picking up a few things to keep up appearances. Adam paid cash for everything, smiling at Raina when she held up the most hideous thing at every stand. She was testing him or something, but Adam couldn't scrounge up any emotion.

They left the craft fair with far more crap than they should have bought. Raina was still angry. Adam was still beating himself up. He could deal with her anger. It was better that she was mad at him for doing the right thing than mad at him for being an asshole.

After the craft fair, Adam drove to a parking lot for a scenic overlook and pulled into a spot near a snow-covered trail he had no intention of walking.

"What are we doing here?" Raina snapped.

"We need to check in." Adam turned the borrowed phone on and dialed F-BOMB, hoping Liam was the one who answered.

"Hello, newlyweds. How's it going?" Liam's voice held a grin.

"Great. What's the news?" Adam wasn't in the mood for small talk.

"Are you safe?" Liam asked, his tone raising the small hairs on the back of Adam's neck. Whether he picked up on Adam's tension or something was wrong, Liam was worried.

Which meant Adam was worried. He looked out the windows and around the entire car, double checking they were completely alone. "Yes. Why?"

"I'm guessing you already saw the news."

Adam and Raina exchanged a glance. His was coupled with a scowl, hers paired with a tremor. "What happened?"

"The judge is missing."

"What?" Adam barked.

"Okay, I guess you didn't know. The judge is gone. Hasn't been seen since the day he dropped all charges against Street."

"Fuck," Adam groaned.

"Yeah, pretty much what we're all thinking. We found video of him leaving the courthouse, then he vanishes in the city. Never returned to his house."

"Family?"

"None," Liam said. "Ex-wife is remarried and hasn't spoken to him in decades. No contact at all. Seemed as though he didn't have much of a life."

"So where is he?"

"No clue. We're looking, but the assumption at this point is Street made him disappear so he couldn't be questioned about dropping everything."

"Is the FBI involved?"

"Yeah. Street is a person of interest, but they have no proof he's involved so there's no warrant. All the judge's cases are being investigated. It's only a matter of time before warrants are issued for Street again. The charges being dropped by a corrupt judge means no new evidence needs to show up for the warrants to come back out."

"Just need to find him again."

"There's that," Liam said.

"No bail this time."

"Agreed. Dunn's been working on that and sharing all the video and other information we have on Street. As long as we get a fair judge, it'll be an easy one."

"They might need protective custody."

"Yeah, we're working with a private security firm to handle that."

"Good. So, where does that leave us?" Adam asked with a glance toward Raina. As much as he hated the idea of going back, staying wasn't good either.

"Nothing changes. Keep moving every few days. Pretend you're in love. Play the roles."

Raina snorted, looking out the window instead of at Adam.

"What was that?" Liam asked.

"Nothing," Adam said.

"If someone thinks something's up with you two, Street will find you. You can't fuck this up."

"I know," Adam snapped. He ran a hand over his head, willing the pounding headache he'd had all day to stop. He was still healing from Street knocking him out two weeks ago. Now he was pretending to be in love with the woman he was secretly falling in love with, and wanting to kick his own ass every time he thought about touching her.

"Obviously you made it to wherever you are safely. Decent place?"

"Yeah, it's great," Adam said with zero emotion.

"Okay. Good. Listen. Stay safe. Don't draw attention to yourselves. If this place is getting too nosy, move on."

"We will," Adam said. "One more night."

"Sounds good. Make sure you check that phone at least once a day. Call every other day at least. Let us know what's going on. You can leave it on, too, just make sure you're checking in regularly."

"Got it."

"Adam."

"What?" His frustration rang through in his voice, something Adam couldn't control.

"I love you. Be careful. Take care of Raina."

"I love you, too. Hi to Caitlyn. We'll be in touch."

"Yep."

Adam hung up and closed his eyes. Liam was worried. For him to say he loved Adam meant he was worried he might not get the chance to say it again.

Which was why Adam didn't want to go on the crazy fucking trip in the first place. They should have stayed put. Where there were more people to watch Raina. Instead, she was in even more danger with just Adam as her personal protector.

"Are you okay?" Raina asked.

Adam shook his head slowly, lights exploding behind his eyes with each move.

"Your head hurts. Why didn't you tell me? I could have driven. Or we could have had a quiet day."

Adam snorted. "If we ended up back in that bedroom, we both know it would not have been quiet."

Raina sucked in a shocked gasp.

Adam realized what he said and swore. "I shouldn't have said that."

"It's fine."

Great. She was pissed at him. Again. Which meant it was time to go. And time to stop fucking talking.

He drove them back to the B&B, convincing Raina to leave their purchases in the back of the vehicle since they were checking out in the morning, anyway. He hurried her up to their room instead of letting them get caught by Norma again.

Adam sank into the chair in the corner of the room and put his head in his hands. His head throbbed. All he wanted to do was sleep, but he needed some of his meds first. As soon as he worked up the energy to get them.

"Here," Raina said softly.

Adam looked up and found her in front of him with a glass of water and two of his pills. Adam swallowed the pills dry, then drained the glass of water. "Thanks."

Raina took the glass back and returned it to the bathroom. She settled on the bed and turned on her side, away from him.

Adam wanted to say something to make it all okay, but he didn't know what to say. He knew he was giving her mixed signals. It wasn't fair to her.

"I'm sorry about today," he said after a minute, when the meds started to kick in and the throbbing reduced to a pulsing.

"For treating me like I was nothing or for ignoring me or maybe for telling me we would have had sex after you practically shoved me out the door? Because all you have to do is tell me you're not interested. Just because I thought I felt something when we kissed doesn't mean it was real. Or that it was mutual."

She said all of that without moving, her back to him.

Adam hated not looking into her eyes. He hated not

being able to see her when he said what he needed to say. He forced himself up, but the room spun. He dropped to his knees and crawled over to her, kneeling in front of her next to the bed.

"For all of it," he said. "For wanting you badly enough that I was willing to sleep with you without thinking about how vulnerable you are. For shoving you out the door and acting like an ass because I feel guilty for wanting you. And yeah, for admitting I wanted you. Then and now. Because you deserve better than a cheesy B&B with a man pretending to be your husband. You deserve romance and fancy dinners and seduction."

Raina snorted. "You don't have to say things like that. I told you to just tell me you're not interested."

Adam cupped her jaw and leaned forward. He stopped when he was a breath away from her.

She finally opened her eyes. They were shiny with unshed tears and apprehension he knew he had put there.

"The number one rule is don't sleep with the witness. Getting involved would be a bad idea. I'm not saying that because I don't want you. I'm saying that because I do. I've been an asshole because I let my guard slip, then hate myself for it."

"Why would you hate yourself?"

"Have you been with anyone since Street?"

She nibbled her lower lip and shook her head.

"You should have a chance to fall in love with someone good. Someone who deserves you."

"What if I never get that chance? What if I'm never free?"

Adam closed his eyes against her fear. He knew what she was asking. And answering the question was going to take something from him.

But she deserved the truth.

"I'm not going to let that happen," he said softly, firmly. "I'm going to kill Street if he gets anywhere close to you."

"I know it's your job—"

"No, Raina. You don't understand. If I see him, I'm going to kill him."

11

———

RAINA HAD NEVER SEEN THAT LOOK ON ADAM'S FACE. Ferocious. Angry. Protective.

It should have scared her when he said he was going to kill Damon. It should have upset her. He was telling her he intended to commit murder. Premeditated would be thrown around if he told anyone.

But the bright blue eyes she stared into weren't evil. Adam wasn't evil. He was doing it for her. He was willing to risk his entire life, his career, his future, to protect her.

"Adam," she breathed.

He shook his head, then winced. "You deserve better than this. Better than being stuck with me and wondering if you'll live long enough to meet a man worthy of you."

"What if I already have?"

"Raina." He sighed heavily.

She exhaled a laugh. "I don't know what's going to happen tomorrow. Or what's going to happen when all of this is over. I used to be a planner. There were things I wanted in my life. But right now, all I want is for you to kiss me."

He stared into her eyes long enough that she grew uncomfortable. The hope inside her faded, and she withdrew, moving to roll away from him.

He caught her wrist before she could turn over. She fought him, but he held firm. "Please. I know I shouldn't, but..."

She looked at him, the war behind his eyes visible for a second before he closed his eyes and shut himself off from her.

"I don't want to hurt you, Raina. I don't want to lose focus and lose you."

"You won't." Her words didn't waver, and neither did she. She trusted him with her life, and she ached to trust him with her body. The last man she was with was Damon. She wanted to change that for months, to remember the feel of someone else against her skin. She could have slept with anyone. She could have gone to a bar and picked up any number of men before she went into hiding. That never held the appeal that being with Adam did.

Adam tugged her wrist, encouraging her to roll toward him again. He brushed her hair back and tucked it behind her ear. He kissed her cheek right in front of her ear, lingering with his lips pressed to her skin. Then he kissed her forehead. Then her eyelids.

Raina stopped breathing, waiting for Adam to decide if he was going to press his lips to hers. He continued the achingly sweet kisses around her face. When she tilted her chin up, he inhaled a breath and sealed his lips over hers.

For a second, they were both still. Adam groaned softly in his throat and licked her lips. She opened for him instantly, her lips parting before he even asked permission. He growled, a low sound of approval and desire, and claimed her mouth like she'd never been kissed.

His fingers tightened against the back of her neck, bringing her closer to his kiss. His tongue thrust in and out of her mouth, tantalizing her with the possessive kiss that wasn't about fooling anyone and all about giving her exactly what she wanted.

Raina lifted her hand and grabbed his wrist, needing to feel the warmth of his skin against hers. He started to pull back, but she held tighter, silently letting him know she didn't want him to stop.

He sighed, his breath fanning across her cheek. He gentled the kiss, easing the force of his tongue and pulling back with reluctant kisses. He kissed her forehead, then sank to sit next to the bed. He groaned.

"Shit. Your head. Are you okay?"

"Yeah," he said, groaning again. "No. I'm sorry."

"You should lie down."

"Yeah," he said, letting go of her and sliding to the floor.

"Get in the bed. You can't sleep on the floor again."

"I'll be fine."

"Then do it for me. If you sleep in the bed, I'll feel safer."

"Are you just saying that?"

"Does it matter?"

He was silent for a few seconds. "The way I feel right now, no, I don't think it does. Are you sure?"

"Yes. Please."

He took his time getting back to a seated position, then onto his knees so he could crawl onto the bed. He climbed on right where Raina was, nudging her over so he was on the side closer to the door.

He winced when he laid back, his eyes closed and the lines on his face tight with pain and tension.

"You need to tell me when your head is bothering you."

"They're both bothering me right now."

Raina looked to where his jeans were tented and gasped. "I'll be fine in a few hours."

"Okay," she whispered, unsure what she was supposed to do.

It wasn't long before Adam was snoring softly, still wearing his clothes from the day. Outside, darkness took over and Raina felt herself fading as Adam's steady, heavy breathing soothed her to sleep.

ADAM COULDN'T BREATHE. Something, or someone, was on top of him. He slowly came awake, keeping his breathing steady so whoever was there didn't realize he was awake.

He could tell it was still dark on the other side of his eyelids. He opened one just enough to get a look at where he was.

The B&B. Honeymoon Suite. Raina.

It all came back to him like a dream, pieces of the last few weeks falling into place before the previous night tried to sink in.

Street got rid of the judge, Raina knew Adam wanted her, they kissed.

And she said he could share the bed.

The erection pressed hard against his zipper had Adam opening both eyes to find the source of his breathing struggles.

He grinned.

Raina had somehow managed to get him under the covers. She was laying almost completely on top of him, the covers pulled up to her chin and tucked tightly around them. Like the filling inside a bed burrito.

Adam moved his hand and found it full of flesh. He

groaned. She was smooth and warm and perfect. His dick hardened even more, his ability to resist her slipping further out of grasp with her firmly in his grasp.

"Morning," she said, her voice raspy and sleepy and sexy.

"Morning." He tried to keep his body still, but it was almost impossible to not enjoy the feel of her on top of him.

"I must be crushing you," she said, making a move to get off of him.

He held her tight. "Not even a little," he lied, preferring not breathing to not holding her. She wasn't that heavy now that the panic of someone being there was past him.

She chuckled softly, knowing he was lying but letting it go. She tucked her head under his chin and laid there with him, their breath the only sound in the room.

"We're leaving today?" she whispered.

"I think it's for the best. No more than two nights. Anywhere."

She nodded. If he hadn't been holding her, he would have missed the way her entire body tensed at the reminder of their plans.

After a minute, she sucked in a breath and rolled off him. She kept rolling, climbing out of the bed on the other side and walking around to go to the bathroom. She closed the door but didn't lock it.

Adam laid there another minute. His head felt better, no lingering pain, but he was starving. He skipped dinner the night before since he passed out and wondered if Raina left the room on her own or if she missed dinner, too.

When she came out of the bathroom, he took his turn. She was sitting on the edge of the bed when he came back into the room.

"Are you okay?"

She nodded. "Just thinking."

"What are you thinking?"

She smiled up at him and shook her head. "Nothing. Are we getting breakfast here before we head out?"

"We might as well. Did you eat dinner last night?"

She shook her head. "I didn't want to wake you up, and I laid down and ended up falling asleep, too."

"I'm sorry. I'll do better to watch how I'm feeling so I don't get that bad again."

She nodded slowly, then looked up at him. "I think we need to do better about talking to each other."

He chuckled. "Yeah. Sorry about that, too."

"I don't regret kissing you, Adam. And I wouldn't have regretted anything else."

"Raina."

"No. You've been treating me like I'm fragile. I can't handle that. Not from you. I hate all of this, but I have to feel like I have some control over things. I haven't had that in far too long, so I need you to treat me like I'm your partner instead of someone who can't handle everything happening right now."

"You're one of the strongest people I've ever met," he whispered.

"Thank you."

"I mean it. And I don't regret kissing you, either, Raina. Just in case you were wondering."

She smiled shyly at him, her cheeks pinking. "I'm going to get in the shower, if that's okay."

"Yeah, of course. I'll stay over here if you want to leave the door cracked."

She nodded, grateful for the suggestion. "Thanks."

She grabbed clothes and went to the bathroom, leaving the door slightly open to let out the steam.

And proving she trusted him. That made Adam smile.

When they were both showered and dressed and their bags were packed, including a few of the freebie condoms Adam hoped to be able to put to use one day, they turned toward the door.

"Raina," Adam said before she opened the door.

"Yeah?" She looked up at him with a question in her beautiful hazel eyes.

It was a punch to the gut. She was so beautiful it hurt to resist her, and as they were about to leave the bubble they'd created in the tiny B&B with nosy, and borderline rude, hosts, he found himself unable to walk out without one last kiss from her.

Adam let go of his suitcase and stepped into her personal space, crowding her against the wall and taking what he hoped she was offering him. Her hand tunneled into his hair, eagerly kissing him back with the same madness he felt pumping through his veins.

He covered her body with his and didn't hold back the way he'd done for weeks. He leaned into her, smiling when she gasped at the feel of his hardness against her stomach. He kissed her harder, his hands dropping to her hips to hold her in place. She held on to him, her barely audible whimpers turning him on and making him want to toss her onto the bed and use the room for exactly what it was intended.

Sex. Lots of sex. Dirty sex with the woman he was pretending to be married to.

Adam's stomach let out a strained growl, reminding him neither of them had eaten since lunch the day before. He backed away from Raina with a sheepish grin. They smiled at each other and panted.

"I guess food wins out," she said.

Adam kissed her again, determined to prove her wrong, and his stomach growled again.

"Fuck," he hissed.

Raina chuckled. "It's okay. I'm hungry, too. And we'll be somewhere new soon."

"Soon isn't now," Adam whispered.

"No," Raina said, laughing at him. "But we've resisted each other this long. I think we can make it a few more hours."

Adam glanced down at his erection straining his zipper and muttered, "Speak for yourself."

Raina cupped his jaw. "Do you want me to...?"

"Suck my dick? No."

"Oh." She sounded hurt and ducked her head, shifting away from him even though he was pressed against her.

"Fuck, Raina, not like that. Want you to? More than I want food right now. But there's no way in hell I'm going to fuck your mouth before I have you fucking mine. You're going to have a few orgasms before I even think about having one."

"Oh." That was a very different sounding *oh*. One that had Adam cursing under his breath for a very different reason. "I wouldn't object."

Adam cupped her jaw. "When we get these clothes off, I'm not going to rush to put them back on."

"Oh."

"Let's go get breakfast and get back on the road," Adam said, picking up his suitcase before he filled his hands with Raina again.

Raina nodded and followed him downstairs.

Norma and Tom were at the front desk when Raina and Adam made it downstairs. They gushed over them and thanked them for staying. Adam carried their suitcases to the SUV, leaving Raina inside to get coffee and order breakfast.

They ate quickly, sharing their food again. Before they finished, Norma approached and asked them to come back sometime.

"We'd love to," Raina said, setting her fork down. "Thank you for being such amazing hosts."

"See?" Norma said to Tom, who'd just come out of the kitchen. "I told you that room would work. He said I needed to keep my nose out of it, but I was sure that room would work its magic and you two would be acting like newlyweds are supposed to. He hasn't looked at you like that since you've been here."

Adam tore his gaze from Raina. She sucked in a breath when she looked over at him, but Adam focused on his food instead of revealing even more of how badly he wanted her, especially in front of Norma.

"Leave them to their food, my love," Tom chastised gently.

Norma grinned and clasped her hands together before going back to the desk to speak to another couple who came down for breakfast.

"Maybe next time we keep the newlywed part to ourselves," Adam whispered.

Raina chuckled. "Yeah, but then where would we get free condoms?"

Adam choked on his coffee, sputtering and coughing and trying to figure out how she knew he stole the condoms from the basket.

"I had the same thought," she confessed, her cheeks turning red.

Adam grinned, nodding and chuckling as he thought about the night ahead.

It was going to be a damn good night.

THE SIX-HOUR DRIVE down the coast was much better with them talking to each other. It passed quickly for Adam, learning more about Raina in a few hours than he'd learned in more than two months of him living with and protecting her.

He also shared a few things about himself. By the time they pulled into a B&B east of Richmond, Virginia, near the Atlantic Ocean, he knew things had changed between him and Raina. For the better.

"Good evening," a woman said when they walked into the bed-and-breakfast. "Welcome to Shady Garden Bed and Breakfast. I'm Bobbi. How can I help you?"

"Hi, Bobbi," Adam said, stepping forward with his hand on Raina's back, ignoring his own earlier advice about not telling the host they were newlyweds. "I'm Mark, and this is my bride, Lisa. We're hoping you have a room for two nights."

"Bride? Are you newly married?" Bobbi asked.

"We are," Raina said, setting her right hand on Adam's chest and leaning her head against his shoulder. "We eloped last weekend and are making our own honeymoon trip."

"Oh, that's so sweet. I don't think we've ever had honeymooners here before. But all our suites have private bathrooms, so you're not sharing with other guests."

"That sounds perfect," Adam said. "Thank you."

"Oh, no, thank you. My late husband, Leonard, always said it would be nice to have honeymooners here. He was a romantic."

"I'm sorry for your loss," Raina said.

"Thank you, dear. It's been almost a year. But our oldest son lives here with me and helps me out. He loves this place as much as Leonard did. We had thirty-two years together."

"Wow. That seems like such a long time," Raina said.

Bobbi nodded. "When it's right, it's never long enough."

Raina grinned at her, then looked up at Adam. The smile on her face made him want their lies to be true. Honeymoon, in love, romance, all of it. He wanted it with her.

And the way she was looking at him made him wonder if she felt the same.

Bobbi gave them all the information about breakfast the next morning and handed over the key to their room. She offered to carry their luggage upstairs, but Adam waved her off. He grabbed their suitcases while Raina talked to Bobbi for a few more minutes. Raina hugged the older woman before looping her hand through Adam's arm and walking up the stairs side-by-side with him.

"She's very sweet," Raina said when they were closed in their room. They'd stopped for dinner on the road, leaving them nothing but each other for the night.

And Adam did not want to talk about their host.

"She said we were a cute couple. Not like Norma and didn't believe us."

"We were less than believable for Norma and Tom."

Raina nodded. "True."

She met his gaze with a smile, one that faded as the tension between them thickened.

Adam watched as unease and uncertainty filled her gaze. "Nothing has to happen, Raina."

She shook her head. "It's not that."

"It doesn't look like you're thrilled right now."

"I'm nervous. It's been a while, and with Damon..."

She trailed off, leaving Adam to fill in the gaps. He realized it was possible Street was far from gentle or loving with her. Something that made Adam want to kill the other man all the more.

"Raina, I never—"

"Don't. Don't make this about him. I'm ready to more forward with my life. I need to move forward. But I'm nervous."

"I'm not going to hurt you."

She smiled, the appreciation shining in her eyes. "I know. That's how I know I want this. I want you, Adam. I trust you."

That meant more than anything else to him. She was trusting him with her body and believing he would take care of her.

It had never been so important to Adam to make sure the woman he was with enjoyed every minute. And it never would be again. Because no woman would ever be Raina.

No woman would ever be the first woman he loved.

12

RAINA HAD NEVER WORRIED ABOUT MAKING THE FIRST MOVE with a man before Damon. She approached him, picking him out of the crowd and finding him intriguing. Ever since, she felt like her instincts were off. Broken.

She was fairly sure Adam wanted her, but she still waited for him to make the first move. For him to cross the room to where she stood on the far side. Beyond the king sized bed that took up the majority of the space in the small room. Unlike their previous B&B, this room was more like a hotel room. Nicely decorated, but simple in appearance and amenities.

Meaning there was no overflowing basket of condoms for them to enjoy.

Raina knew Adam had taken some from the last room, and so did she. She figured the last thing they needed was to be unprepared or to have to go into a convenience store that undoubtedly would have cameras.

Adam watched her for a long minute, his gaze skipping over her body like he couldn't decide where he wanted to look.

She waited, her breath held, until he took a step toward her. Then another.

He stopped in front of her, the tension in his jaw matching that in his balled fists.

"Nothing has to happen," she echoed his earlier statement. Worse than her being a convenience would be him feeling forced into bed with her.

He shook his head slowly. "I'm sorry for everything he did to you."

Raina's breath caught in her throat. That was the last thing she expected him to say. Most people felt bad for her, but few were so direct. And even fewer knew the extent of the torture she'd been through.

"Thank you," Raina breathed, the words barely a whisper. A tear broke free and took the scenic route down her cheek.

"You deserve better than him. Better than me. I will never do anything to intentionally hurt you, but I don't want to hurt you by accident either."

"You won't," Raina said.

Adam shook his head again. "What if I hold your hands or tug your hair or grip your hips? What if I do something that hurts you or scares you? I'd never forgive myself."

"Damon was not the first man I'd ever slept with. I know sex can be good. Really good. And I want to feel that again. I want to enjoy the sensations of my body. I want to feel the weight of a man on top of me and not worry that he won't get off of me. I want to be fucked and have sex and make love. I want to kiss and touch and taste. I want Damon to not be the last man I slept with. I know it isn't fair to put all of that on you, and you can say no. I will understand if you're not interested in me after learning all of that—"

She didn't get a chance to finish her sentence before Adam erased the gap between them and attacked her. His hand slid into her hair and tugged so her head tilted back as he lowered his mouth to hers.

She squeaked at the sudden move, then moaned into his kiss and wrapped her arms around his neck.

Adam's other hand went to her hip, pulling her closer. It slid around her back and held her in place as he searched for a separation between her jeans and her top. When he found it, he pressed his hand widely against her back, searing her skin with his warmth.

Raina speared her hands through his short hair, throwing herself into the kiss. It was as far as they'd gotten before, and Raina was going to enjoy the hell out of it in case he pulled back again.

He did pull back, his lips wet and red from their aggressive kiss. "Are you okay?"

She nodded. "I'll be better if you tell me your head doesn't hurt tonight."

He chuckled. "Good to go."

She grinned, gently tugging him down to kiss her again.

He smiled just before their lips touched again. He parted hers with little effort, slowing their frantic kiss with the same knowledge she had.

They had all night. And nothing was going to stop them.

Adam backed Raina up to the bed, keeping his lips to hers as he helped her ease onto the mattress. He followed her down, crawling over her and settling between her parted thighs.

A second of panic hit her when Adam's weight pressed her to the bed. He stopped instantly, making a move to get off the bed, but she held him in place.

He stilled, not breathing as she sucked in breath after breath and convinced herself she was safe.

"I'm sorry."

He shook his head. "Nothing to be sorry for. We can stop whenever you want."

"I don't want to stop. But I don't want to make you crazy."

He smirked. "Too late on that one, but for a very different reason. You can say no at any point, Raina. I will always stop."

She nodded, her damn throat tightening again. "Thank you. Will you kiss me again?"

He nodded and eased his body over hers, supporting himself on his elbows to keep from pressing her to the mattress. She inhaled deep, drawing his scent in and reminding herself Adam would never hurt her.

Slowly, he let her feel more and more of his weight until he cupped her cheeks with both of his hands and pulled back. "Can I take off your shirt?"

She smiled, feeling like a teenager getting felt up for the first time. She pushed him back, sitting up when he scrambled off her. She lifted her shirt at the hem and pulled it off before she thought twice. She reached back and unhooked her bra, sliding it down her arms and tossing it toward her suitcase, then reached for the waistband of her jeans.

"Let me," Adam said in a shaky voice, stilling her hand before she could ease her jeans off.

Raina met his gaze, surprised to find pure lust reflected back at her. Her entire body flushed hot with desire of her own. She nodded.

"You're so beautiful, Raina," Adam whispered. He tore his shirt off and leaned down to kiss her. He held his body entirely off hers, but heat radiated from him and made her ache for him to cover her again.

He pulled back from their kiss and trailed his lips down her jaw to her collarbone. He nipped at the skin on her neck before continuing his path. He pressed featherlight kisses on the upper swells of her breasts, ignoring her nipples as she writhed beneath him and tried to position herself for his mouth.

"We said we needed better communication. Tell me what you want, Raina."

Her eyes snapped open. He was watching her with eyes so dilated they looked navy. His muscles rippled as he held himself back, letting her decide what she wanted from him.

Even if it was for him to stop. Which was the last thing she wanted.

"Lick my nipples. Please." She whispered the request, feeling more exposed by asking for what she wanted than her naked torso made her feel.

"Gladly," Adam said, lowering his mouth to her nipple while he held her gaze.

Watching his tongue dart out and flick over the tip of her nipple was one of the most erotic thing Raina had ever witnessed. She moaned, her core tightening with need.

Adam licked her nipple, circling the tight peak before biting gently. He brought his hand up to hold that breast and moved his mouth to the other one, licking and teasing that one until Raina wanted to beg him to make her come.

Adam went back to the first nipple, sucking and licking it, again letting her decide what she wanted him to do.

"Adam," she whispered.

He looked up at her, his mouth full of her oversized breast. He didn't look bothered in the least as he smiled around her flesh.

"I need more. I need you."

He nodded once, unbothered by her request as he

continued to suck on her nipple. She shifted, frustrated he wasn't moving things along, and he finally let go of her nipple. He kissed the underside of her breast, then licked her belly.

Only when he reached the edge of her jeans did she realize he'd already unbuttoned and unzipped them and was pulling them down as he moved closer to her.

"Adam," she whispered.

He kissed her thighs and knees and calves. He stood at the side of the bed and dropped his jeans and boxer briefs, exposing himself entirely before he put her in the same position. He didn't say it, but she knew he was making sure she felt safe. It made her want him even more.

He leaned over her, cupping one breast as he kissed her. She reached for him, wrapping her hand around his thick erection, and he jerked in her palm.

"Fuck, that feels good." His hissed words were the first sign he was as close to the edge as she was.

"Fuck me, Adam."

"Raina."

She shook her head. "I want you. I've wanted you for weeks. I don't need sweet and gentle and romance right now. I need to be fucked."

He growled and stalked away from her. "Take off your panties," he ordered as he tossed his suitcase over and yanked the zipper open. A minute later, he ripped into the foil and turned to face her.

His cock twitched. He grabbed it and stroked, his gaze locked on her exposed entrance as he took his time getting back to the bed.

He stood beside the bed and flicked his gaze from her to his cock, hurriedly rolling the condom down his length.

Raina giggled when she saw the neon pink condom.

Adam looked down as though he didn't realize that was the one he chose. "As long as it gets the job done."

Raina giggled again, but Adam ended that when his hand went between her thighs.

"You're soaked."

She nibbled her lip and nodded.

"Communication, Raina."

"Fuck me, Adam."

He slammed his fingers inside her, the move making her cry out. The sharp pain she felt faded almost as soon as it made her wince, like the first time she had sex.

He thrust his fingers deep, rubbing his thumb over her clit as he fucked her hard with his hand. Her breath faltered, the sensations overwhelming her.

"Adam," she cried, just before she fell over the edge. It was like being set on fire. She felt everything all at once, her skin hot, her core sucking his fingers deeper, her entire body begging for more and more and more.

He withdrew his hand, sending tremors through her, then lined himself up and plunged into her. She screamed, forgetting how delicious it was when a man filled her to bursting.

Adam stopped. "Raina?"

"More," she breathed, begged. "More, Adam. More."

Her demand set his hips to a steady, punishing rhythm. He hooked one knee over his forearm and opened her up wider so he could drive deeper into her.

The added depth hit Raina in the right spot, and she flailed at the intensity, grunting and moaning as her body felt like it was splitting down the middle.

Adam grabbed her hand, forcing her to look at him. The way he looked at her stilled her wild arms but kept her heart pounding, throbbing, aching as her orgasm raced toward the edge and sent her flying.

"Oh, fuck me," she cried as it hit her full force.

Adam pounded into her as she came. His face twisted, his jaw tight, before he let out a satisfying groan and stilled deep within her.

He twitched inside Raina, the feel of him intimate and so damn good Raina didn't want him to take a step back and slide from her body. She wanted to wrap her legs around him and pull him on top of her, on the bed, and go through all the condoms they stole from Norma and Tom.

But Raina let him go when he stepped back. She lowered her leg to the floor when he slid his arm from underneath it. She watched him walk away and told herself it was just sex.

ADAM GRABBED a handful of condoms from his suitcase and tossed them onto the nightstand while Raina was in the bathroom. He wasn't sure if he was going to stop smiling like an idiot anytime soon, but he hoped not.

Sex with Raina was ten times better than he dreamed it would be, and his dreams were vivid and inventive. But nothing compared to feeling her tighten around his dick as he pounded into her. He was getting hard again just thinking about the way it felt.

Raina came out of the bathroom and looked at him. Her gaze danced around his naked body, pink brightening her cheeks at the lazy way he stretched out on the bed without caring about his nudity.

She walked around the bed, and he held his breath. Was

she going to get dressed or was she going to join him in bed, naked, like he was?

Adam sighed heavily when she bypassed her suitcase and lifted the covers to lie next to him.

He shoved the covers down and maneuvered himself under the sheets to pull her body flush to his. "Are we okay?"

She looked up at him. "Very much so. Thank you."

"I enjoyed every minute of that. Trust me."

"I see you're prepared for more."

At his confused look, she pointed to the pile of condoms on the nightstand. He chuckled. "Not willing to wait if you decide you need more orgasms."

She chuckled. "I'm so greedy about them."

"Music to my ears," Adam teased. "I'm happy to supply you with as many as you'd like."

She laughed softly. "Has this happened to you before?"

He stilled at the seemingly innocent question that felt far from innocent. "Has what happened?"

"Someone you're protecting gets orgasms from you."

Adam shook his head slowly. "No, Raina. I've never been involved with someone I've protected before. I've also never been on my own with a witness. Or liked one as much as I like you."

She nodded, putting her head on his chest again. She was silent for a long moment.

"Do you feel like I'm taking advantage of you?"

She shook her head and sat up, the sheets sliding to her waist.

It took everything in him to keep his gaze on her face.

"I feel like... I feel like I forced you into this."

Adam laughed, then realized she was serious. He flipped over her, covering her body with his. He let her feel how hard he already was again. "Trust me when I say you didn't force anything on me. Those condoms are there because I'm hopeful I'll be able to make you come a few more times tonight, and tomorrow and for as many nights as you want me to share your bed, but if you tell me this is one-sided, I'll go back to sleeping on the floor. I'm an asshole for fucking you, Raina, because it's against the rules and puts you in more danger, but I couldn't resist you."

"You didn't like me enough to talk to me last week. You were pissed about this trip."

He shook his head slowly. "I didn't think I could resist you if we were alone. Pretending to be married. Acting like we were in love. I knew touching you would shatter all the walls I tried to put up between us."

"What?" she breathed.

Adam swore. "I've wanted you for weeks. Since we met, actually, but the more I learned about you, the more I wanted you. I stayed away from you so I didn't make you uncomfortable. So I didn't do something stupid. But it was never because I didn't like you, Raina. It was the opposite. Completely the opposite."

"Oh," she whispered.

Adam wasn't sure what that breathed word meant, but he was going to wait for her to tell him.

"Adam?"

"Yes?"

"I think I need another orgasm."

His cock twitched against her thigh at her proper tone and dirty words. "I would be happy to supply as many as you'd like." He rolled to the side, sliding his fingers into her without resistance. "Jesus, you're wet."

"Maybe I need more than one?"

Adam groaned. "You can have as many as you want,

gorgeous. All night long. And if we run out of condoms, I'm willing to get creative."

Raina moaned as he slid his soaked fingers over her swollen clit. "Yes, please."

Adam kissed her hard and got very, very creative, with and without condoms.

13

DAMON PARKED IN FRONT OF THE BED-AND-BREAKFAST AND looked up at the seafoam green house and bright white trim. The place was too fucking happy for him. But if it led him to Raina, he would deal with that.

He smiled at the woman behind the desk and asked for a room. Thankfully, she wasn't the chatty type. She handed over his key and pointed to the stairs on the other side of the lobby after she told him about breakfast and the activities they offered.

He wouldn't be joining them for any of that. He had one purpose.

Damon unlocked his room and let himself inside. The only bag he brought with him had his favorite assortment of knives and guns, more than enough ammunition to take care of his enemy, and a few changes of clothes.

He tossed the bag on the queen bed and went to the window. The room was decent enough, but he didn't care about the place he was staying in. It was simply a place to lie low and gather information. The window from his room overlooked the place he was really interested in.

Shady Garden Bed and Breakfast was currently the home of Bobbi and Lenny Granada. Mother and son owned and ran the place, and were hosting Raina and the dumb-fuck agent who was supposed to be protecting her.

Damon snickered. Not only did the agent suck at his job, but he was misguided. There was no keeping Damon from Raina. She belonged to him, and she was going to be his again.

Damon looked out the window into the backyard of the neighboring home. Both places backed up to the water, cutting off one escape route. He grinned. It was like the guy had no training. He didn't even realize he was putting them at greater risk.

Worked for Damon, though.

He watched out the window until the sun dipped low behind the house, casting long shadows over both properties. He was a patient man, but only for so long. He was officially out of patience with Raina.

Damon stared, knowing the place next door offered dinner at six for guests and a happy hour on Thursday nights. It was cold outside, but for two people from farther north, the beach was enticing.

At least, that's what he was counting on.

Almost an hour passed, and Damon was beginning to doubt his instincts. Then he saw what he was waiting for.

Raina walked onto the grass beyond the patio, her hand stretched behind her and holding onto the asshole. They'd both dyed their hair, but Damon already knew that. He kept his focus on Raina, the smile on her lips and the light in her eyes. She looked like she was happy.

Not acceptable.

She wouldn't be happy with any man but Damon. He would make sure of that.

His gaze strayed to the man she was with. He moved closer to Raina, his hands going to her waist like she belonged to him.

Their previous hosts told Damon they said they were married. But the agent didn't look like he was acting. He looked like he was in love with Raina.

Damon's Raina.

Not the agent's.

He would pay for touching her. He would pay for thinking he had a right to touch her.

Damon's grip tightened, squeezing his fists until his fingers ached. No one touched what was his. No one played with his toys.

And if they did, they died.

Damon smiled. Tonight, the agent would die. And Raina would be his again. For good this time.

RAINA SPUN IN A CIRCLE, arms up, letting the last rays of sunshine soak into her for the day. It was cold, but the beach was sand instead of snow, and she loved it.

Adam stood a few feet away from her, watching her.

Her pulse skipped and her body heated at the look in his eyes. She didn't expect to feel so close to him, especially after just one night together, but she did. She wanted to be able to imagine a future together. After Damon was gone and Raina had her life back.

She shook her head and rolled her eyes at herself. They'd had one night. She was getting too far ahead of herself. Which was exactly what got her into the situation she was in. She jumped in with both feet. She convinced herself everything was fine, even when something inside her screamed that wasn't true.

She couldn't do it again, even if she knew Adam was nothing like Damon. She had to be cautious with her heart.

"What are you thinking?" Adam asked. He came up behind her and wrapped his arms around her waist. He kissed her neck, his lips warm against her chilled skin.

"Just wondering what's going to happen when this is all over."

"Whatever you want," Adam whispered.

Raina shrugged. "I want to feel like I'm safe all the time. Like this. It's beautiful here, and I know we're safe. I don't want to have to change locations every few days to have this feeling. You know?"

"I do. And once he's gone for good, you won't have to."

She shivered at the hard promise in his tone. One day, Damon would be gone for good, but Raina didn't like the idea of Adam having to kill him. Of Adam choosing to take a life. Even if that life was Damon's.

"Are you getting cold?"

Raina nodded in reply, even though that wasn't what made her tremble. It had been too long since she'd been able to enjoy being outside, but she was having fun being inside with Adam even more.

Adam held her close as they turned to go back into the B&B. Bobbi and her son, Lenny, had been easier to handle hosts than Norma and Tom. Bobbi and Lenny were friendly and kind, but they didn't ask too many questions and hung back out of the way more than inserted themselves in front of everything.

As soon as they were in their room again, Adam spun Raina and pressed her back to the wall. He locked the door and turned all of his focus to her.

Raina didn't fight him as he eased her clothes off and helped her step out of them. He kissed every inch of her body and kneeled on the floor in front of her, looking up at her as he leaned closer to her center.

Damon hated oral sex. He was a big fan of receiving it, but he refused to give it. Before him, Raina hadn't been with anyone regularly in years and had convinced herself she wasn't a fan.

"You don't have to," she said before Adam could press his mouth between her legs.

He kissed her inner-thigh. "You don't enjoy it?"

She shrugged and shook her head. "I... uh, no?"

He kissed her other thigh, and her knees weakened. "You don't sound so sure."

"Um..."

"You can tell me to stop. Any time. Until you do, I'd really like to suck on your clit and make you come."

He ended his declaration with a lick through her folds that made Raina moan. "Oh, God."

He hummed and tapped her ankles.

She widened her stance, looking down past her round belly to where his dark head disappeared. One of his hands wrapped around her leg, and the other teased her folds with gentle touches that had her gasping.

He licked her clit gently, setting a slow pace that had her easing into the orgasm she knew was building. Then he pressed his fingers inside her and jumped a few steps up the ladder.

"Adam," she whispered. Her head fell to the wall behind her, her legs shaking from supporting her weight while she fought the urge to buck against his face.

He lifted one of her legs, putting her off-balance, then

draped it over his shoulder. The leverage it gave her set her hips in motion.

His fingers pressed deep inside her, sending jolts through her body and rushing her to the top of the cliff. His slow, steady licks became quick flicks of his tongue, followed by long sucks on her already sensitive clit.

"Adam, fuck, Adam," she moaned, her orgasm right there at the edge. She reached for it, beyond ready to fall.

He curled his fingers inside her and sucked hard on her swollen clit, and sent her flying. She moaned and rode his face, not caring if all the other people under the same roof heard her.

Adam kept one hand between her thighs and helped her lower her foot to the floor. "Bed," he growled, teasing her as they struggled together to make it the few feet with her weak knees and second orgasm building.

As soon as she laid down, he was sucking on her clit again, making her cry out almost instantly as another orgasm raced down her spine and burst out of her body.

The sound of foil tearing brought her back to the moment just before Adam plunged home. She moaned with him, wrapping her legs around his hips and holding him tight inside for just a minute.

He leaned down and kissed her sweetly, the taste of her come on his lips. She thought it would turn her off, but sharing that with him only turned her on more.

As they kissed, he stroked in and out of her. She was determined to let him come before she did again, but her sensitive skin and well-primed body had other plans. Before she knew it, she was begging him to fuck her hard and barely holding back the screams clawing at her throat to come out.

"Fucking hell, Raina. You're the sexiest fucking thing

when you come. More, come for me some more, beautiful," Adam growled, his hips pistoning deep and hard and helping just as much as his words to send her right back to the peak before she leapt again.

"Oh, God! Yes! Yes!"

"Fuck me," Adam choked out, slamming hard into her before he stilled and emptied himself inside her.

Raina shook with the aftershocks racking her body, wondering how she missed out on sex that good for so long.

Adam slumped over onto her, staying inside her as they both struggled to catch their breath. He kissed her neck and nuzzled her jaw, making himself at home right there against her.

She didn't have any argument against it.

They laid there without speaking for a long minute, then Adam kissed her soundly and pushed himself up. He went to the bathroom, laughing when he came back and Raina hadn't moved.

"You wore me out," she groaned.

"I think I wore us both out," he said, lifting her legs and spinning her so she could lie down on the bed. He crawled under the covers with her and pulled her close to him.

She was silent, thinking about the choices she made that got her to where she was and how she was going to do things differently. She'd already made some decisions, if she survived long enough.

"You okay?" Adam asked, brushing her hair aside.

Raina nodded. "More than you know."

"Yeah?"

"Yeah. I don't want to scare you when I say this, but I feel like you're giving me my life back. I'm starting to remember who I used to be. Before Damon. I wouldn't have been able to do that without your help."

"Why would that scare me?"

She shrugged. "I don't know. I don't want you to think I'm going to tell you I'm falling in love with you or trying to trap you or something. That I'm not going to let you go back to your life when all of this is over. I have no intention of causing problems in your life. You don't have to worry about that."

"I wasn't, but that's good. I know you have a lot to figure out."

She nodded. "I do. And I'm starting to get there. I thought leaving him would be the hardest part, and it was hard, but I had no idea who he was. I know everything will change when he's no longer a threat to me."

"Soon, Raina. Soon."

Adam kissed her jaw and curled his body around hers from behind. She let his heat warm her and soothe her, and she drifted to sleep knowing the safest place was in his arms.

ADAM LAID in the dark and listened to Raina's steady breath. When she told him about her nightmares, he wasn't sure how to help her through them. But after the first night, she hadn't had any.

Adam tried to convince himself it had nothing to do with them sharing a bed, but he couldn't. He slept better with her in his arms, too.

He replayed their last twenty-four hours and knew he was completely gone. When he kept his distance from her, he was still falling for her, but it was slow. He fell for her strength and heart. Being alone with her, and loving her with his body, Adam was done. She was smart and funny, compassionate and passionate, beautiful and sensual, and made him absolutely insane.

She was it for him.

He almost laughed when she promised him she wasn't falling in love with him and wouldn't cause problems in his life when everything was over. He'd do just about anything for her to take those words back.

Adam pressed his nose to her neck and inhaled. She smelled like him. Like sex. It made him hard again just to breathe her in, but he wasn't asshole enough to wake her up just to appease his lust for her. They had more time. And Adam was fairly sure there would be no end to his wanting Raina.

He drifted to sleep, holding her tight the entire time. Something kept him from sinking too deep, making him wake up every time she stirred.

Adam got up after midnight and used the bathroom. Raina didn't move while he was gone. He smiled as he crossed the room to join her, but stopped when he heard a buzzing noise.

He paused long enough to remember he never turned off the phone they carried. Liam promised him it was secure and no one could access anything about the phone, so after the first day, Adam left it on in case F-BOMB or Lorelei needed to reach them.

The buzzing stopped before Adam could dig the phone out of his suitcase. He finally closed his hand around it just as it started to ring again.

"Yeah?" he answered.

"Thank fuck. Are you okay?" Liam asked.

Adam looked at Raina, naked in the bed they were just sharing. "Yeah. Why?"

"FBI got a call an hour ago. A guest went to check in at a

B&B where they had reservations. Found the owners beaten and close to death."

Fear tightened Adam's throat. "Where was the B&B?"

"Cooke Bed and Breakfast. The owners are—"

"Norma and Tom."

"Yep. They identified Street as the man who attacked them. Said he asked about you and Raina. Had a picture of her. Pretended to be law enforcement and said you two were fugitives, but Tom didn't fall for it. Asked for identification, and Street took him out."

"Jesus."

"Yeah. When we couldn't get in touch with you…"

"We're fine. We obviously left there."

"Which is good, but it's not good enough. Are you still using the same names?"

Adam ran a hand through his hair. "We don't have another choice. So, yeah."

"Norma told him the names you were using. She told him who you are. If he has someone who can trace cards, and we know he does, he can find you."

"Fucking hell. Are you serious?"

"Adam, you need to get the hell out of wherever you are. Now. He could already be there. If not, he's coming."

14

———

ADAM LOOKED AT RAINA, SOUND ASLEEP IN THE BED THEY'D been sharing. Peaceful. Beautiful. Naked.

"Adam!" Liam shouted in his ear.

"Yeah."

"Did you hear me?"

"Yeah, I did. Um, we'll leave first thing."

"You can't wait until morning. Go now. It's very possible he's already in the same town as you. We will have someone there tomorrow and will settle up with the owners and make sure they're safe. Local agents are heading that way, but they won't interfere unless they see evidence Street's there."

"We haven't... I haven't seen him."

"You wouldn't. He's too fucking good. Get out of there, Adam. Now."

The words finally sank in. It was what Adam was afraid of. Getting involved with Raina took his focus. Was Street there? Did Adam miss it?

"I'll be in touch when we stop somewhere," Adam said. He heard the change in his voice, the harshness. The agent was back. Not the man who wanted to wrap himself around the curvy woman in bed. The agent who knew hell was about to rain down if he didn't get them the fuck out of there. Immediately.

"Good. Be safe. Love you."

"Love you, Liam. Thanks."

Adam hung up the phone. The bubble around him and Raina was popped. No longer could they pretend they were married. They were on the run. And they needed to hide. Now.

Adam stalked to the bed, forcing his footsteps to be silent on the carpeted floor. If Street was already there, they didn't need to alert him to anything, even something as simple as them being awake.

"Raina," Adam whispered. He glanced back at the door, almost expecting Street to be standing there. "Raina."

She stirred, her beautiful eyes fluttering open. A smile lifted her lips when she saw him kneeling in front of her. "Hey."

"I need you to get up, Raina."

"I thought that was your department." She reached for him, but Adam rose to his feet and avoided her hand.

"We have to go."

She jerked back, like his tone and words were a physical blow. "What happened?"

"I'll tell you when we're out of here. We have to go. Pack everything. Don't leave a thing. Quickly. Quietly."

Raina nodded, the movement sharp and jerky. But she did it. She tossed back the covers and went to her suitcase. She reached into it and hissed, "I can't see."

"Here," Adam said. "Use the flashlight on the phone, but keep it low so it can't be seen outside the window."

"He's here, isn't he?"

"He might be."

Raina sucked in a breath. She turned back to her suitcase, keeping the phone almost inside it while she searched for something to wear.

Adam yanked on boxer briefs, then jeans and a long-sleeved tee. He shoved the rest of his clothes into his suitcase, not bothering to take the time to make sure things were packed neatly. There was no time.

Adam went to the bathroom while Raina kept packing. He grabbed everything in the shower and on the counter, tossing all of it into the bag they used for bathroom products. He scanned the nearly black room to make sure he had everything and knew there was no way to know for sure without checking with the light.

He closed the door and turned on the light. Raina's brush sat on the far side of the vanity next to the wall. He grabbed it, checked the shower and under the vanity, then grabbed the bag of trash and tied it up. He turned the light off and opened the door.

Raina was standing outside the bathroom door, her suitcase in her hand and a panicked look on her face.

"Bathroom's clear," Adam said.

Raina nodded. She handed him back the phone and shifted the suitcase in her hand. "What now?"

"I'm going to double check the room. We need to take the trash with us. Hold this."

Raina took the bag from Adam and nodded again. It seemed that was the only thing she could do.

Adam understood the fear she felt. It had slithered deep inside him, too. Not for himself, but for Raina. If something happened to her, again, he'd never forgive himself.

He checked the room quickly, grateful it was a small room, and grabbed the trash bag full of condom wrappers.

He stuffed the bathroom trash bag into the new one and tied it up so they only had one to carry. He left the room key on the table in the corner.

"Let me go first," he said when Raina made a move toward the door.

She nodded and pressed herself to the wall so he could get by. Adam grabbed the bag with their bathroom stuff and threw it over his shoulder. He drew his gun and opened the door.

It squeaked loudly enough to wake up the entire fucking house. Adam cursed and peeked into the hallway. Empty. Thank fuck.

He opened the door the rest of the way, quickly so the squeak wasn't as bad. He stepped out, pointing his gun toward the staircase they had to walk down to get out of the B&B.

Adam trusted Raina to close the door behind them, keeping his focus on the direction they were going. She rolled both of their suitcases down the hallway close enough behind him that he could feel her heat.

When they got to the stairs, Adam checked that it was clear. The light in the entryway and sconces on the walls created a soft glow all the way up the stairs. A glow Adam hoped would make it harder for Street to hide and easier for them to get the hell out of the building.

Adam grabbed his suitcase and nodded to Raina. Together, they carried their suitcases down the stairs, one step at a time, moving as one. Adam kept his gun in his hand, but pointed down at his side.

The next blind corner was when they made it to the bottom of the stairs. The front door was right there, but there were rooms on each side. Rooms that someone could easily hide in.

Adam went first, keeping his back to the wall as he crept toward the rooms. He cleared one, then the other, and breathed a sigh of relief when no one was there.

He motioned for Raina to come to him, then opened the front door. He turned the lock on the doorknob to lock the building again, then eased out into the darkness.

Darkness swamped them immediately. The porch lights were out, something Adam didn't remember from when they arrived. The hairs on the back of his neck stood up. Street was definitely there.

"Go," Adam whispered.

Raina didn't hesitate. She grabbed the suitcases and ran toward their SUV. Adam followed behind her, watching the area for any movement. She made it to the SUV and loaded the suitcases into the back with Adam guarding her. When she hit the button to close the back, they both moved to the front seats.

Adam had a moment of hesitation before he turned the key, but Street wanted Raina alive. The chances of a bomb on the SUV were small.

The vehicle purred to life, and Raina exhaled like she had the same thought. Adam backed out of the parking spot, wishing he could turn off the automatic lights. They lit up the other cars in the lot, but thankfully, all of them were empty.

Adam pulled out of the lot and onto the road. He turned west, keeping his gaze on his rearview mirror as much as it was focused out the windshield.

They weren't safe. They weren't in the clear. But they got away. That was the only thing he could do at that moment. And he hated it because everything in him screamed to turn around and find Street and end Raina's hell.

But he couldn't risk Street not being alone. He couldn't

risk Raina's safety. He couldn't risk losing the woman he loved.

DAMON LET himself into the patio door just after three in the morning. After Raina and the agent disappeared from the beach, Damon took his time planning out his attack. He had a knife strapped to his thigh, three guns, and his fists. His fists were his favorite weapons, but the agent was strong. Damon knew how to prepare to fight off an opponent.

The stairs to the rooms were in front of him, lit up all the way to the top. He wasn't sure which room Raina was in, but if he was right, the stupid owners kept their guest book out in the open.

Damon rolled his eyes when he found the book and easily figured out what room they were in. He went back to the stairs and crept up them, listening for movement in the silent house.

The door to the room was closed. Damon turned the handle, not surprised when it was locked. He made quick work of the lock and slipped inside in less than twenty seconds.

The room was pitch black with the blackout curtains drawn and no lights on. Damon drew his gun and moved into the room. Two lumps in the bed amped up his anger. The agent was sharing a bed with Damon's woman. That was not okay.

He moved closer, listening for their breath, wanting to hear when the agent took his last one. The room was silent.

Damon crept to the edge of the bed and reached for the blanket. He grabbed it and yanked, exposing the pillows laid out in the bed.

"Fuck!"

The word burst from him without thought, but in the silence of the house, it was possible it woke others up. Damon had to get out of there.

He turned to leave when he saw something in the bed. He reached for it, grabbing the foil wrapper. Opened. Used.

Damon growled and crumpled the condom wrapper in his hand. A gun was too easy for that son-of-a-bitch. Damon was going to cut him to pieces and make him beg for death. The fucker not only touched Raina, he fucked her. He took what was Damon's.

Death was too good for the agent.

RAINA WATCHED the dark blurs of trees pass by the window and tried to be calm. They were safe. They got away. Damon didn't find them.

But he was there. He would have found them if they didn't leave when they did.

Her stomach twisted in knots. Her body felt too big for her skin. She wanted to claw it off and let the fear and anxiety she felt out. She wanted to scream and cry and kick and fight.

But she just sat there and watched the trees go by. Hour after hour, Adam drove. Silence filled the car, a strange contrast after the way they'd been the last few days. He'd made her come in more ways than she'd ever experienced. He was a fun and creative lover, and she was looking forward to spending more time together, but they weren't on a vacation. They weren't enjoying each other. He was protecting her.

Because she was unable to protect herself.

Raina hated that truth, but it was the truth. Lorelei was a strong, badass woman who protected others. Karli and Jessica both went on the run alone and took care of themselves. Stacey outed a killer. So did Frannie.

But poor, defenseless Raina was being kept in a cage because she couldn't do a damn thing herself.

She hated it. And she was sick of it.

No more. She refused to hide anymore. She...

Adam slowed down and eased into a gas station. The place was lit up inside and out. "We need gas. Bathroom? Something to eat?"

Raina shrugged. She needed a backbone, but she didn't think they sold those in the gas station convenience store.

"Stay here until I finish pumping gas, then we can go inside."

Raina nodded.

A few minutes later, Adam opened her door and reached for her hand to help her out. One more sign she couldn't take care of herself.

She let Adam stick to her side because the reality was, she couldn't take care of herself. If Damon stopped them, Raina had no idea what to do. She couldn't disarm someone. She couldn't stop an attacker. She couldn't do anything.

They walked inside. Adam smiled at the clerk and guided Raina toward the bathrooms. He told her to stay in the bathroom until he knocked on the door so she knew it was safe to come out. Again, she nodded. Again, she was helpless.

He bought them both coffee and snacks, paid cash, and they were back on the road.

The sun was barely coming up behind them when Adam stopped again. They were somewhere in West

Virginia, six hours from the B&B where she felt safe and loved and good for the first time in far too long.

Adam pulled into the parking lot for a motel that had definitely seen better days. Raina did not want to stay there. If Damon didn't catch up to them, one of the others guests might kill them, or whatever disease they'd catch from being there.

Adam paid cash for a room and gave the guy behind the desk a new fake name. They got a key and went to a room that was definitely not clean and probably hadn't been clean in a few decades.

"Try to get some sleep. Lay the towels on the bed if you want. Most places are good about cleaning towels."

Raina stared at him like he had lost his damn mind. "Do you really think I'm going to sleep?"

Adam ran a hand through his hair, looking more exhausted than Raina had seen him. "I don't fucking know. I'm just trying to keep you safe."

"And sleeping will keep me safe?"

"Nothing is keeping you safe! I didn't know he was there. I didn't know he'd found us. I was so busy fucking you that I forgot to do my fucking job!"

Raina wrapped her arms around her belly and sucked in a breath, backing up a step away from the man she was falling in love with. The man who made her feel like shit.

"I didn't mean it like that," Adam whispered. "This is why it's a rule." He checked the window, then moved across the room to where she was standing next to the bed. Adam cupped her jaw and tilted her head back to meet his gaze.

She fought him for a second. He didn't force her.

"I care about you. Too much, Raina. Being with you... I don't care about the fucking rules. I don't know what this is or what it's going to be when all of this is over, but I don't regret being with you. What I regret is putting you in danger again. Losing focus and letting Street get close enough to us that we had to get out of there like we did."

Raina nodded. She felt like she was going to break. Like she'd shatter if something else happened. "I'm scared."

Adam pulled her against him and wrapped his arms around her body. He kissed the top of her head and rubbed his hands up and down her back. "I am, too."

She breathed a laugh. "I'm not sure that makes me feel better."

Adam chuckled with her. "I won't let my guard down again."

Raina sucked in a breath, hearing what he wasn't saying. They were over.

She backed out of his embrace and moved to the bed. It wasn't stained and there were no bugs crawling around, but it smelled musty. She grabbed the towels from the bathroom and stretched them over the comforter. Then she curled on her side, facing away from Adam's spot at the window and tried not to let him hear her cry.

ADAM'S GUT twisted as Raina turned away from him. He knew he said the wrong thing again, but he couldn't risk Street finding them. He couldn't risk Raina getting hurt. He should still be taking care of his head from his TBI, but he was driving through the night and loving Raina all night and ignoring his health.

For her.

Which was exactly what was going to get them caught.

Adam swallowed two painkillers and washed them down with a bottle of water. From where he sat, he could see the parking lot and any cars that pulled in. The curtains were closed, so no one would see him, but he was watching between the wall and the curtains.

Raina appeared to sleep while Adam watched people leave their rooms, load their vehicles, and leave. He hated having Raina in that place, but the guy at the desk didn't care who they were or why they were there. It was a good place to lie low.

Around noon, the phone Adam hadn't set down yet rang. He answered it quickly, even though he knew Raina would wake up when she heard him talking.

"Yeah?"

"He was staying at the B&B next door. Checked in yesterday."

"That's too fucking close."

"I agree. Are you safe?"

Adam snorted. "Relatively."

"What's your plan?"

"Fuck if I know."

"Can you get to Pittsburgh?"

Adam did some mental math and nodded. "We're about four hours away."

"I'll text you an address. We'll meet you there tonight."

"With backup."

"Lots of it. If Street's going to stick his head out to find you, we're going to make sure he pays for it."

"I'm definitely on board with that plan."

"See you in a few hours."

Adam hung up and looked up. Raina was looking at him, red-rimmed eyes that gutted him. "Where are we going?"

"Pittsburgh. You up for a few more hours in the car?"

"As long as it gets us closer to ending this, yes."

"That's what I hope."

Raina held his gaze for a long minute, then nodded and climbed off the bed. She grabbed the suitcase she never bothered to unpack and followed him out the door and back into the SUV.

Back on the road.

15

More trees, more roads, more anger. Raina was getting close to the end of her sanity. She tricked herself into thinking everything was okay when she and Adam were playing married couple. She let herself believe the lie.

The truth always comes out.

Adam checked them into the new hotel, under a new name with a prepaid reservation and a card on file that wasn't from them.

"They're already here," Adam explained as he guided Raina away from the desk at the hotel.

It was a nice hotel. The kind of place that hosted happy hours in the afternoon, had room service around the clock, and employees who were not only discreet but paid well for it.

The elevator whisked them quickly to the eleventh floor. Two people were waiting for the elevator when they stepped out. Raina tensed until they both stepped on the elevator and the doors closed between her and the strangers.

Adam checked the room number written on the room key envelope and turned to the right. When they reached room eleven-twenty-two, he held the key in front of the pad on the door. It blinked green, then clicked with the release.

Raina stepped inside the room ahead of Adam. He locked the door behind them and left his suitcase at the door. Raina dragged her suitcase across the room and sank onto the bed, feeling more exhausted than one night of not much sleep should make her.

She opened her mouth to ask Adam if she could lie down for a while, but Adam was at the door to the connecting room, his ear pressed to the door.

"What are you doing?"

He cut his eyes at her and shook his head just enough for her to understand.

He needed silence.

After a minute, he knocked on the door. Another minute went by before there was an answering knock.

Adam opened the door connecting their room to another one while Raina held her breath.

Liam stood on the other side of the door, with a tentative smile. "You good?"

Adam nodded. "As good as we can be."

"Good. Hi, Raina."

"Hi, Liam," she said, struggling to smile. Adam's cousin was a nice guy, but the last thing Raina felt like was small talk. She wanted a bottle of wine to herself and a bubble bath. Then ten or twelve hours of sleep without dreams about Damon.

"What's the plan?" Adam asked.

Liam glanced at Raina like he was gauging if he wanted to speak openly in front of her.

"She needs to know everything," Adam said, answering the unasked question.

Liam nodded, then moved into their room. He stood

near the TV and looked between her and Adam. "The judge is still missing. We don't know if we'll ever find him. The new judge is under the protection of Rose Protection Agency."

"Who's that?"

"Montgomery Rose served with Dex for a few years. Dex vouched for him. Said he's top notch. His company is growing, and they have an excellent record." Liam held Adam's gaze, waiting for approval.

Adam nodded once.

"Street came out of hiding to go after you two. He got close, but the biggest problem we have is how he knew where to find you."

"I thought you said he found the people from the first B&B," Adam said.

Liam nodded while Adam's words sank in for Raina. Damon found Norma and Tom. They were nice people, but Damon found them. And if they stood between him and her, he wouldn't hesitate to kill them.

"Are they okay?" Raina blurted, ignoring whatever Liam was saying.

Liam looked at Adam, letting him answer.

Raina didn't care who answered her as long as she found out. She'd been too afraid to ask before, but she had to know. She had to know if more people died because of her. Because Damon was obsessed with her and she ran. "Norma and Tom. Did he kill them?"

Adam shook his head. "No. Thankfully, another guest found them and was able to call for help."

"They're going to be okay?"

Adam looked at Liam. Liam nodded. "They should be. The husband—"

"Tom," Adam growled.

Liam nodded once. "Tom. Street knocked him out pretty quickly. Caught him by surprise. The wife..."

"Norma," Adam supplied.

"Norma put up a fight. Street wasn't gentle, but neither of them had life-threatening injuries."

"That's not like him," Raina whispered.

"It's a good thing," Adam said. "Whatever the reason."

Raina nodded, but she knew it was bad. When she was with Damon, he toyed with her. She learned his moods, and if he didn't get to inflict some kind of pain on her every so often, it would only be worse when he did.

She hated herself for staying there as long as she did. The broken bones weren't the worst of it. That was the part she talked about, but the rest... That was what kept her up at night.

Adam and Liam talked, making plans like she wasn't there. She wanted to care, but she didn't. She knew she was done. It didn't matter what they tried, Damon found her. No one knew how he was finding her, and it didn't matter. He did. And he would keep chasing her until one of them was dead.

Tears built in her eyes until they overflowed. Raina stumbled to the chair in the corner of the room and sank into it. She tucked her feet up against her butt and wrapped her arms around her knees. She put her head on her knees and let the tears come.

She sat there crying for a few minutes, barely noticing when the men's voices faded and stopped. A door closed, and the next thing she knew, she was being lifted from her seat and carried to the bed.

Adam laid her down and stretched out next to her, pulling her against his chest and holding her close while she cried.

She cried until she exhausted herself. Her body felt heavy, like she couldn't move if she tried. Sleep tugged at her, but every time she got close to fading, Damon popped into her mind and jolted her awake again.

"You're safe, Raina. I got you," Adam whispered.

"I'm never going to be safe. He will find me and he will kill me. I need to stop pretending that's not my future."

"Raina," Adam groaned.

"No." She pushed away from him and shook her head. "I've tried to be strong. I've tried to have faith. Damon is the worst of evil. He is going to delight in torturing me. It won't be the first time. But I can't just sit here and wait for it to happen."

"We're not sitting here and waiting for it. We're going to find him. We're going to stop him."

She sucked in a breath and sat up. She knew her words were going to hurt him, but she had to say them. "I know you're trying, but I don't think that's possible. I don't think anything will stop him, Adam. I can't trust that I'm safe. I'm not as long as he's alive. No matter what you do."

Raina looked at him just in time to see the shutters fall and the defeat take over.

ADAM WANTED to argue with her. He wanted to tell her she was wrong. He'd never faced someone like Street before. None of them had. He had more resources than any of them knew about. He was charming when he needed to be, but he was manipulative and didn't care if he killed people. He was a dangerous combination of the worst of humanity.

"We're trying," Adam confessed. It wasn't good enough. He knew it, and she knew it. He wanted to keep her safe. But fighting against a man who seemed to know everything you were going to do before you did it made the fight not just unfair, but impossible to win.

Raina looked up at him, the resignation in her gaze gutting him. He hated that she knew there was nothing more he could do. That it was only a matter of time before someone else was put in charge of protecting her because Street had outsmarted him one too many times.

"I want you to teach me self-defense," she whispered.

"What?"

"I need to know how to defend myself against him. I know it'll probably only delay the inevitable, but I need to have some knowledge. I need to have a chance."

"Raina."

She shook her head. "I have spent the last year hiding from him. In the shelter, with Karli, now with you. I've been running. He's been in control of my life because he's bigger and stronger and more deadly. Even if he's caught again and somehow the charges stick, he has people. It's very possible he'll have someone kill me. I need a chance."

Adam closed his eyes, hating that she wasn't wrong, but she also wasn't right. Her best chance was to stay in protective custody. But until Street was brought in, their options were limited. And she was in danger.

"Please, Adam," she whispered, the pain and fear she felt sinking into her words.

He nodded, knowing he had to put his bruised pride aside for her own good. She deserved the best chance she could get to stay safe. To stay alive. It didn't matter that he'd failed at his job, that he hadn't kept her safe like he was supposed to. He owed her.

"Thank you," she breathed, like she thought he was going to refuse her.

She clearly didn't know he couldn't refuse anything she asked for.

"I have one more request," she said, her voice even more unsure.

"Okay," Adam said, prompting her to explain. His shoulders tightened, his body preparing for whatever else she wanted him to do.

"I want to go back to Niagara Falls."

"What? Why? We know he'll be there soon. He'll go back, if for no other reason than to get more information."

She nodded. "I know. But it's home for me. It's where I feel safe. I want to be there. And I know with so many people looking for him, it's the best chance we have of finding him."

Her gaze didn't waver from his. There was something hidden in it, something he couldn't figure out. Something he knew would mean he'd regret agreeing to take her back to Niagara Falls.

"He's going to find us no matter where we go. We might as well go home and have all the resources we have. We're stronger there, too."

Dammit. Again, she wasn't wrong. She was smart, and she knew Street better than the rest of them. "We will talk to Liam and come up with a plan. We're only here tonight. He talked about switching vehicles tomorrow and going west."

"No," Raina cried. "Adam, I can't. I can't do this. He's taken everything from me. He took my job, my life, my entire world. He's isolated me from everyone and everything. He's completely destroyed me. I can't keep running. I'm tired. I'm done. I can't. I just..."

"Okay," Adam said, crossing the room to hold her close. She vibrated, from anger or anxiety, he didn't know, but it didn't matter. He was going to do everything he could to erase all her fears.

Street wouldn't stop. He'd proven that. He was going to get Raina, no matter what anyone else did to stop him. The only choice was to kill him.

Adam knew it weeks ago. He knew it when he looked into the eyes of that monster right before Street knocked Adam out. Adam couldn't stop him. No one would be able to stop a man like that. His mind worked in ways Adam would never understand.

The only choice was to think like Street. Adam knew Street would go back to Niagara Falls. That's why he and Liam were talking about them going west. Putting more distance between them. But through it all, they both knew it was a risk. It meant less support, more unease around who to trust, and putting more civilians in danger like Norma and Tom.

None of that sat right with Adam. He wanted a solution that meant bringing Street in. Dead or alive, Adam no longer cared.

That wasn't true. He did care. But he couldn't bring himself to admit it to his cousin.

"Adam," Raina whispered. She pressed her lips to his throat.

Liam and two of his guys were on the other side of the wall. None of them had any idea Adam had fallen for Raina and had been sleeping with her.

But one whispered plea and one brush of her lips and he was willing to throw everything away to make sure she knew she was the most important person in his world.

Adam didn't say anything. He didn't ask her if she was sure. He didn't hesitate. He didn't do any of the things he should have done. He just ducked his chin and caught her next kiss on his lips.

Raina's arms came up and wrapped around his neck. She felt as desperate as Adam was. For a connection, something good, to erase their reality. All of the above? Adam wasn't sure what Raina's motivation was, but he wanted to believe it was simple.

His was simple. He wanted to slide inside the woman he loved and believe there was something good left in the world. Something good worth fighting for. Something that would make up for what he was going to do.

Adam lifted Raina's shirt, abandoning the task when his knuckles brushed against her soft skin. He dragged them up her belly to the underwire of her bra. She pulled back just far enough to tug her shirt off, then made quick work of her bra while he lifted the cups over her full breasts and got his hands on them.

She groaned and pressed her breasts into his hands. She vibrated with need, her leg wrapping around his calf as she brought herself closer to him.

"Bed," he growled, pushing her toward the mattress while he licked her nipples and throbbed with lust and love and luck.

Raina pulled away from him to sit on the bed. She shifted her body across the mattress, but Adam caught her ankle and yanked her back toward him. She yelped in surprise, but grinned up at him.

"You're not getting that far away from me," he whispered into her ear, licking the shell and hardening at the shiver that traveled through her entire body.

"I'm not going anywhere," she whispered back.

"Good. But you have to make sure you're quiet. I'm not

sharing the sounds you make with the men on the other side of that door."

Raina glanced past him to the door that connected the two rooms. Her eyes sparkled with desire. "I'm not sure I can be quiet."

"You have to be, Raina. I'm going to lick you and suck you and fuck you, but we can't let them know what's going on."

She moaned.

Adam unzipped her jeans and helped her shove them down, leaving his hand between her thighs while she tried to get her pants and panties off. She gave up when he thrust two fingers into her entrance. He swiped his thumb across her clit, and she bucked against his hand, biting her lip to keep from crying out.

"You want to scream, don't you?" he teased her.

She nodded.

"I love watching you come. I love making you come."

"You're not all that quiet yourself," she teased him back. "You've—Oh, God."

"Quiet," he hissed.

"That's so good."

He smiled and pressed his thumb to her clit again. She moaned, but he was ready for her this time, swallowing her cries with a kiss. He didn't let up, stroking her until her body milked his hand and trembled through an orgasm that he ached to feel on his dick.

Adam eased his hand from her, loving the way she shivered, then rushed to get naked. He stalked across the room to where he left his suitcase at the door, not caring that he was naked in a hotel room with three other men on the other side of the door. All he cared about was Raina and making her feel good.

He found the condoms they had left and grabbed three of them, tearing into one on his way back to the bed. Raina kicked her jeans off and was lying on the bed with her head propped on a pillow, a satisfied grin on her face as she watched him roll the condom down his length.

"I love the way you look at me," Adam admitted.

"Same," she said, meeting his gaze with her own lust-filled one.

"I should be more considerate of your feelings right now, but—"

"The only feeling I have right now is that I need you inside me, Adam. I need to feel good."

Adam didn't hesitate another second. He covered her body with his and slid inside in one hard stroke.

Raina's eyes fell closed and her mouth fell open. She lifted her knees, spreading herself wider so Adam could sink deeper into her.

Then he moved. He held himself above her, easing his hips back and plunging in, his head and heart and body all working as one to bring Raina to the same place he was.

Adam watched the bliss lift her lips. He watched the way her eyelids fluttered as she climbed closer to the peak. And when she opened her eyes and found him watching her, he felt their connection from his fingers to his toes and everywhere in between.

Raina lifted her hands to cup his face, sliding her hands down his arms to where his hands supported him on the bed. Adam lifted one hand, wrapping his fingers with hers, and brought their joined hands above her head. He did the same with the other, bringing a smile to her pink lips.

Their joined hands above her head changed the way he stroked inside her, dragging his pelvis against her clit. She moaned with each thrust, her body tightening around him as he drove into her.

Adam was so busy watching her come undone he didn't notice his orgasm sneaking up on him until it tightened his balls and slammed into him.

"Raina," he grunted.

"Yes," she whispered. "Fuck, yes."

Adam pressed his weight onto her and lost his mind, slamming hard and deep into her while she cried out again, her release triggering his as they fell together.

16

RAINA LAID IN ADAM'S ARMS AND LISTENED TO HIS STEADY heart beating under her ear. She worried she was being unfair to him. Using sex to get her way. It felt far too close to the way Damon treated her for her sanity.

"When I met Damon, I was out with work friends. I hadn't been there long and didn't know many of them. They'd invited me out a few times, but I'd always said no. They were all younger than me. I felt like they weren't sincere."

Adam didn't respond, but he kissed the top of her head, confirming what she already knew. That he was awake, too.

"I agreed that night because I'd had a good day. Working as a massage therapist was not exciting or thrilling, but I loved it. I loved working on a client and helping them feel good when they walked out the door. One of my longtime clients was my last appointment of the day. For the first time in months, she was smiling. She felt good. Her pain was less intense, and she was glowing. She said it was because of me. After our previous session, she felt a shift. She was doing physical therapy and had a personal trainer, and all of it was making her stronger, but she was positive it was the massage therapy that made her feel so good. She hugged me and thanked me, and I wanted to celebrate."

Adam grunted his understanding.

"The bar was a mix of people and I felt better about being there. Less like the old lady and more like I belonged. I was at the bar, closing out my tab, when I saw Damon. I said something to him, catching his attention because I thought he was good looking. He was funny, and I was feeling good, and when he asked, I gave him my number."

Adam sucked in a breath, his chest lifting, then settling again.

"He called me the next day and invited me out over the weekend. He took me to dinners and shows and acted like I was the only woman he could see. He completely charmed me. It was so precise that I didn't even notice that he was isolating me from everyone I knew. He convinced me the people I worked with were only being nice. Then he convinced me my family wasn't really interested in what was going on with me. Then he asked me to move in with him. My lease was up, and I was spending most nights with him, anyway. As a surprise, he moved all my stuff to his place while I was at work one day."

"He's an expert at getting people to do what he wants," Adam whispered.

"He is. Not long after I moved in with him, he told me I didn't need to work if I didn't want to. Said he made more than enough money. I laughed it off and told him I liked my job. He dropped it, but a few weeks later, things started happening at work. Break-ins. The office was trashed one night. Cars were vandalized. One of my coworkers was mugged on the way to her car when she was leaving by herself. I started to get scared."

"He was behind it all." It wasn't a question, but Raina nodded.

"I didn't know it at the time, but yes. When he pushed me to quit, this time for my safety, he said he could support me until I found something else. He didn't want me in danger. It sounded so reasonable. Smart. Caring."

Adam tensed beneath her.

"A week went by, then two. By the end of the first month, I was having a hard time searching for a new job. Not only weren't there many, but I'd gotten comfortable. My independence was gone, and I didn't even realize I'd handed it over to him. I woke up one day and had no idea when I'd last spoken to someone other than Damon. When I'd left his place."

Adam tightened his grip, then relaxed his arm and stroked her back. The soothing gesture gave Raina the confidence to share the rest.

"I called one of the other therapists and asked if I could join them for a drink that night. It was Friday, and I figured they were all getting together. She was less than encouraging, but I assumed it was just because it hadn't been a while and maybe things were still tense. But when I met them, they all acted like I was part of the problem. They told me the attacks stopped after I quit, and that someone left a threatening note to not contact me again."

"Jesus."

"I was so embarrassed. I still didn't see that it was Damon. When I went home that night, he was there. He was angry that I'd gone out and not told him ahead of time. He demanded to know where I'd been and who I was with. Said I wasn't allowed to see people without his approval from now on. I laughed at him."

Adam's breath stopped, his lungs holding it in. Tension radiated off him, and she continued quickly.

"He didn't appreciate that. He told me I belonged to him. That I was his. I argued. Said I didn't belong to anyone. He threw it in my face that I lived in his house and let him provide for me. That he wasn't going to let me make a fool of him. He... I stormed off to the bedroom, intent on leaving. Even as I walked away, I knew there was nowhere for me to go, but I felt like I had to regain a little of my independence. He followed me into the bedroom."

"Raina," Adam breathed.

Tears ran down her cheeks, soaking his chest. But she had to tell him. She had to get rid of the hold Damon had on her. "He told me he loved me as he forced himself on me. Told me I belonged to him. Said he was never going to let anything happen to me, but that I needed to listen to him so he could protect me. I cried and tried to get him to stop, but he wouldn't. He left bruises on my hips from where his fingers dug into me. And when he was done, he told me he was sorry for having to teach me a lesson, but that it was for my own good that he was keeping me safe."

Both of Adam's arms circled her, holding her close and making her feel safe as she recounted one of the worst moments of her life.

"I took a shower and opened one of the drawers he gave me. I realized he'd slowly replaced my old clothes with things he'd chosen for me. Even down to the underwear he wanted me to wear. As I stood there and looked at what my world had become, I repeated the words he'd been saying to me. That he loved me. That he wanted to protect me. That it was all for my own good. I convinced myself it wasn't rape because we were in a relationship. I told myself I loved him, and he loved me, and I was safe with him. I'd never had anyone else ever care much about me. I... I knew leaving him meant walking away from a man who wanted me. He wasn't perfect, but being with him was better than being alone." Raina sucked in a shaky, watery breath. "Then I got dressed in the clothes he bought me and laid down in the bed he provided in the apartment he shared with me and knew my life would never be the same again."

Adam was quiet for a long minute. He held her, his heartbeat the only sound Raina could hear as she waited for his reaction.

Tears continued to pour down her cheeks for the woman who decided to stay with Damon back then. The woman who thought she wasn't worthy of someone better than Damon. Living in Shelter in the Storm and working with Francesca and Stacey taught Raina she wasn't that person anymore, but believing she deserved better was harder than knowing she'd changed.

"I would never hurt you," Adam whispered, fierce and firm, like the words were painful to say.

"I know," Raina told him.

Adam shook his head. "I'm not without my own demons, Raina. I've killed people. In my line of work, it happens. And this... I want to kill Street. I want to watch the life leave his eyes and know he'll never touch you again, never hurt you again. I've never felt this way before. I've chased down some of the worst humanity has to offer. People who've killed kids, shot up schools, tortured their victims. With Street... I won't rest until he's dead. Death means he won't pay for his crimes, but it's the only thing that will stop him. I want—"

"Adam," Raina whispered. He was so tense he was almost hurting her in his grip. She knew it wasn't intentional, but she also knew he was better than that.

"I'm sorry. I just..." Adam trailed off and inhaled deep, his breath shaky like hers.

Raina lifted her head and looked up at him. Tears stained his cheeks. He didn't hide them from her, just met her gaze and held it. Raina lifted her hand to his cheek and wiped his tears away. She crawled on top of him and kissed him softly.

It was more than a job for him. She believed that before, but seeing the emotion on his face confirmed that his feelings for her went to the same depths hers did for him.

"Adam," she whispered, sliding down his body as his erection tapped her ass.

"No," he said, halting her progress. "I want to feel you. I want to be inside you."

Raina nodded, reaching over to grab a condom from the nightstand. She helped Adam roll it on, then lowered herself onto his erection while he held it still.

His fingers gripped her hips, then loosened and slid to her thighs.

Raina rocked over him, lifting up and sinking down with each move and feeling him fill her more with each stroke.

Adam surged up as she sank down, making her cry out at the depth he hit.

"Adam," she whispered.

"Don't hold back. Please, Raina. All I want is to see you happy."

"So good," she moaned.

Her gaze caught on his and held. They moved together, their bodies in sync, like they'd been together more than just a few days.

Her hands slapped down on his chest as exhaustion started to take over. Adam rolled them, grabbing her hands and lifting them above her head and bringing himself over her body. He kissed her gently, loving her mouth with his as he stretched and filled her body until she couldn't hold back the orgasm bursting from her.

He swallowed her moans, then gave them back to her as he followed her over the edge, both of them trembling, splitting, and coming back together as one instead of two separate people.

Adam lowered his weight onto Raina, and she held him close, fighting the emotion she felt. She was counting on him for everything, just like she'd done with Damon, but being with Adam was nothing like being with Damon. Adam was good. He was kind. And Raina was falling hard and fast for him.

She just hoped one day she could tell him and be free to love him the way he deserved. The way they both deserved.

Because for the first time since she left Damon Street, Raina believed she deserved love. The kind of love Adam was showing her every time he touched her. The kind of love she always dreamed of finding.

ADAM SAT in the backseat of the SUV with Raina, holding her hand. Liam drove, and his teammates took the SUV they'd loaned to Adam and Raina, just in case Street was following that vehicle.

Liam gave Adam a look when he climbed into the backseat with Raina, but Liam didn't make a comment about it. Adam was sure he'd get questions when they got back, but until then, he wasn't going to worry about anyone other than Raina.

The almost four-hour drive from Pittsburgh to Niagara Falls felt far too quick. As they got closer to the city, Adam's tension increased. He felt like they were walking back into the lion's den, after starving the lion.

Liam parked the SUV in the garage beneath the F-BOMB building. His team was waiting for them, surrounding the vehicle as they all got out and went to the elevator. Once they were inside F-BOMB's secure office, the silence that fell over the group stopped.

"What's the plan?" Dunn asked. Even though he was the leader, they all worked together and made decisions independently.

"Raina wanted to come back here." Liam nodded at Raina and Adam, waiting for them to nod before continuing. "Adam and I talked about going west, but Raina said Street won't stop. Being here means the most resources, the most people looking for him."

"We still need her in custody," Dunn said.

"Agreed," Dex said. He was one of the two who met Adam and Raina in Pittsburgh with Liam. He'd been a part of the decision to come back.

Archer, the other F-BOMB teammate who met them in Pittsburgh, stood in the corner of the conference room, looking menacing with his large arms crossed and a pissed off look on his face.

"Above all that, we need to find this fucker," another guy said. He was the biggest one in the room. Adam was still figuring out who all of them were, but he trusted them implicitly.

"Mason's right," Dunn said, nodding to the man who spoke. "None of this matters if we don't bring Street in again."

"I think I know a way we can do that," Raina said. Her voice was small and quiet in the room full of large men with even bigger opinions on how to handle a criminal.

Raina was a massage therapist. She was smart, but she wasn't trained the way the rest of them were.

Adam's entire body tensed. He knew Raina. He knew the way she thought. If she had an idea, Adam was fairly sure he knew what it was going to be.

"No," Adam said before she could speak. "Raina, no."

She spun in her chair and leveled him with a look. "You don't even know what I'm going to say."

Adam stepped forward. Raina sat at the table in the center of the conference room. Some of the men sat with her, others stood. Adam had chosen to stand behind Raina. Guard her. Protect her.

"You're going to offer to use yourself as bait," Adam said.

Raina held his gaze while everyone else in the room held their breath. When she nodded, she tore her gaze from Adam's.

His heart dropped to his feet. She couldn't do it. She couldn't risk her life. She couldn't walk into a situation where Street could win.

"No," Jack said. His normally smiling face was angry and set. "My wife did the same when we were trying to catch her asshole ex, and he almost kidnapped her."

"But he didn't," Dunn argued.

"But he could have. How in the fuck can you possibly consider that option again?" Jack barked.

"Because Pilar was fine," Archer said. "And because the only thing Street wants is Raina."

"It's dangerous," Dex said.

"So's letting that fucker stay above ground," Mason argued. "I'm all for coming up with Plan B, but we've been at this for weeks. He's evaded custody for decades, and when we finally brought him in, he was free in hours with all charges dropped."

"He'll probably see right through it," Liam said.

"He might, but if we're smart about it, it won't matter," Dunn said.

"This is a bad idea," Jack growled.

"We don't have any good ideas," Mason said.

"But this? Putting her in danger? Putting her in his view and dangling her like a carrot in front of a hungry horse? I can't believe any of you are even thinking about this." Jack slammed his fist on the table and stood, his rolling chair crashing into the wall behind him.

"I'm with Jack. I think it's too dangerous," Dex said.

"I agree," Adam snapped.

"I think it's our best shot," Mason admitted.

"Me, too," Archer said.

Dunn looked around the room at the others. It was clear they operated as a democracy and he was giving them all a voice.

Rocky looked at Raina. "Have you ever been in a situation where you need to defend yourself?"

Raina shook her head. "I asked Adam to teach me self-defense. It's only been a day, so I don't know much, but I know Damon better than anyone else. I know what he'll do."

"That might be so, but if he takes you, it won't matter. He'll kill you," Rocky said.

"And if he stays out there, he'll kill others. He's not going to stop until he gets me back or dies. Those are the only options for Damon. He thinks I embarrassed him by leaving. He wants to teach me a lesson. He wants to prove he can control me. He's going to kill me. I know that. If he gets his hands on me, I'm dead. I've accepted that. I don't want that to be the outcome because I know what he'll do before he kills me will be so much worse than death, but Damon won't stop. Ever. This is the only way."

"She's right. We need to let her do it," Slade, who'd been silent to that point, said.

"I disagree," Rocky said. "It's too dangerous."

Dunn looked at Liam. "You're the last vote."

Liam exhaled a shaky breath and met Adam's gaze. Before he spoke, Adam knew what he was going to say and swore.

"Are you fucking kidding me? What if this was Caitlyn? Would you send her up against a sick son-of-a-bitch who wanted to kill her?"

Liam's face morphed into a scowl. His eyes slid to Raina, then back to Adam, a disapproving sigh escaping. "You know Caitlyn would make the same decision. She did make the same decision."

Adam growled and glared at his cousin. The one person in the room he thought would have his back. But he didn't. Liam betrayed Adam, throwing Raina in front of the speeding train with the hope she could stop it.

She was going to die. Street would kill her. And Adam's hope of changing that was gone.

He shoved his way out of the conference room and stomped down the hall, slamming the door of one of the offices hard enough to rattle the walls. He pounded his fist against the door, then sank to the floor and tried to come up with a better idea. One that wouldn't mean sacrificing the woman he loved.

17

Raina couldn't move. Her entire body felt like it was made of glass and movement would shatter her entirely. She knew she should go after Adam, but he was angry. More than she'd ever seen him.

"I'll go talk to him," a voice said.

Raina finally looked up. All the men were watching her, but Liam was moving toward the door. He must have been the one who spoke.

"No," Raina said, forcing herself from the chair she wanted to sink into and never leave. "I'll talk to him."

"Are you sure?" Liam asked.

Raina nodded, even though she was far from sure. "He wouldn't be upset if I hadn't convinced him to come back here without telling him why. It's my mess."

Liam smiled at her and squeezed her hand as she walked by.

Raina turned in the direction Adam went when he slammed out of the conference room. The hallway wasn't that long, but she had no way of knowing where Adam went.

The first two offices were empty. Raina was about to check the third when a woman walked out of it. "Oh."

The woman smiled. "Hi. You must be Raina. I'm Kyra. I'm the office manager, which means I do my best to keep these men in line. Of course, Slade's the easy one for me since he's my husband."

"I didn't realize," Raina said, unsure what she was trying to explain away. She didn't realize Kyra existed at all, either as Slade's wife or as the office manager or that she was in the building.

"It's okay. I'm not the one you're here for, but I thought you'd like to know Adam is in that office. It's Rocky's, technically, but Adam ducked in there and closed the door."

Raina drew a breath and stared at the door like it was going to attack her. "Thank you."

Kyra smiled. "You're welcome. And good luck. These men are amazing and kind and passionate about what they do. I've heard a lot about Adam from English, Liam to you, sorry. He's a big fan of his cousin's. I can see you are, too."

Raina blanched, unsure how the woman she'd just met knew anything. "I, um... Adam's been great."

Kyra grinned. "Don't worry. I'm not here to judge, and I know how it feels to fall for a man you tell yourself not to fall for. I'm cheering for you two."

"Thanks," Raina whispered. She didn't know how to feel about that, but she figured it couldn't hurt to have an ally.

Kyra walked past Raina, leaving Raina to approach the office where Adam was.

Raina drew a deep breath and let it out slowly, then knocked on the office door. Silence greeted her. She knocked again, but still heard nothing from inside. She turned the handle, relieved when it didn't catch.

The office was dark, but the high windows let outside

light in. Raina stepped inside and closed the door, giving her eyes a minute to adjust before she found Adam sitting on the floor, his back to the wall behind the door.

"What do you want?" Adam growled. He was back to snapping at her and acting like she was the enemy.

Instead of answering, Raina sat on the floor next to him and put her head on his shoulder.

As if it was an instinct, Adam wrapped his arm around her and kissed the top of her head.

Raina let out a sigh of relief. He was angry, but he wasn't going to pull back from her. It meant more to her than he could possibly know that he was willing to support her, even though he disagreed.

They sat there in silence for a few minutes. Raina wanted to explain to him what was going through her mind, but she knew he wouldn't be willing to let her risk her safety to save him. If Damon found out they'd slept together, he would kill Adam without a second thought. She couldn't let that happen. And she couldn't let Damon keep hurting people.

This had to end.

"I don't want you to have to face him," Adam whispered.

Raina nodded. "I know."

"He'll try to kill you."

"I know."

"He might succeed."

"I know."

Breath shuddered from Adam like he was giving it all up. He surrounded her with his other arm, pulling her tighter into his grasp. He pressed his cheek to the top of her head and held onto her.

"I can't keep living like we have been. Neither can you. That's not to say I didn't enjoy spending time with you, but he's not going to stop. It's been a year since I left him. In that time, he hasn't stopped. He's still trying to get me back."

"You can't go back to him."

Raina shook her head. "I'm not. I don't want to die, Adam."

"Then why are you doing this?"

She laughed mirthlessly. "You really don't get it, do you?"

"Get what?"

"I... care about you, Adam. Damon has taken a lot of people from the ones who cared about them. Not just him, but the people who work for him. He's not going to stop until he has what he wants. What he wants most right now is me."

"You said you're not going back to him."

Raina shook her head. "I'm not. I refuse. But I can't let anyone else die because of me. Norma and Tom... He would have killed them. Same with Bobbi and Lenny. How many more people would die if we kept running?"

"I don't know," Adam admitted.

"We can't do it. I can't do it. I can't risk anymore lives. I don't want to die. I don't want to end up with Damon. I want a life after all of this. But I can't trade mine for the lives of innocent people who happen to meet me along the way. You. Lorelei. Edie. Her cousin died because they thought she was Karli. Karli would have died. Jessica, Stacey. Mackenzie. Francesca. Damon would kill all of them if he thought it would get him closer to me. I'm not willing to risk it. Not another day."

Adam's body was tense, his arms locked around Raina. She could feel his uneven breath and the anger pouring off of him.

He buried his nose in her hair and inhaled deep. As he

breathed, his grip on her loosened. "You're right," he finally said. "I still don't like this, but I know you're right."

"Thank you."

"I can't lose you, though."

"You won't. I'm not going anywhere."

He kissed her hair, then her neck, then tilted her head back and claimed her lips. He urged her on top of him, straddling his lap, and kissed her until they were both panting and desperate to finish what they started.

"Think this door locks?" Adam asked with a smile.

"I think it doesn't matter if it does."

He chuckled with her and nodded. "Then we need a place to stay tonight. Preferably with one bed and lots of condoms."

"Agreed."

ADAM WALKED with Raina back down the hall to the conference room. F-BOMB were still in there talking, but there were two new additions when Adam and Raina joined them.

"Lorelei!" Raina exclaimed, rushing to hug Adam's partner.

Lorelei hugged Raina and looked over her shoulder at Adam. The one raised eyebrow was enough to tell Adam Lorelei didn't miss that he and Raina were holding hands when they walked in.

Adam shrugged, not bothering to hide it and knowing Lorelei wouldn't judge.

Her answering smirk said she was happy for them.

"Edie, what are you doing here?" Raina asked when she let go of Lorelei, going to Edie and speaking softly to her.

Adam fist-bumped his partner. "You good?"

"Yep. I've been keeping Mooney up to date on what's going on. He's itching to get us back, but he knows if he demands it, we're going to take vacation." Lorelei rolled her eyes.

"It's only been a week. He gave us two."

Lorelei shrugged. "We'll make it work. Just glad to see with my own eyes you two are good."

"Thanks," Adam said.

Raina and Edie were talking, and their conversation caught Adam's attention. He hadn't gotten to know Edie well in the short time she stayed at the safe house, but what he did know of her, she was a smart and kind woman who'd lived through hell and was brave enough to not only escape but to fight back.

Edie sat next to Raina looking stronger than last time Adam had seen her. She offered him a tentative smile, then turned back to Raina. "I've been helping. Providing information and doing what I can to try to take down Damon and the rest of the Company."

Raina sucked in a breath, her shoulders tensing for a long minute before they relaxed with her exhale.

Adam waited for her to speak. Without seeing her face, he wasn't sure if she was upset or grateful.

"It's going to take all of us," Raina said. "I know this isn't easy for you, though."

Edie shook her head. "It's not, but neither is knowing there are other women there. Others who've been forgotten and ignored and left behind. I don't know why I was lucky enough to get away, but I'm not going to waste the chance I have to stop what they're doing to people."

"Thank you."

The two of them shared a look as they held hands.

Everyone else watched them. The trained members of the group knew the knowledge Edie and Raina had about Damon was invaluable, but the people in the room who carried guns and fought evil on a regular basis had to be in charge.

Dunn stepped forward, as if reading Adam's mind, and cleared his throat. "Ms. Warren was nice enough to agree to help us come up with a plan. We've filled her in as far as what we've talked about so far in terms of dangling Raina out in the open so Street will notice her. After that, we're still working on it."

"Damon isn't the type to jump first," Raina said. "It might take him seeing me a few times before he thinks he can get the upper hand."

"She's right," Edie said. "He's smart and sneaky. When he took me from where I was held, I thought he was helping me. He got my trust quickly and easily. I really thought I was going to be safe with him."

"We know this is going to be a tough sell. We can't just have Raina show up someplace and think he's going to fall for it. This has to seem natural or he'll know we're onto him," Dunn said.

"So, what do we do? Our priority has to be keeping Raina safe," Jack said, his scowl saying he still didn't agree with the plan.

"It will be. We aren't going to let anything happen. We will have people everywhere and we will make sure anytime she goes out there is someone close enough to keep her safe," Dunn growled toward Jack.

Jack leveled his boss with a look that made Adam tense. The two of them looked like they were going to fight. Adam appreciated Jack fighting the plan and wanting to confirm Raina would be safe, though. After the way Adam stormed out of the conference room, he wasn't sure any of them would be willing to listen to him.

Jack finally looked away, and Dunn continued.

"We need a few locations where Raina would be. Places he would see you that wouldn't be unusual."

Raina nodded. "When we were together, I didn't go a lot of places, but I would think he'd expect me to be at a grocery store or something like that. Maybe out to dinner or at a bar."

"Wherever she's staying has to be far from where we plant her," Dex said. "We don't want him to figure out she's in the area and catch us off-guard."

"We have a block of hotel rooms set up, and we'll be switching off vehicles and moving her around. We're going to make this a long game and as complicated as possible." Dunn held Dex's gaze until Dex nodded.

Adam wanted to trust Dunn as much as the others did, but it wasn't Dunn's wife in danger. Adam knew she'd been on the run once, from her own dangerous ex, but she was safe now. Raina wasn't.

"I don't think Damon is going to be at a grocery store. He doesn't do his own anything," Raina said.

"I agree," Edie said. "He keeps himself isolated. That's how he's been able to stay under the radar all this time. He's like a ghost."

"Do you remember where you were being held?" Archer asked Edie.

Edie shook her head. "Not really. Sometimes I was at a house with the guy who decided I was his. When he wasn't interested, I was with others at a different house."

"When Street took you, where did he take you?" Archer asked.

"Mackenzie might know. I ended up at her station, so not far," Edie said.

"Do you think you were close to where you'd been held before?" Archer asked.

Edie closed her eyes. "I know the house I was in most of the time was big. We were kept in the basement. When someone was there for us, we were brought upstairs into a bedroom. There were at least four bedrooms, but probably more. It wasn't far from that house to the other one. Maybe ten minutes at the most. When Damon took me, I was coming down from my high and barely conscious. I was pissed, and he promised me drugs. I was in and out of consciousness, but I think it was still fairly close."

"You were always in a house?" Dex asked.

Edie opened her eyes and nodded.

"We've already done a search around the rescue station, but we can expand out," Liam said. "We might get lucky."

"In the meantime, we'll target places in that area for our adventures," Dunn said. "You okay with that, Raina?"

Raina sucked in a breath and nodded, not looking sure at all.

They planned a few outings, then let Raina, Adam, Lorelei, and Edie leave. Dex and Archer went with them, riding down to the garage with them in the elevator.

Archer stayed with Lorelei and Edie, and Dex took Raina and Adam to a hotel. He walked right past the desk, heading to an elevator that could only be accessed with a key card.

"We didn't want any chances," Dex said when they were in the elevator. "This place is secure, and we've had someone staying here for a few days. Haven't seen anything odd."

Adam nodded, grateful for their advanced planning.

Dex escorted them to a two-bedroom suite and cleared it with Adam before declaring them good to go. He handed over a key card and assured them someone would be posted outside at all times, someone else in the lobby, and more people watching the building from the outside.

"Isn't that overkill?" Raina asked.

Dex shook his head. "We aren't taking any chances. The suite across the hall is ours, so it's not like someone will be standing in the hallway and drawing attention to you. The others will blend in and not be noticed. We want you to feel safe, and to be safe."

"Thank you," Adam said.

Dex nodded and left them alone in the suite that already had their luggage, in separate bedrooms. Adam was a little impressed F-BOMB had pulled all of this off without him even noticing what was going on.

Raina stared at the door while Adam stared at Raina. He wasn't sure where her head was, and he didn't want to push the boundaries of what she wanted.

After a minute, she looked over at him with a sad smile. "I'm scared."

Adam nodded and moved closer to her. He reached for her hand and held it loosely in his. "I am, too. But we're safe here."

She nodded. "I know. But I'm not safe out there." She exhaled a shaky breath. "I'm not ready to face him."

"I'm not going to leave your side. I'll be with you every step of the way."

She smiled up at him. "I know you want to, but you'll have to leave me alone if Damon's going to approach me and try to get to me."

"I won't go far."

She stepped closer and wrapped her arms around his waist, resting her head on his chest.

Adam inhaled the scent of the shampoo he massaged into her hair that morning before they left Pittsburgh. It felt like far too long ago. Like a lifetime had passed since then.

"I know you're upset with me, but I am grateful you're going along with this."

"I'm not mad at you. I'm scared for you. I don't want to lose you. Now or after all this is over," he admitted.

Raina pulled back to look up at him, a ghost of a smile lifting her lips. "I feel the same."

Adam leaned down slowly, kissing her lips gently. Sharing breath and life and love, even if neither of them used the word. It hung right there, between them like it was a part of them.

"I'm not leaving you," he whispered against her lips.

"I'm going to hold you to that," she whispered back.

He kissed her again, then carried her to the large, soft bed in the room farther from the door and showed her how much he loved her all night long.

18

———

Did they think he was an idiot? For fuck's sake, a rookie would be able to tell they were setting a fucking trap. And Damon was no rookie. But nothing had changed. Three weeks and Raina was still at the same store at the same time on the same day of the week.

How fucking stupid did they think he was?

Damon shook his head and snickered. They'd probably get bored eventually and try something new, but he was going to have a little fun. Raina's protector was always right by her side, not going far enough away to give Damon a chance to grab her, if he was dumb enough to try. But they were getting comfortable. Lazy.

Sloppy.

Damon was a fan of sloppy work, as long as it wasn't from someone he was in charge of. His employees didn't get second chances. They learned how to take advantage of sloppiness in others. Which was exactly what Damon was going to do.

He moved closer to Raina, careful not to draw any attention to himself. The Agent was paying more attention to

Raina than their surroundings, but there were others. The guy in the baseball hat two aisles over, the guy with the bulge in the back of his jeans at the end of the aisle, and the couple one aisle in the other direction. And that didn't count the ones in the parking lot outside or the ones near the exit.

Damon wouldn't be able to get Raina out of the store without someone stopping him, but that wasn't the goal today. Today was about letting her know he wasn't falling for it.

Raina and the Agent moved to the end of the aisle. Damon watched from ten feet away, knowing he'd get his chance soon. He smiled when Raina pointed to something and the stupid agent went to grab it for her, leaving Raina without anyone watching her as she turned down the new aisle.

"Hello, Raina," Damon said, stepping up behind her so she was trapped.

The breath she sucked in hardened his dick. He inhaled the fear rolling off her and had to force himself not to slam her against the aisle and claim her right then and there.

"Damon," she breathed, turning to look him in the eye.

Damon smirked at her, enjoying the panicked look in her eyes. "So nice to see you, my love. How've you been?"

"How have I been? Are you fucking kidding me? What is wrong with you?"

Damon's smirk hardened to a glare. He didn't tolerate her swearing at him. He stepped closer, backing her up against the metal shelves that separated the aisles. "Don't you dare use that language with me."

"What are you going to do about it? We're over. We have been for a year. You're the only one who can't understand that."

"We're over when I say we're over," he growled. "And I don't say we're over. You're still mine, and that agent who thinks he can touch you will learn again that it's a bad idea to cross me."

"Adam is twice the man you are," she spat.

Damon reached up so fast she didn't have time to react before his hand was around her throat, tightening. He grinned at the bravado slipping from her gaze, replaced by terror. It was his favorite look. The one that kept him going. The one that brought a smile to his face.

"Be careful what you say, Raina. It's not nice to insult the man with his hand around your fucking throat." Damon squeezed, feeling her airway shrink. It would be so easy to squeeze hard enough to kill her, but he didn't want her dead yet. He had plans for her. Plans that involved his bed and handcuffs she'd never get off and a punishment that would teach her never to try to leave him again.

"Fuck... you," she hissed, the words barely audible through her closing throat.

Damon chuckled. "Yes, that's the plan. But not now. Your agent might be too stupid to stay by your side, but your other protectors are too close. I'll find you again. Maybe at that hotel where you're staying on the eighth floor. Or the house you go to in the city. Or maybe I'll just crash into that black SUV they drive you around in and grab you from the backseat before any of them know what's going on. If I'm lucky, I can kill two birds with one stone and get rid of your agent at the same time I bring you back to me."

Each threat came with a widening of her eyes and a tensing of her body. The realization that he not only knew her routine, but he had planned ways to get her away from the people who were supposed to protect her made Raina stiff as a board.

She wasn't the only one. If Damon had it his way, he'd shove her to her knees and fuck her mouth until she choked on his dick, but the bitch would probably bite it off.

A single tear trailed down Raina's cheek, and Damon leaned in, licking it as she shivered in his hand. He kissed her cheek and whispered in her ear. "You're always going to be mine, Raina. Until the day you die."

Damon's time was up, so he released her and walked away as she collapsed on the floor and gasped for breath.

He'd rounded a corner before the yelling started. Damon smiled as he walked down the aisle, away from Raina and her stupid agent who finally found her.

He was almost to the front of the store when someone caught his eye. He knew those legs, and the eyes.

Damon smirked and changed direction, knowing he had another minute to say hello to an old friend.

She gasped when she saw him heading toward her, but her instinct had her freezing instead of fleeing.

"It's good to see you again, Edie. How have you been?"

She shook, her hands balled together in front of her. Her gaze was locked on his, not looking around. Too scared to do anything else.

"I see you didn't die in that storm. Shame. I was hoping you had. Well, really, I was hoping we could have spent some time together. It's been a while. But then Trevor claimed you as his, and I was out of luck. I would have treated you better than he did. I would have made sure you had all the drugs you wanted. I never would have let you lose your high so you were willing to leave with another man. Then again, your cousin was causing trouble. I'm glad I could take care of her, even though it wasn't her I was after." Damon laughed and shook his head. "Lucky accident, you know?"

Edie continued to stare at him.

Damon looked down at her hands and saw a knife clenched in her fist. He leaned closer so no one else would hear his words. "Aw, Edie. What do you think you're going to do with that? We both know you'd never hurt me. Not after how good I was to you. I even let you orgasm when we were together. Didn't punish you for it because your tight pussy felt good on my dick. And then I saved you from Trevor. Why would you hurt me?"

He pulled back and watched as tears streamed down her cheeks. Her eyes were clenched tight, her hands shaking again.

Damon patted her cheek. "It was so good to see you, Edie."

He kissed her forehead, then turned and walked out of the store without anyone stopping him.

Just like he always did.

RAINA COULDN'T STOP SHAKING. She thought she was so fucking brave. But she wasn't. She nearly peed her pants when Damon wrapped his hand around her throat.

And then she cried, and he licked the tear.

The whole thing made her sick. God, how stupid was she? She thought Adam teaching her a few self-defense moves and being surrounded by people would make her feel safe, but she didn't. Not even a little.

Especially when he made it clear he'd been watching her and knew her every move.

Everyone in the room was shouting over each other. They were angry. Damon made them all look incompetent. He made Raina feel like they were incompetent. She trusted the men and women who were yelling at each other. She thought they'd keep her safe.

She wasn't safe. She'd never be safe. Damon told her that. He was more patient than she ever gave him credit for. He would wait until he could get her and then he'd take her.

He made it sound easy. And Raina knew it would be for him. Nothing had ever stopped him before. Even being the most wanted man in the city hadn't stopped him from walking into a public place and wrapping his hand around her throat and squeezing until Raina almost blacked out.

She rubbed her neck, wishing she could erase the feeling of Damon's hand on her. It wasn't the first time he'd put his hands around her throat. She hated him.

"I'm sorry," Edie whispered from the seat next to Raina. The two of them were huddled in the corner of the conference room, present but not involved in the discussion that didn't include listening.

"Why would you be sorry?" Raina asked Edie.

Edie shook her head and swiped at her cheeks. "Because I let him get away."

"There was nothing you could do."

"I had a knife. But I froze." She looked over at Raina, her eyes wide with fear and pain. "I knew him."

Raina nodded. "You said he's the one who got you out of that other house. Before Mackenzie and Holden found you."

"No. I mean, yes, but no. I knew him before. He was... I recognized the way he smelled."

"What?" Raina gasped. She turned in her chair to face Edie fully. "You slept with him?"

Edie looked at the others as the shouting quieted. Her gaze lowered to her hands, twisted in her lap. "It's not like I was given a choice, but yeah. He was walking out of the store, but he turned toward me. I guess he recognized me. He said..."

"What did he say?" Raina whispered. She wasn't sure why she needed to know, but she did.

"He said he remembered me. Told me... things."

"What things?" one of the men barked.

Edie closed her eyes. "We would get punished if we had an orgasm during sex. We were supposed to just lay there and let them do what they wanted. Damon said he would let me... That he enjoyed it. Said he would have treated me better than Trevor if I'd stayed with him."

"Jesus," someone breathed.

"I'm so sorry, Raina. I don't remember him. I was so drugged up that I barely remember anything. But I... I knew his scent." Edie sucked in a scared, shaky breath.

"Scents are powerful," Lorelei said. "We have a lot of memories tied to scents, and they're used to recover memories, too."

Edie nodded.

"Is that why you didn't kill him?" one of the men asked. "Because he was good to you?"

Raina turned to glare at whoever asked the insulting question, but Edie answered before Raina could figure out who asked.

"Being pumped full of drugs and raped repeatedly is not my version of being treated well. No one involved in that organization treated me well. Death would have been welcome at times. I prayed for it. For the drugs to be laced with something that killed me or... something. Have you ever been so broken, so scared and sick and disgusted with yourself that you prayed to die? Have you ever thought death was a better option than life?"

"Yes," some of the men answered.

One stepped forward. Slade, Kyra's husband. "I was taken prisoner. For two weeks, I was tortured. Every single day, I thought I was going to die. I'd wake up and wonder if I was dead or not. It was a time in my life I wished for death. But it was only two weeks for me. I'm sorry for what you've been through. For what you're still going through."

"Thank you," Edie whispered.

Slade looked around the room at the others. "Street knows our tactics. He knows what we've been doing. He knows more than we realize, far more."

"But how?" Archer barked.

"It doesn't fucking matter," Dex said. "He knows. Which means we need to change everything we do to keep Raina and Edie safe."

Edie looked up at them. "Me? I don't have anything to do with this."

"Street knows you're involved now. He may have known before, but he definitely knows now. Whether he intends to do anything about it or not, it doesn't matter. You were let down in the past. We're not going to let it happen again." Dex waited until Edie nodded at him to meet the gazes of the others in the room.

"Dex is right. The hotel isn't an option. Coming here or going to English's place are out. All the places we've had you going recently are not options," Dunn said.

"Why would he tell her all of this? Why would he tip his hand and let her know he's been following her? Why wouldn't he just use the information he has and grab her?" Liam asked.

"Are you saying it's a bad thing? That him admitting all of this so we can protect Raina is a disappointment?" Adam snapped.

Liam shook his head. "No. I'm saying it doesn't make

sense. He likes to be in control. He's smart. He's been ten steps ahead of us this whole time. Why tell us what he knows? Why eliminate the options he has for grabbing Raina? Obviously, he knew there were more people there today. He didn't even try to take her." Liam glanced at Raina. "Not that what he did was okay, but you're here. It doesn't make sense to me that he would show his cards."

"Liam's right," Mason said. "He wants us to scramble. He thrives on creating chaos. He gets off on knowing that we're all here trying to come up with new plans that he's going to figure out again. New plans that might not be as well thought-out and might give him a new opportunity."

"What are you suggesting?" Dunn asked.

Mason shrugged. "Don't change a thing."

"Are you fucking kidding me?" Adam shouted. Tension and anger radiated off of him. Raina wanted to soothe him and make him calm down, but he wasn't wrong. "What the hell is wrong with you? Why the hell would we do that?"

"He might be right," Dunn said, rubbing his jaw. "I know that's not easy to swallow, but if Street knows what we're going to do before we do, he's ahead of us. If he tells us all the things he knows, and he thinks it's going to force us to change tactics, he can anticipate what we're going to do. He's been studying us, all of us. He knows how we think and who we are. He probably has someone on all of our houses, plus all the safe houses we have access to. His network is bigger than we know. Officer Bernard was working for Street for years and no one had any idea. Bernard used another officer to murder someone in police custody. Street didn't share what he knows because he fucked up. He did it to send us into a fit."

"And you think continuing with things as they are is the best option?" Raina whispered.

Everyone in the room looked at her. She met their gazes, wishing she could sink into her chair and disappear.

"I think it might be, yes," Dunn admitted. "We know what he knows. We can be more vigilant. We can add people to our routes and have an extra team stationed at the hotel. Street isn't giving up, but neither are we."

"Better not be. But we need a new plan. He knows we were watching. He knew we were there, but we didn't know he was there. Putting Raina at risk and having that fucker walk up to her and put his hand around her throat is not an option again. You're all the best of the best. Fucking fix this," Adam yelled at the others.

"Adam," Raina said.

Adam spun on her. "No. Don't tell me you're going back out there. That you're willing to have that sick fucker get close to you again. I agreed once. We've been doing this for weeks. We all got complacent. And he pounced. I can't... I won't let anything happen to you. And neither should the rest of them."

Adam glared at the others around the room, letting them all see and feel the anger pouring off him. When he finally looked at Raina again, all she felt was his love.

Adam would die for her. He would die to protect her. Raina was not going to let that happen. There had to be another way. Another way to get to Damon before he got to them again.

Raina just had to figure out what it was. Fast.

19

RAINA CHEWED ON HER LIP AND WATCHED THE CLOCK. SHE had to make a decision. Betraying Adam would mean keeping him safe. But it would mean he'd never forgive her.

It wouldn't matter if she didn't survive, though. Every time she came face-to-face with Damon made her think the chances of her surviving were slim, at best.

Adam was still angry when they made it back to the hotel. The entire team agreed to keep things as they were for now. The whole point was to get Damon to come after Raina, but now that he had, and he got away again, everyone seemed confused and overwhelmed.

Raina was just scared. She could feel the clock ticking down on her life, and it broke her heart that she wouldn't get to live out all the dreams she once had.

A knock on the door had Adam looking at Raina, his agent face on as he drew his weapon and went to the door. Raina watched him, just as scared as the bunched muscles in his back said he was.

He leaned in close and looked through the peephole on

the door, then sighed and tucked his gun away before unlocking and opening the door.

"Hi," Edie said, walking inside while Adam checked the hallway. "Dex said I could come over here." Edie smiled at Adam, then focused on Raina. "I was wondering if you wanted to come over to my room for a little while. Lorelei, Frannie, Stacey, Jessica, Karli, and Mackenzie are on their way. I thought you might want to see them, too."

Raina could barely contain her excitement. It was the first time she felt like a normal person in far too long. Time with friends? Hell yes.

"Who's going to be there?" Adam asked before Raina could agree.

Edie turned to face him. "Dex, Dunn, and Mason are all staying in the suite right now. They've been moving me around, so I just got here today. They said you're welcome to join us, too."

Adam nodded, as though that was good enough for him.

Edie turned back to Raina with an expectant smile.

Raina nodded. "I'd love to. Thanks."

"You can come back over now while it's still quiet in the hallway. If you want. They'll all be here in about fifteen minutes, I think."

Raina unfolded herself from the corner of the couch and slid on her sneakers, not bothering to tie them or add socks. She was too excited to see friends. She grabbed a sweatshirt from the bedroom she and Adam shared and tugged it on over the tee and sweatpants she was wearing.

Adam went into the hall first, knocking on the door across the way. Dex opened it within a few seconds, beckoning them all inside. Adam made sure Edie and Raina were in the other room before he checked that their door had locked behind them.

Edie pulled Raina toward the seating area in their suite. It was toward the windows, just like the room Raina and Adam were sharing.

Dex led Adam to the dining table near the kitchen, where Dunn and Mason were seated. The four of them spoke in low tones while Raina and Edie settled on the couch. Raina wondered what they were talking about, but she didn't have long to think about it before Edie dropped a bomb on her.

"I know what you're planning," Edie murmured.

"What?" Raina asked, knowing there was no way Edie knew anything.

"I saw it in your eyes earlier today. You're going to ditch these guys and let Damon take you."

"I don't know what you're talking about." Raina crossed her arms and tucked her feet under her.

"The day I was taken, I was at a bar. I told the guy I was talking to that I didn't have any family in the area and that I lived alone. He was funny and cute and I didn't think about what I was admitting."

"Edie," Raina whispered.

Edie shook her head. "He put something in my drink. When I woke up again, I was in a room with four other women and I was high as a kite. I'd never done drugs before in my life, but I knew I was high. I could feel the need pulsing through me already. I don't know how many days had gone by, but it was more than one. I was still wearing the same clothes, but I was sore and I was dirty. I could tell I'd been raped, but I had no memory of it. I thought that was a good thing."

Raina put her hand on Edie's arm. She admired the other woman's strength, but Raina wasn't sure she had enough to hear the story.

"Someone kept giving me drugs. They wanted us hooked because then we would do anything they wanted. Every time I woke up again, I knew I'd been raped again. One time, I woke up during. I screamed and cried, but the man didn't care. He taunted me with it, said he liked it. After that, the drugs would wear off more quickly. I remembered more, and I was conscious for more." She scratched at her arm. "I can still feel the needle going into my arm. The pierce of my skin and the welcome relief of numbness. I began to crave it because it meant I'd get a reprieve from the nightmare I was living."

Raina's tears rolled down her cheeks, horrified and scared for the woman who'd become her friend.

"I'm telling you this because Damon was one of the men. I don't remember him, but I know he was. And if he did that to me, when I didn't piss him off or leave him, when he said he liked me, I can't even imagine what he'll do to you if you go back to him."

Raina's throat tightened. She looked across the room at Adam. His arms were crossed, tension in every line of his body. He didn't like whatever it was the others were telling him, but he wasn't arguing. He was following the plan.

"I can't let Damon hurt anyone else."

"And you honestly think he's going to what? Walk away? Once he has you, he'll forget about Adam? And me and Stacey and Jessica? He'll just pretend none of us existed?"

Raina closed her eyes. Edie was right. She was so focused on Damon's obsession with her that she forgot about the rest of it. Damon approached Edie in the store. He framed Jessica for Karli's death. He tried to kill Karli. He threatened Adam.

Damon wouldn't stop. Even if he got his hands on Raina, he wouldn't stop.

Knowing Damon, he'd enjoy killing every last person she loved before he finally killed her. Sharing his successes with her in punishment for putting all the people she cared about on his radar.

Raina got it. She finally got it. She had one option. She had to kill Damon.

The acceptance of it felt freeing as much as it terrified Raina. She'd said she wanted Damon dead, and she'd said she wanted to kill him, but it was all in thickly shrouded fear. Not only did she not know how to kill someone, she wasn't sure she could actually do it.

Adam had been teaching her self-defense every day for the last few weeks. He'd shown her how to disarm someone, how to break free if someone had a hold of her, how to get someone off her if she was pinned down. All things they both knew Damon was likely to do.

One thing Adam hadn't done was teach her how to use a gun. Raina had been too afraid to ask, and Adam hadn't offered. But now that Damon told her how close he was, how much he knew about her routine, it was time for her to learn how to kill someone intent on killing her.

Before she could voice her thoughts, a knock on the door drew the attention of everyone in the room. Dex and Adam went to the door, guns in hand. Dunn and Mason were right behind them, blocking Raina's view from her spot on the couch. When the men tucked their guns away and opened the door, Raina nearly cried with gratitude.

All the women hugged, and some tears were shed. Raina hadn't realized how much she missed the connection to other women until it had been taken away from her. Spending time with Adam had been good, but it was different than being around friends.

When the women all settled on the couches and chairs

in the living room of the suite, Raina realized the men had moved to the first bedroom in the suite. The door was open, so the men would hear if they were needed, but the separation gave the women privacy.

"How are you?" Karli asked, taking Raina's hand in hers. "I've missed you."

"I've missed you, too. Although I'm happy you're safe now and Damon hasn't come after you again," Raina told her friend.

Karli nodded. "I just wish he'd leave you alone. That he'd accept that things are over."

"She wants to go back to him," Edie told the group.

Gasps and shocked faces met Raina's gaze.

"Why would you do that?" Stacey asked. Stacey knew more about what Raina had been through than the others. As the counselor at Shelter in the Storm, Stacey was the one who helped Raina feel strong enough to live without Damon. She helped Raina believe in herself again.

But that was before Damon started killing people to get to Raina.

"I don't want to go back to him. I just want this to be over. And we talked." Raina looked over at Edie. Edie wasn't telling everyone out of ill-intent. She wanted the others to know what Raina was dealing with. "Edie helped me see Damon is never going to stop. He's going to come after all of you, eventually. Whether I'm alive or not."

"That sounds about right," Francesca mumbled. "I've never known evil like him. I wish I'd been able to bring him in decades ago, but he's continued to destroy the city. He's smarter than any of us ever thought. And the way he manipulates people is horrifying."

"I know," Raina said, having been a victim of Damon's manipulation.

"What can we do?" Stacey asked.

Raina looked around the room at the women she considered her closest friends. She'd known Karli for years, but the others she'd only met recently. All of them were women who were strong and brave and would stand with her if she asked them to.

But she couldn't. She couldn't risk their lives.

"She wants to face him herself," Francesca answered for Raina. "She needs to do this alone."

Raina looked at the woman who was a confidant and supporter. Francesca was not afraid of anything. She'd faced more than one angry ex and more than one threat to her life. But she understood the need for closure. The need to deal with your shit in your way or it would haunt you forever.

"I know he's likely to kill me. He'll definitely try. I was thinking about trying to sneak out tonight, but Edie convinced me not to. What I don't know is how to stop him."

"He won't go down without a fight," Karli said. "He told me he enjoys breaking bones."

"He also likes knives," Jessica said. "And secret poison."

"And dominating," Edie added. "Anything he can do to be in control."

"So maybe that's it," Mackenzie said. "We take away his control."

"How would we do that?" Lorelei asked.

Mackenzie looked around the room at the others. "What makes you feel most in control?"

"My family," Stacey said.

"My Shelter," Francesca said.

"Cade," Karli said.

"My job," Jessica said.

"My skills," Lorelei said.

"You guys are doing that for me right now," Raina told them. She smiled at the others and realized Edie hadn't answered. "What about you, Edie?"

Edie slowly shook her head, her gaze vacant and trained on the coffee table. "I don't ever feel in control. It was so easy for them to take me. For them to make it feel like I chose that life. It was so easy to beg for drugs and ache for the numbness. And since I stumbled into the fire station," she lifted her gaze to Mackenzie, "and met you and Holden, I still haven't felt like I'm in control. I'm not being controlled, but I'm also not in control. Does that make sense?"

Everyone nodded.

"That's a big difference," Mackenzie said. "Damon liked to be in control. He wants to tell someone to do something and know it'll be done. We don't have to control him, we just have to take away his control."

"And again, how do we do that?" Lorelei asked.

"By taking away his most important asset," Mackenzie said.

"Which is?"

"His network." Mackenzie met the gazes of everyone else.

Everyone was silent as Mackenzie's words sank in. Raina sat back and considered what Mackenzie was saying. They knew Damon had a network, and that it reached far and deep. Police officers, judges, and a collection of criminals all worked for Damon. Possibly others. If they were running scared, they wouldn't be available to help Damon. It was a good plan. There was only one problem.

"We don't know who's in his network," Lorelei said, voicing Raina's thought.

"Maybe not everyone," Mackenzie said. "But we know some of the people. The cop Damon killed had other cops he worked closely with. Marcus looked into them and went through everything he could find on Bernard, but it's likely there's more. I have listened to hours of calls and heard dozens of names. Maybe Edie can help me figure out if any of them might be connected. And we have a radius of where a lot of things have happened. We can figure out where Damon is likely to be, and where he might be hiding out."

Raina was beyond impressed with what Mackenzie had put together. Not only did it make sense, but it almost sounded possible.

"There's a room full of military experts, an entire police force, and the FBI looking for Damon," Jessica said. "What makes you think we're going to find him when all of them haven't?"

Mackenzie smiled. "Because they're looking for the criminal mastermind. They want to bring down the leader of the organization. We just want the man. He's far more simple and basic. He is not as smart as the organization. And we know a lot more about him."

Lorelei stood and paced the room. "I think she's right. If we come up with anything, we need to tell everyone else, but this isn't about Damon Street, the leader. It's about Raina's ex-boyfriend, who's trying to kidnap and kill her. It's a lot smaller than what everyone else is looking at."

"So, you actually think we can find him? That we can take him down?" Raina asked.

Mackenzie and Lorelei shared a look and nodded.

"I think we can," Lorelei said. "I really think we can."

ADAM WAS only half listening to the conversation going on around him. He knew he wasn't being very friendly to the other men, but his mind was on Raina. Something was off with her. She was acting jittery and unsettled earlier. She jumped at the chance to spend time with Edie.

Adam wasn't sure if that meant she was sick of being around him or if she was sick of being stuck in a suite under guard, but either way, he didn't like it.

Raina was more relaxed when they got out of town. Adam didn't love the idea of going again, of leaving the extra support and protection behind, but after seeing the fear in Raina's eyes after her encounter with Street, Adam hated that he listened to her and the others and let her use herself as bait.

"You good?" Dex asked softly.

Adam looked over at him, wondering how many times Dex had spoken before the words came through. "No, but there's no alternative."

Dex nodded. "We've all been there. My fiancée had someone after her, too. It's how we met, and it was terrifying. To wonder if you're capable of fighting off something you know is coming but don't know when or how. Sorry you're going through this."

"Raina's not my fiancée or anything," Adam argued.

Dex exchanged a look with Mason and Dunn. All three of them smirked.

"She might not be your fiancée, but she's a hell of a lot more than nothing to you," Mason said, raising one eyebrow. "And none of us care about the lines you're not supposed to cross. We all crossed them. I slept with Slade's sister when she surprised him and showed up in town. Didn't tell him when I found out she was pregnant and didn't stop sleeping with her. Slade's got a hell of a right hook." Mason rubbed his jaw.

"My ex showed up on my doorstep asking me to protect

her. It had been more than fifteen years since I threw away what we had and left her to join the service, after planning a future with her that I never intended to share. She was also married, or thought she was," Dunn said.

"I thought you had a kid," Adam said, trying to make sense of the story.

"Yep. Messed up on that protection," Dunn said with a smirk.

The other two snorted their laughter.

Adam looked at the three men. They were all confessing their secrets. Telling him it was okay if he was falling for Raina. That they didn't blame him.

"I'm in love with her," Adam admitted out loud for the first time. "It scares the hell out of me. Not just falling for her, but the idea of losing her."

"That'll never change," Dunn said. "Hell, it'll probably get worse if you have a family."

"Agreed," Mason said. "But in a good way."

"How is it good to be more terrified than I am right now?" Adam asked.

"Because that's how you know it matters. Do you want to be a robot? Going through the motions and not really caring about what you're doing? Or would you rather know that all of this is important?" Dex asked.

"It's all important," Adam argued.

"Sure, but what we're saying is you fight differently when you're not on your own. When you have someone else who shows you the good in the world," Dex explained. "We all get a little lost in the hell we see. We focus on that instead of seeing the brightness. But when you have someone at home who's showing you the brightness every day, you have a better chance of not letting the evil get to you. It's all important, but fighting for the woman you love is different than fighting for a faceless organization because you know it's the right thing to do."

Adam nodded slowly. They were right. Protecting Raina was different. It was bigger. If something happened to her, it wasn't just losing a witness. It was losing a piece of himself, too. Everyone he'd ever protected was important to the case he was working at the time, but none of them were important to Adam like Raina was.

He had already changed. Months of protecting her meant months away from his regular duties. Months of focusing on the woman he'd fallen hard for. Months of wishing for something different, and having it in his life.

Adam wasn't sure he could go back to the FBI after all he'd been through with Raina. He wasn't sure he wanted to. Because his fight was different. His choices were different. And he was different.

He'd always heard falling in love could change a person, and he was living proof. But first, he needed to make sure the threat against Raina was over. Then he could figure out what was next. And if she wanted him to stay in her life.

20

Raina felt better after talking to the other women. She'd always had friends in her life, until Damon, and knowing she had new friends gave her back some of the confidence he took from her.

"You okay?" Adam asked when they were back in their room.

Raina nodded, fingering the mask Francesca gave her. Frannie, she insisted. She said her friends called her Frannie, and she thought of Raina as a friend. Raina couldn't stop smiling. And she couldn't stop thinking about everything they told her.

"I was going to leave tonight," she confessed to Adam. "I was going to wait until you were sleeping, then sneak out and go find him. Convince him not to hurt you or the others."

"He'd never—"

"I know." Raina nodded. She cupped his jaw and stroked the rough stubble there. "That's why Edie came over. She knew what I was going to do."

"How did she know?"

Raina shrugged. "She said she saw it in my eyes. She's observant and smart, and I think it's what she might have done. But she convinced me, reminded me, that it wouldn't change anything. Damon would say or do anything to have me, and he would never keep his word."

"No, he wouldn't."

"I just..." Raina's lip quivered with the emotions running through her.

"Hey, it's okay," Adam whispered, pulling her into his arms. He kissed the top of her head and held her tight. "You're safe. Dex and Dunn checked the room before we came back and found nothing. There's been no sign of him since you saw him earlier."

Raina nodded and forced her emotions down. "But he's out there. He's not giving up. That's why I thought about going. I'm never going to be safe. No one I care about is ever going to be safe."

"Don't worry about me, or anyone else."

"I can't help it," Raina said. "I care a lot about you, Adam."

Adam pulled back and wiped the tears from her cheeks. His blue eyes met hers and held.

Raina's breath caught in her throat at the look in his eyes. Passionate and understanding, loving and sympathetic. She didn't know all of those could co-exist, but they were right there, watching her.

"I love you, too," Adam said with a half-smile.

Raina exhaled on a smile and closed her eyes, wrapping herself around Adam again. She couldn't say the words, not through the fear clogging her throat and not until she knew they could be together.

But she could show him.

Raina lifted the back of his tee and splayed her hand on

his skin. He was warm and comforting, solid. Nothing bad could happen with Adam. He was good. So good. She finally fell for the right guy.

Adam didn't rush her or push. He let her lead, lifting his arms when she raised his shirt, then tugging it off to give her full access.

Raina kissed his neck, moving her lips across his chest. The dusting of hair tickled her cheeks. She flicked her tongue across his nipple, and Adam groaned, his fingers sliding into her hair. Not controlling, just touching.

Raina lowered her hands to his waist and pushed at his sweats. They got hung up on his erection before sliding down his legs. She kissed her way down, licking and teasing him as she sank to her knees.

She stretched his boxer briefs over his erection and freed him. She let the fabric fall and wrapped her hand around him.

His hands were still in her hair, but his eyes were locked on her face. She smiled at him as she leaned forward and took him into her mouth. His lids fluttered closed, but he forced them back open and watched her.

She held his gaze the entire time, loving the way he surrendered to her. Raina felt desirable and powerful and sexy as she kneeled before him. Whenever she did the same with Damon, she felt controlled, but Adam was letting her lead. Letting her do what she wanted to do. He was just going with it, and enjoying it, if the noises he made were any indication.

Raina focused on her task, ignoring the ache between her thighs. She wanted to show Adam how she felt, and getting herself off at the same time wasn't part of the plan, even if giving him pleasure was turning her on.

No, that was only part of it. Watching his face and seeing

the way he wanted her had her nearly panting around the thick head of his erection. She wanted to share everything with Adam. Not just sex, but their lives.

"Raina," he groaned, tugging on her hair.

She resisted him, using her free hand to hold him in place. He grunted, and his eyes widened. She moaned, sending a vibration through his cock, and sucked harder on him.

"Fuck, Raina. I can't hold back. Raina."

She kept going, needing to taste him. He'd always pulled her off him in the past, but she wasn't going to stop. She pumped her hand and her mouth together, her other hand holding his leg from stepping back.

He swore, then leaned into her, giving up his side of the fight. His fingers tightened in her hair, his orgasm taking over for his brain.

Raina moaned as he pumped his hips, nearly hitting the back of her throat before he stilled in her mouth and exploded. She held still, licking the underside of his dick and trying to keep her hands exactly where they were.

"Holy fuck," Adam hissed.

He eased back, and Raina let him slide from between her lips. She held his gaze while she swallowed and licked her lips. "Thank you."

He sank to the floor with her and kissed her hard. "Thank you. That was not what I expected."

"I couldn't stop myself."

"If that's the only excuse you need, then I have a little catching up to do because I feel that way every time I'm in the room with you."

Adam surprised Raina by yanking her to her feet and tossing her over his shoulder. She yelped, then laughed as he carried her to their bedroom. He lowered her from his shoulder slowly, her body sliding down the front of his until her toes hit the floor.

One hand went into her hair, tangling in the already messy strands. He tilted her head and kissed her until she was panting and his hands were dipping beneath the edge of her sweatpants.

"Adam," she whispered.

"Let me love you tonight, Raina."

She nodded, the emotion again tightening her throat.

Adam pushed her toward the bed, smiling when she laid down. He drew her sweats down her thighs, then helped her remove her tee. His eyes heated at her stretched out in only her panties on the bed.

He ran one finger up her leg, the touch gentle and teasing. He hooked it around the edge of her panties, but he didn't tug them off. He dipped below the fabric, teasing her overly sensitive skin.

She shivered and twisted, trying to get his finger to where she wanted it.

He slid it away, making her groan. His soft chuckle said he wasn't doing it by accident.

Adam's teasing touch and Raina's frustrated groans chased each other. She ached for him, and when she was just about ready to take matters into her own hands, he pressed a hot, wet kiss to the soaked fabric between her legs.

"Adam," she breathed.

He sucked her, the fabric adding a rasp to his touch that was new and different and shockingly erotic. Raina twisted and writhed, begging him to make her come.

He yanked her panties to the side and slammed three fingers deep into her, using the fabric pulled over her clit to make her come hard and fast.

Raina cried out, riding his hand. It wasn't enough, but

Adam seemed to know that. As she came down, he pulled her panties down far enough that he could get his mouth on her and send her right back up to heaven a second time.

Adam rose up and kissed her, letting her taste herself on his lips. She wrapped her arms around him and kissed him back soundly. As they kissed, Adam settled between her thighs, his erection rubbing against her slippery skin.

"Condom," Adam hissed, pulling away from a reluctant Raina.

"Crap," Raina breathed. It had been a while since the last time she slept with anyone else, meaning Damon, but she didn't want to take any chances.

While Adam found a condom, Raina kicked her panties off. When he came back to the bed, condom on, he didn't waste any time sliding into her.

They both groaned at the perfect feeling of him inside her. Adam stilled for a minute, his loving gaze on her face. Looking at him brought tears to Raina's eyes. She'd never had a man look at her the way Adam did. Even if it didn't last forever, she was lucky to have found love once in her life.

Adam moved slowly at first, dragging out each stroke and letting Raina feel every inch of him as he moved in and out of her body. She tightened her channel around him as he stroked in, and he sped up.

He leaned over her, his pelvis grinding against hers with each stroke. His pubic hair rubbed her clit, and she didn't have to tighten her channel. It was an automatic response to the building stimulus.

Raina shuddered as her orgasm drew closer. She watched Adam, staring into his blue eyes. He looked between them every few seconds, watching as he slid in and out of her body. She wanted to see it, too, but she couldn't over her belly.

"Tell me what it looks like."

"What?"

"To see you slide into me. Tell me."

"So fucking good, Raina," Adam said without hesitation or embarrassment. "Your pussy stretches wide to make space for my dick, drawing me in with each stroke. When I pull out, your skin follows, like you don't want to let me go."

"I don't," she whispered.

"Fuck," he growled.

He pounded into her, all control gone as their skin slapped together, their bodies meeting and rushing toward orgasm.

"Raina," he hissed. A question, not a gasp.

"Close," she replied, understanding.

He didn't falter for a second, and he didn't give up. He slammed hard and deep, rubbing her clit with each thrust into her body, and within seconds, she was crashing, falling, dying.

"Oh, God. Adam. Yes. Adam. Yes!"

He grunted his approval and chased her over the edge, his body stilling with his cock buried deep inside her for a second before it swelled and burst. "Fuck. Raina."

Her heart was like their orgasms, at the edge and tumbling downhill. She loved him. So damn much it scared her. Not because she thought he could be anything less than perfect, but because he was perfect. He was everything. He showed her what it meant to be giving and loving and supportive and everything a man should be. He loved her with his entire being.

She just hoped loving her didn't kill him.

Because that would kill her.

ANOTHER WEEK WENT by since Adam told Raina he loved her. She still hadn't said the words, but he could feel it in the way she gave herself to him every night.

They were still on high alert, still waiting for Street to make his next move. They hadn't seen him again, but Adam knew Street was out there. Watching. Waiting. Plotting.

F-BOMB insisted they stick to the routines they'd set. Adam bristled at the thought of walking back into the same store where Street put his hands on Raina last time, but his woman was strong and determined and she wanted to go.

This time, Adam was not leaving her fucking side. No matter who told him to walk away for a minute and leave her exposed. They could fucking fire him. He didn't care about anything except Raina being okay.

They walked the aisles like they did every week, picking up items they might need. Even though they were staying at a hotel, the suite had a full kitchen and they were using it. Eating out every meal was exhausting, and it meant putting on clothes. Adam preferred to use Raina as his plate some days, and to offer himself up as hers. Most restaurants frowned on that behavior. So, they cooked.

When they approached the aisle where Street trapped her last time, Raina's tension radiated from her. Adam kept one hand around her back and the other on top of hers on the handle of the cart they pushed. When they turned the corner, the aisle was empty.

Raina breathed a sigh of relief, but she didn't lose all her tension until they were in line at the checkout. The cashier was friendly, but efficient, and within a few minutes, Adam and Raina were on their way out of the store with Archer and Jack not far behind them.

A car slowed down as they walked out of the store, letting them cross the street in the crosswalk. As soon as they were clear of the car, it crept forward, stopping right behind Adam and Raina, who were still in the crosswalk.

"Nice day for some shopping, huh?"

Raina went still. Adam put himself between Raina and the car. The voice belonged to Street.

Adam spun, his hand reaching for the gun he kept tucked at his back in the holster. Before he could draw it, Street was pulling away, tires squealing as he tore out of the parking lot.

"Oh, my God," Raina breathed.

Adam focused on her, moving their cart out of the cross-walk so other cars could pass. Adam cupped her jaw and pulled her against his chest, watching in case Street came back.

"What happened?" Archer barked when he reached them.

"Street. He was out here, timed it perfectly to drive by when we were walking out of the store."

Archer and Jack exchanged a glance. Jack stepped away, already on the phone.

"What was he driving?" Jack asked.

"Dark blue sedan. No plates."

Jack turned away again, talking into the phone.

"Let's get you two out of here. English will find Street."

Adam nodded, leading Raina to the SUV they used to get there. Archer took care of the cart, loading the groceries into the back before handing off the cart to Jack to return. Archer climbed into the driver's seat and turned on the SUV, waiting for Jack before taking off to the hotel.

"He's never going to stop. Every time we think he might

leave us alone, he shows up again." Raina shook as she spoke, her gaze straight ahead and unseeing.

"We'll get him. He couldn't have gotten far," Jack assured her.

No one else spoke the rest of the drive back to the hotel.

They parked in the lot next to the hotel, silent as they removed the bags from the back and trudged inside. The day started out with Raina naked and crying out his name, but Adam had a feeling the rest of the day would just be crying.

He didn't blame her. He wanted to scream out his frustration. Go for a run and pound it out of his body. Or better yet, pound his frustration into Street.

"Want us to help you carry stuff inside? Or check the room?" Archer asked.

Raina shook her head.

Adam thanked the other men. He tried to silently convey that Raina needed a minute. Or an hour.

Their nod of approval said they understood. They'd both been through the same hell with their wives, and they got it in ways few others could.

Adam took four bags and left Raina with two. She waved the keycard in front of the panel on the door, waiting for it to turn green and unlock before she turned the handle.

Raina held the door open for Adam to walk through first. He carried the groceries past the bedrooms to put everything in the kitchen, but stopped short at the intruder leaning against the counter.

Both Adam's hands were full. His gun was at his back. Archer and Jack were in the room across the hall. None of them thought Street could be there.

But Adam was looking at the man. The scar cut across his eyebrow was the only proof Street wasn't invincible. If he could scar, he could bleed. And Adam intended to make him do just that.

"Raina, get out," Adam barked, his voice harsh and deadly, his gaze not wavering from the man in front of him.

The bags in her hands shifted. She was barely inside the door to the suite, the door still open. She could escape. She could leave. She could be safe.

"What—" she began, then stopped abruptly, the words cut off like a hand was wrapped around her throat.

"She's not going anywhere," Street said, looking past Adam to Raina. "Because if she walks out that door, she'll never see you again."

Adam looked back at her. He couldn't lose her. Facing Street was bad enough, but doing it with Raina in the room would mean his every move would be more about protecting her than stopping Street. She had to go. Even if it meant the gun Street had pointed at Adam would end the fight between them before it began.

Adam didn't think Street would do that. The gun was for show. He was a bruiser.

"Raina," he whispered.

She didn't look at him. Her gaze never wavered, even though her lip did. She was focused, determined, and not walking out of the room.

21

———

DAMON'S LIPS CURLED UP IN A SNEER WHEN RAINA STEPPED forward into the hotel room. "Good girl."

She blanched at the words, but he didn't care. The more she did what he said, the more she'd do what he said. He knew that from experience.

"Now, put those bags down and come over here," Damon told her. He kept the gun on the agent, but he had no intention of using it. That was too quick. Too easy. The agent was going to be punished for putting his hands on Raina. He was going to break. Literally.

Raina put her bags on the floor and walked down the short hall, past the two bedrooms in the suite. One room was untouched, the bed not slept in and the room completely empty. It hadn't escaped Damon's notice that the other room's bathroom trash was full of condom wrappers and there were men's and women's clothes in the closet. Damon took his time going through the suite when he let himself in, choosing what Raina was going to wear when she left with him.

"Sit on the couch," Damon told Raina.

She spared a glance at the agent, who still stood in his place with his bags in his hands. The longer he held them, the more strain on his muscles. And the more strain on his muscles, the harder it would be for him to fight back.

Damon wasn't an idiot.

Once Raina was seated, her hands folded in her lap and her gaze bouncing between Damon and the agent, Damon lowered the gun.

As expected, the agent dropped his bags and reached for his gun at the same time. But Damon was ready for him.

The agent didn't know Damon had a knife in his other hand. When he reached for his gun, Damon took advantage of the move and jabbed his knife into the agent's stomach.

"Adam!" Raina screamed.

Damon twisted the knife, then pulled it out, smiling when the agent sank to the floor.

Damon pointed the knife at Raina when she moved. "Don't you fucking touch him."

Tears rolled down her cheeks. She stared at the agent, but she lowered herself to the couch again.

Damon crouched in front of the agent, scanning the man. Blood oozed from the wound in his side. Eventually, he'd bleed out, but it would take a while. All Damon wanted was to make sure the man couldn't fight back. Mission accomplished.

"You touched her," Damon growled. "You put your hands on my woman. You fucked her!"

The agent fucking smiled. He fucking smiled. "And I'm gonna do it all again as soon as I kill you."

Damon reached back and swung, his knuckles landing with a solid blow and satisfying crack on the man's nose.

The agent grunted and fell back, rolling from his side to his back. Blood poured over his face, choking him in his position. He rolled again, spitting blood out onto the carpet and coughing.

"She's mine. You're never going to touch her again. No one is. She's going to learn right now that she belongs to me."

Raina whimpered, but Damon ignored her and kept his focus on the agent. His face, despite being covered in blood, showed his anger. He made a move to get up, telling Damon he still had a little fight left in him.

Time to erase that.

Damon stomped on the agent's hand, bones crunching beneath his boot. Then he kicked the man's knee, another crunch. The agent howled and rolled in pain, his face twisting in agony.

Damon crouched in front of him again. "Nothing else to say?"

He grunted in pain, bracing his shattered hand against his body. His leg didn't move.

"Good. Every word out of your mouth will get another broken bone."

The agent glared at Damon, but he didn't speak. He was learning.

Just like Raina had to.

RAINA'S BREATH STOPPED. Her heart dropped. Everything inside her screamed to run.

But that option was gone. She chose to stay. She chose to lot leave Adam to die.

Instead, she was going to have to watch him die.

The only sound from Adam was a groan. One that said he was barely hanging on to consciousness. Raina wanted to help him, to stop the bleeding or something. But if she moved, Damon would kill her.

Fuck. He was going to kill her, anyway. Did it matter? Sitting on that couch and waiting for death didn't feel like a better option. She spent too many months doing exactly what Damon told her to do. When she left, she promised herself she'd never get involved with another man like that. Another man who wanted to control her and force her to do things.

And here she was, right back where she started. Listening to the man who broke her spirit and almost killed her. The man who was going to kill her. Today. Right now. In this room.

Unless she stopped him.

Raina stood, drawing Damon's attention.

"What the fuck do you think you're doing? I told you to sit on the couch."

"Fuck you," Raina growled. She shook as she forced the words out. She'd only once talked back to him when they were together. When they started dating, she would joke around with him and sass him, but it wasn't long before he would withhold attention when she did. He told her he didn't find it funny and would ignore her if she spoke out against him.

Now, she didn't care what he thought or did. If the end result wasn't going to change, Raina was not going to go to her grave ashamed of her behavior and trying to appease the man who intended to kill her.

"What did you say to me?" His voice was menacing, dangerous. Just her words were enough to anger him.

Good.

Raina took a step in his direction. She stayed out of his reach and repeated what she said. "Fuck. You."

Damon moved fast, catching her off-guard. He slapped her hard enough to send her back onto the couch.

She bounced on the cushion and nearly fell off the couch to the floor.

Damon towered over her, his face inches from hers. "Do you think you're big and bad now, Raina? That fucking this piece of shit made you stronger? A year ago, you were begging for me to fuck you. You did anything I asked. I touched you how I wanted, fucked you how I wanted, and you whimpered for it."

Raina swallowed her shame. He was right. He had her so convinced he was the best she'd ever do that she let him do whatever he wanted. And she told herself she liked it.

But Adam did make her stronger. Adam showed her what love meant, what love could be. He helped her believe in herself.

"Yes, fucking him made me stronger," Raina whispered.

Damon grabbed her arm and yanked her upright, then kept pulling until she was on her feet. He dragged her to where Adam laid on the floor, puddles of his blood soaking into the carpet.

"This is what you want? This bloody fucking mess? You think he's good enough for you? That he can give you what you want?"

"I know he can. He's a good man."

Damon laughed, the sound loud and grating. It bounced around the room and echoed inside Raina's body. It wasn't a laugh of humor. It was a laugh that was evil, cruel, dangerous.

"He's a fucking pussy, Raina! I can't even imagine how he satisfied you. Good." Damon scoffed. "Good means nothing. It means weak. Look at him. Look at him!"

Raina flinched at Damon's shout. She squeezed her eyes

shut. But that left her vulnerable. And Damon took advantage.

Damon wrenched her hair, the pain forcing a cry out of her.

"Look at the man you think is so good. He's nothing, Raina. He's not even fighting back. He's just laying there, bleeding all over this beautiful white carpet." Damon tsked as if disappointed in Adam. "Such a mess he's leaving for housekeeping to clean up."

"You're evil."

Damon's laugh started small, like it surprised him she would say such a thing. It grew with each passing second, like her words buoyed him and encouraged him.

Raina knew she had to do something. He would yank her hair out if she gave him the chance. He'd do whatever he wanted to her. She had to get away from him. Get a weapon. Get his weapon, if possible.

She moved quickly while he laughed, reaching up to karate-chop him in the throat like Adam taught her. She was lucky, and it worked, shocking him enough that he released her.

"You bitch," Damon snarled.

Raina hurried out of his reach, debating going to Adam, but he couldn't help her and there was nothing she could do for him until she got away from Damon.

Escape was the next thought in Raina's mind. She raced toward the door, knowing if she could get out, she could alert Archer and Jack that Damon was there. In their room. With Adam.

She was almost to the door when an arm wrapped around her waist and lifted her effortlessly from behind. "No! Help me! HELP!"

"Did you really think you'd be able to get away from

me?" Damon hissed in her ear. "Did you think it would be that easy? This is going to be fun, Raina. You never put up a fight before, but I like this side of you."

He ground his erection against her backside and licked her ear.

"Do you feel how much that turns me on? I'm going to fuck you so hard you beg for me to let you come. I can't wait to feel your tight fucking pussy around my dick again. It's been too long."

He shoved his hand beneath the waistband of her jeans, his fingers brushing the edge of her panties before she grabbed his arm. She dug her nails into his skin, scratching and pulling until she drew blood.

He pressed harder, slamming his hand between her thighs. He bit the edge of her neck, hard enough that she saw stars.

"You're not going to be able to fight me off, Raina. I'm going to take everything I want from you. And your good agent is going to lie there and watch it. He's going to see me fuck you every way I want, and then you're going to watch him die. And when he's dead, you and I are leaving this hotel room and no one will ever see you again."

Tears poured down Raina's face, obscuring her vision of Adam. She fought against Damon's touch, but he was too strong. He pushed a finger into her. She bucked against the intrusion, hating the feel of him surrounding her. His erection pressed to her back, his hand in her panties, his hot breath on her neck.

Her stomach rolled, nausea buckling he knees. She fell, Damon's hand mercifully yanked from her. She dry-heaved, nothing coming up except the shame and regret that filled her entire body.

"Raina," Adam whispered.

She forced her eyes open and looked at him. He was close to her now. Only a few feet away. He was still blurry from her tears, but she could see his gaze, locked on her and steady.

"I love you," he breathed.

"I love— Gah!" Raina reached up to stop the painful yank on her scalp.

"You don't love him. You love me. He's a poor substitute."

"He's not a substitute," Raina snapped. All her rage exploding at the insinuation that Damon could ever be better than Adam. "You were the substitute. You're not even a man. The only way you can get a woman is to drug her or kidnap her or trick her? How does that make you powerful? You're a weak, pathetic excuse for a man. I don't know what I ever saw in you, but my eyes are open now. You are worthless, Damon. Nothing. I will never love you. I will never willingly allow you into my body. You might fuck me and touch me and hell, you're probably going to kill me, but you will never have my love. You will never have my heart. That belongs to Adam. He's the man I love, the only man I love."

Damon tossed Raina to the side. She stumbled and fell into the edge of the armchair, her rib slamming against the solid frame barely covered with cushioned fabric.

A crunch and oof had her spinning around. Damon was over Adam again, his boot lodged in Adam's ribs.

"Stop it!" Raina screamed.

Damon kicked Adam again, squarely in the gut.

Adam rolled and heaved, vomiting blood. He sank against the floor, his gaze glassy and dazed. He wasn't going to last much longer without medical help.

"Stop it!" Raina screamed again, jumping on Damon's back before he could kick Adam again. She pounded on him, hitting and punching whatever she could reach.

Damon swung at her, landing more than one blow to her head and back. He reached behind him and grabbed her hair, jerking her up his body until she toppled over his shoulder. She landed hard on the couch, her leg hitting the solid wood coffee table.

Raina yelped in pain, but she knew that wasn't the worst of it when Damon covered her body with his.

He pressed his lips to hers and forced his tongue into her mouth. She bit him, and he pinched her nipple so hard she cried out. She brought her knee up to his crotch, and he tore her shirt down the middle, leaving her bra-covered breasts exposed.

"I've missed these tits." He leaned down and bit one, eliciting a scream when he bit down hard. "Oh, yeah, let me hear how much you like that."

He bit the other one, and she screamed louder.

He had her arms pinned against the couch. His upper body covered hers, making it impossible for her to move.

"I love you," she heard from the floor.

Adam. He was still giving her strength. Telling her not to give up. Encouraging her.

And distracting Damon.

Damon shoved Raina down and roared as he stomped the few steps to where Adam laid, barely moving and barely conscious. Damon kneeled in front of Adam and sneered at him.

"Do you think you're going to ever touch her again? Do you think I'd ever let you? All the things you did to keep her safe were useless. And this is just one more." Damon made a fist. He held it up in front of Adam's face.

Raina sucked in a breath, not wanting to watch Damon hit Adam.

But Damon didn't punch Adam. He took his fist and pressed it to the stab wound. Hard.

Adam shouted.

Damon pressed harder.

Adam screamed.

And Raina saw the gun. In Damon's waistband.

She'd forgotten about it. But there it was. And he was focused on Adam.

She pushed off the couch before she could think twice. She launched herself at him. She tackled him, the metal brushing against her fingers.

Adam grunted when the pressure was released from his wound.

Damon shouted when Raina landed on him.

Raina tightened her grip on the gun and scrambled away from Damon. She held it up in front of her, a barrier between them that shook with her fear and uncertainty and pain.

Damon looked from Raina to the gun, then back to Raina. "What are you going to do with that?"

"I'm going to kill you."

Damon snorted. "With hands that shaky, you'll be lucky if you don't hit your agent instead of me. Come on, Raina. We both know you're not going to shoot me."

Raina steadied the gun with her second hand, knowing he was right. She could hit Adam. "Get out," she growled.

Damon smirked at her. "I told you you'd never shoot me. Now, be a good girl and give me the gun."

Damon took a step toward her, and Raina squeezed the trigger.

22

RAINA COULDN'T MOVE. IT WAS TOO MUCH. THE SHOT boomed, echoing all around her. Her ears rung, the sound drowning out everything else, if there was anything else.

She stared at the man she thought she loved once upon a time. His face registered shock when he looked down. A single spot on his shirt turned red. Like ink from a broken pen. The red grew, more pumping out of the hole in his chest.

Damon fell to his knees, the jolt of his fall hard enough that he clutched for his chest. Or maybe that was because of the bullet hole.

Then he collapsed onto the floor. His blood created a stain right next to Adam's blood. Twin holes. Two men unmoving. Ringing. Echoes. Silence.

Something touched her. A hand. Raina screamed, trying to lift the gun against the person she never noticed in the room. Damon had an accomplice.

"Raina!" the man shouted.

Everything was too loud. Shouting. Footsteps. More shouting.

"Raina, can you hear me?" Archer. It was Archer in front of her. Trying to take the gun from her hands.

Raina shook. She stared at the carnage in front of her. It was her fault. Adam was dying because of her. Damon was dying because of her. Two men she'd loved. One she now hated. One she still loved.

"What did I do?" she breathed.

"Let's sit down," Archer said, his voice low and soothing. He glanced at someone, but Raina could only focus on putting one foot in front of the other. With Archer's help.

He guided her to a bar stool in the kitchen. Away from the blood. From the two men lying on the floor of her suite.

"Are you hurt?" Archer asked, his gaze scanning her, lingering in some spots.

Raina shook her head. "Adam."

"Jack's with him. He's still alive. An ambulance is on the way."

"Damon."

Archer shook his head.

"I killed a man. He told me I wouldn't do it, but I... I..."

"Raina, it's okay." Archer stood and walked a few steps away. He grabbed something, a blanket, and put it around Raina's shoulders.

It was soft. Warm. Comforting against her bare skin.

Bare skin.

She looked down and saw her shirt was torn open. She wrapped the blanket around her body, shame heating her skin.

"You're safe now," Archer said.

He barely got the words out before the room exploded with more noise. Police officers swarmed inside, followed immediately by F-BOMB. Liam spared Raina a glance before dropping to his knees next to Adam.

"What happened?" Liam barked.

"Still working that out," Archer said, his tone equally angry.

"How the fuck did Street get in here?"

"He was waiting for us," Raina answered.

"Waiting for you?" Archer asked.

Raina nodded, the pain of what she'd been through seeping past the adrenaline that kept her fighting until Damon was dead and help arrived. "He was in here when we got back from the store. Adam walked in first. Damon was in the kitchen." She looked at the spot Damon had first stood. "He had a gun on Adam. Adam told me to leave, but Damon said he'd shoot Adam if I did."

"You stayed to protect him," Liam whispered.

"I didn't do a very good job," Raina said on a sob.

"It's okay," Lorelei said, appearing out of nowhere. Or maybe she was there all along. Raina didn't know anymore.

Time felt slow. Everything was muddy.

Lorelei hugged Raina, relieving Archer of his duties. With the arms of a friend around her, Raina's tentative control on her emotions shattered, and so did she.

Lorelei kept Raina pressed to her body and let Raina cry. The sounds around her were confusing and difficult to understand, but Raina couldn't focus on them, anyway.

After a few minutes, or a few hours, Lorelei led Raina across the hall. Edie was no longer in the room, but there were two bedrooms. Lorelei guided Raina into one of them and had her lie down on the bed. Raina fell asleep almost as soon as her head hit the pillow.

Voices filtered into her dream, waking Raina. Her dream was peaceful, soothing. The world was good. She was safe. Everything was okay.

She woke up with a smile on her face, but when she

opened her eyes and saw where she was, the reality of her life came crashing back on her.

She'd killed a man.

It didn't matter that the man tried to kill her and Adam or that he was pure evil. Raina still killed someone. She watched as he bled to death, in front of her eyes. She pulled the trigger, and he died.

"You're awake," Lorelei said softly. She sat on the edge of the bed near Raina's hip. "You slept for a few hours. How do you feel?"

Raina pushed herself up and scooted back to lean against the headboard. She looked from Lorelei to Archer. "Is he dead?"

They exchanged a glance, but Lorelei was the one to speak.

"Adam is in surgery right now. The doctors said he lost a lot of blood, but they were positive about his chances. He had a lot of injuries."

Raina swallowed her emotions and nodded. "Damon stabbed him, then twisted the knife. He broke his nose, stomped on his knee, smashed his hand, I think. Maybe a rib. Damon wanted Adam to watch while he… while he…"

"You're safe now," Archer said, his words from earlier coming back to Raina.

"Thanks to you. How did you know something was going on?"

"We heard the gunshot," Archer said. "The rooms here are good. We were going to check on you guys, but we wanted to give you a little space after running into Street at the store. We had no idea he was in the hotel room until you shot him."

"He told me he was going to… and then he was going to

make me watch Adam bleed to death. Then he was going to take me away and no one would ever find us."

"He's dead," Lorelei said.

Raina closed her eyes, relief and guilt warring inside her. It felt wrong to be happy a person was dead, but Damon was barely a person. He wasn't worthy of being called human. But Raina still killed him. She put a man in the ground.

Tears slipped past her clenched eyelids and rolled down her cheeks. Lorelei was right there, holding Raina close again. "You did nothing wrong. It was self defense. We can tell by the bruises on you that he attacked you."

Raina nodded. "He did. But—"

"No," Archer growled. "Don't feel guilty. I know that's almost impossible to say, but Lorelei is right. You did nothing wrong. He's been after you for months. He killed other people to try to get to you. He would have killed Adam and you if you hadn't killed him. He tried. If there had been a way to stop him, we would have stopped him. We tried. No one wanted this outcome, but none of us blame you for it."

Lorelei nodded at every word Archer said.

Raina knew he was right. She told herself many times that Damon had to die. But it was still hard to accept she was the one responsible.

"You should go to the hospital," Lorelei said. "You need to be evaluated."

"I want to see Adam."

"He's there, too. By the time the doctors check you out, hopefully he's out of surgery."

Raina nodded. "I, um..." She gestured to her body, still wrapped in the blanket Archer gave her. "I need some clothes."

Archer looked at Lorelei. "You good here? I can grab the suitcases and bring them over here."

Lorelei nodded, and Archer walked out.

Lorelei turned to Raina. "Are you okay? Did Damon...?"

Raina shook her head. "He tried. He put his hands... But Adam saved me. He kept telling me he loved me, and it pissed Damon off. That's how I got his gun."

"You shot Damon with his own gun?"

Raina nodded. "He put his fist in Adam's wound and pressed down. He was distracted, and I tackled him, grabbing the gun from his waistband."

"Nice move."

Raina smiled at the approval on Lorelei's face. "Thanks. I just hope it wasn't too late to save Adam. He was pretty hurt. He threw up blood. It was bad, Lorelei. God, I was so damn scared."

"It's all over now," Lorelei said.

THE DOCTORS TOLD Raina she was lucky. Her injuries would take time to heal, but they would heal. They recommended a follow-up for her throat to make sure the swelling went down, but she didn't have any broken bones. Just a lot of bruises.

When she was released, Lorelei and Archer took her up to the surgical waiting room. The rest of F-BOMB was there, along with a few FBI Agents Lorelei spoke to. Raina sat in a corner alone, knowing she was to blame for Adam being in surgery.

Raina kept her gaze on her lap and was surprised when Liam took the seat next to her. He didn't say anything for a minute. When he finally did, Raina was shocked.

"Thank you for saving his life."

"He's here because of me."

Liam nodded. "Exactly. He got into this job long before he met you. He knew what he was signing up for. This could have happened on any number of cases. But because it happened with you, he's alive."

"Have the surgeons come out?"

Liam shook his head. "Not yet, but they said he has a good chance because you saved his life."

"I love him," Raina admitted.

"I know. And I think he loves you, too."

Raina smiled. "He does. He told me."

"Good. All he's going to want to know when he wakes up is if you're okay."

"I have no intention of leaving his side. Ever again, if he'll have me."

Liam squeezed her knee. "I have a feeling he'll agree to that."

"I JUST WANT to sit next to him. Hold his hand so he knows he's not alone."

"I'm sorry, but we can only allow family in."

"I'm... his fiancée."

Adam pried his eyes open, wondering who was arguing. And why?

Uh... where am I?

Adam stared up at the dropped ceiling and tried to understand what he was seeing. He moved his head, groaning at the pain that seemed to come from... everywhere.

"He's awake. Please."

Adam turned toward the voices. Both female. One achingly familiar.

"Raina," he breathed. Jesus, he hurt.

"Mr. Johnson, you need to be resting," another woman said.

Adam forced his gaze toward the other woman. Scrubs. A stern look. Petite but strong. Definitely a nurse. One used to people trying to talk their way past her, likely because she was female and not very tall.

"I apologize, but I don't know your name."

"Sharon," the woman said.

"Sharon. You're my nurse?"

"Yes, sir, I am."

"I know you're doing your job, and if my memory is anywhere close to clear, I know that job hasn't been easy on you. But that woman is the love of my life. Her name is Raina London. The man who did this to me also did that to her. I'd like nothing more than to have her next to me so I can make sure she's okay."

"You need your rest, Mr. Johnson," Sharon said disapprovingly.

Adam tried to nod, but it sent blinding pain through him. "Yes, I do. And I will if she's allowed in here. If she's not, I will make your job hell because I will be out of this bed every time you turn around trying to get to her. Please, Sharon."

Sharon looked between the two of them. The stern expression didn't change, but neither did the hope Adam held on to. When Sharon finally nodded, Raina hurried to Adam's bedside.

He lifted his hand to her face, finding it wrapped in bandages. "Are you okay?" That was the only thing Adam cared about.

Raina nodded, tears streaming down her face.

"What did he do to you?" Adam demanded, fury and fire

igniting inside him. He tried to push himself up, ignoring the pain that twisted his stomach and nearly made him pass out.

Raina's gentle hand on his shoulder took the fight out of him. "I'm fine. He didn't do anything. He tried, but you saved me."

"I doubt that."

She nodded. "You did. You kept telling me you loved me. It distracted him enough that he stopped focusing on me. When he went after you, I tackled him and grabbed his gun."

"Is he...? Did you...?"

Raina's gaze dropped to her hands. "He's dead."

"Holy shit, Raina. I'm so sorry you had to do that. Are you okay?"

She shrugged, her move coupled with a wince.

Adam brushed her hair aside with his un-bandaged hand. The bruises on her neck were dark and ugly. But they were the last mark Street would ever put on her body. "I should have protected you."

She shook her head. "You did. You taught me what I needed to know. And you helped me to believe in myself."

"I'm so sorry you went through that."

"I'm better off than you are. I didn't need surgery."

"Surgery? How long have I been out?"

"A few hours. It's almost eleven."

"Is that why Sharon didn't want you in here?"

Raina nodded.

"So you told her you're going to marry me?"

Raina gasped, her eyes widening. "I thought you were asleep."

"Did you mean it?"

"I, um, I promised I wouldn't trap you."

"That's not what I asked. You said you were my fiancée."

She nodded again. She held his gaze and drew a deep breath, her chest rising before falling slowly. "I love you, Adam. So damn much. I've loved you for a while, but I was afraid to say it. When I thought I was going to lose you, I wanted to kick myself for not telling you every day. I don't want you to feel like you have to say it back. I know you already said it, but the situation—"

"Had nothing to do with how I feel about you," Adam growled. "I fell in love with you in the middle of a shitstorm, but that doesn't make my feelings any less valid."

"Okay." She stared at her hands again.

"Tell me again, Raina."

Her gaze lifted to his. "Tell you what?"

"Tell me you love me."

She smiled and rose from her chair. She sat on the edge of the bed and leaned over him. "I love you, Adam Johnson. I will love you for the rest of my life."

"I love you, Raina London."

"I love you."

"I love you."

Raina stroked his hair until Adam fell asleep with a promise on his mind to make her words the truth as soon as he could get out of the hospital bed and into a jewelry store.

TREVOR DAVIS WALKED into the boss's office without knocking. The men at the door never stopped him. Not anymore.

"Well?" the boss said.

"Damon's dead. The ex killed him."

"Good. What about the one Damon stole from under your nose?"

Trevor wanted to shift his feet, but he knew better than to show weakness. It didn't matter how his relationship with the boss had changed lately. It was still the boss.

"Edie is still under their protection."

"And what are you going to do about that?"

"What do you want me to do?"

The boss stood and leaned over the massive desk that had been in the same office for generations. Many bosses had towered over people from the other side of that desk. "I want you to tie up loose ends. We can't have people out there in the world who know anything about what we do. Damon might have been distracted and dangerous to us, but he wasn't fucking stupid."

Trevor swallowed the retort. He knew better than to ask if the implication was that he was stupid. "Understood."

"You need to put the ones you still have into the pool of candidates."

Trevor grimaced, but he nodded. He liked having his own collection of women at his disposal. Picking someone up at a bar wasn't a good idea in their line of work, but he was a man with needs. He needed those needs to be met.

Trevor turned to leave the office before he was told to give up anything else.

"And Trevor?"

He stopped, facing the boss once more.

"Don't fuck anything else up."

He nodded, knowing he was dismissed.

If the boss had kept Damon on a tighter leash, none of this would have happened. But just like he'd been doing for years, Trevor was cleaning up Damon's mess.

The only good thing was, it was the last one the asshole

would ever make. Trevor's only regret was he didn't get to kill the son-of-a-bitch himself.

RAINA CLIMBED out of the front seat when Liam stopped the SUV outside the garage. Adam's cast started above his knee and immobilized his lower leg, forcing him to keep his knee straight, making it impossible for him to get out of the vehicle inside the garage.

Adam supported himself on the side of the vehicle while Raina grabbed his crutches. When he was stable, she followed him into the garage and up the two steps into the house while Liam pulled the SUV in and grabbed Adam's suitcase from the trunk.

"You're here," Caitlyn said, a smile on her welcoming face.

"Thanks for letting us stay with you guys for a little while," Adam said.

Raina could see the exhaustion and irritation in his eyes. He spent a week in the hospital recovering from his injuries, and even though he was released, he was severely restricted in what he could do. And it was getting to him.

"We wish it was under other circumstances, but we're happy to have both of you here." Caitlyn hugged Raina and squeezed her hand. "Liam said you want to try to go upstairs, so I set up a room for you guys."

"Thank you," Raina said. "We really appreciate it."

"Of course."

Liam came in behind them and carried Adam's suitcase to the stairs. "Are you up for visitors? A lot of people want to come see you."

Adam nodded. "Yeah. I'm good with that. As long as they don't treat me like an invalid."

"Well, you are, so maybe don't hold out for that one."

Adam flipped his cousin off and grinned for the first time in days. "Fuck, I hate this."

"We all do. It's hard to sit still when all you want to do is get back to normal," Liam said.

"Forget normal. I want to be able to make love to my fiancée like she deserves," Adam growled.

"Did you say fiancée?" Caitlyn squealed.

Raina shook her head but couldn't stop the smile that lifted her lips. "I told the nurse I was his fiancée."

"You can't take it back now. Liam's going to take me ring shopping," Adam said. He reached for Raina and lost his balance, catching himself on the counter before he fell. "Fucking hell."

Raina moved into his arms, wrapping herself around him. She didn't care if he needed his arms to keep himself standing, she'd do the hugging for both of them.

"I love you," Adam said.

"I love you. And we have the rest of our lives for all of that stuff."

"Never enough time."

Raina smiled up at the man she loved and wondered how she got so damn lucky. They spent the last week making plans. Adam was transferring to the local FBI office, once he was healed, and he was moving to a division that would keep him home with her every night. They still had to figure out where they were going to live, and Raina wanted to get a job again, but they were together, and that was all that mattered to Raina at the moment.

"Well, you are welcome to stay here as long as you want.

We are happy to have you," Caitlyn said, looking up at Liam for agreement.

Liam nodded just as the doorbell rang.

Within minutes, the house was packed with F-BOMB, local FBI Agents, and the women Raina called friends. Food appeared out of nowhere, compliments of Lily, according to Caitlyn, and everyone ate and drank and caught up on what happened when Damon surprised them in the hotel room.

Raina checked in with Adam regularly, knowing he didn't want the others to take care of him. Thankfully, he let Raina help him get food and drinks and his pain meds when he was due.

Raina had just checked on Adam and was heading into the kitchen when Edie walked up to her.

"I'm so happy you're okay," Edie said. "I can't imagine how scared you were."

Raina nodded. She'd had a lot of time to process what happened with Damon while Adam was in the hospital. The police questioned her, and between her statement and her injuries, they immediately ruled it self-defense.

She still carried the guilt of knowing she took a life. And she carried the nightmares of watching a man die. Both would eventually fade.

She hoped.

"It was horrible," she admitted to Edie. "I really thought I was going to die."

"But you didn't. You saved both of you." Edie wrapped her arms around herself. "I want to be as brave as you."

"I'm not sure what I did was brave. It was... the worst experience of my life. But I knew if I didn't pull that trigger, he was going to kill us both."

Edie nodded, silent for a minute with her thoughts.

When she looked up, Raina saw determination in her friend's gaze.

"Trevor is going to step up. Now that Damon's gone, I have no doubt Trevor will take over. I can't let that happen."

"What are you going to do?"

Edie shrugged. "I don't know yet, but I can't let this continue. I can't let more women get taken and raped and killed. I can't let him do it again."

"What do you need from me?"

"Do you still have that mask?"

Raina smiled and nodded. "It's all yours."

FEAR IS AVAILABLE NOW…

They want the same thing. To stop the drugs flowing through their city. Her way is outside the law. His way is the law. While Edie works to find the criminals selling drugs, Pryce works to find the vigilante putting her life at risk. Wanting the same thing doesn't mean they're on the same side. Until their hearts get involved.

READ **FEAR** TODAY!

Everyone deserves justice. Even when they're no one.

Witnessing a murder was not on Frannie's bucket list.
Marcus had to find out what the curvy dancer knew.
They made a deal. She would help him, and he would find
the murderers. No one would know she was involved. She
hoped.

**Frannie and Marcus's story is available only to
subscribers.**
Sign up at https://dl.bookfunnel.com/y9ms2k2dq8 to get
FORSAKEN now.

Turn the page to read chapter one of FEAR.

FEAR

CHAPTER 1

Edie Warren was done letting fear run her life. She was done being afraid of every damn thing. She'd stared the devil in the face, then snuck out the back window when he wasn't paying attention.

Damon Street wasn't the only devil, though. Not by a long shot. And Edie was going to take down the other ones. The little devils who helped those evil bastards get their hooks into innocent victims. And the devil who held her captive far longer than a few days. The one who held her for months.

That was the one who cost Edie's cousin her life. If Edie had never gone missing, Tonya wouldn't have dug into her disappearance and been in the wrong place at the wrong time and gotten killed for it.

Edie was done hiding and being afraid and letting others fight her battles for her. She was going to fight her own.

She slid the black mask from her pocket and onto her face. She closed her eyes and inhaled deep, ignoring the scents of urine and vomit in the alleyway where she hid. The mask made Edie strong. It connected her to the other women she knew. Her friends. The Curvy Vigilantes.

Edie was just one of them. They were fighting to make their city a better, safer, brighter place. Niagara Falls, New York, was one of the most beautiful places on earth, but the seedy, nasty evil that had taken control of parts of it was ruining the beauty of one of the Wonders of the World.

Edie was ready for it to stop.

A door opened down the alley, twenty feet or so from Edie. She waited until the man leaned against the brick wall and took a drag from his cigarette. He blew out a long breath, the smoke dancing in the air above his face for a second before it dissipated and disappeared into the mild evening air.

Edie moved closer to him, her sneakers silent even in the trash filled space. She wore dark clothes and was all but invisible.

The man froze, cigarette perched between his lips, breath stalled in his lungs. "Who's there?"

Edie was close enough to see the fear in his eyes. "Did you sell drugs to a teenager last week?" she growled.

He laughed. Actually laughed. "What if I did?"

"Then you're going to pay for your crimes," Edie whispered.

He snorted. "And you think you're going to make me?"

"Yes, I am," Edie said, not wasting any time before she rushed the man. Her quick move from the dark caught him off-guard, and the knee she slammed into his nuts had him on the ground in seconds.

Edie pulled a zip-tie from her boot and grabbed the man's wrist before he had a chance to regain his footing. She held his arm against the pipe running down the building and secured him to it.

"You bitch," he spat, half-heartedly tugging on the zip-tie.

Edie got in the man's face. "The kid you sold those drugs to died because they were laced with garbage. You made an extra buck and a fifteen-year-old never woke up again. So use whatever language you want, but trust me when I tell you I'm not the worst piece of trash in this alleyway right now."

Edie walked away, the bastard shouting after her the entire time.

"Nine-one-one. What is your emergency?" Mackenzie Chambers asked. Mackenzie was Edie's friend and confidant, but she was also a professional and had a job to do.

"Alleyway behind Jester's Bar. There's a present waiting if the police can get there quickly enough. He might know a thing or two about that overdose last week."

Mackenzie sucked in a breath. "Can you tell me who you are and how you know this?"

Mackenzie hated when Edie called in her prizes, but Edie wasn't going to go through all the work of finding out who was involved in the drug trafficking in the city without handing the scumbags over to the police. "Just a concerned citizen. Trying to do my part to clean up our beautiful city."

"Be careful, please," Mackenzie said. She couldn't say Edie's name or hell would rain down on Edie. Probably on Mackenzie, too. But Mackenzie knew Edie's voice and always told her to be careful.

Technically, what Edie was doing wasn't legal. But she was willing to work outside the law if it meant delivering justice for the silent ones. The ones whose voices were stolen from them. The ones who'd never speak for themselves, or anyone else, ever again.

Edie hid across the street and waited for the police car to come screeching up the street. The red lights flashed bright and drew the attention of everyone awake that time of night. When the cop walked the man out of the alley in handcuffs, the criminal insisting he was innocent, Edie smiled to herself and knew she did her part for the night.

Tomorrow was another day.

Pryce Murphy knew exactly what he'd find when he got the call that another gift was left for the police. He broke every traffic law in the book to get there before the *present* found a way to get free and get away.

But he was still there when Pryce arrived, the zip-tie holding him to the pipe nearly split in half from the guy's work. His wrist was raw from the effort, but he insisted he was innocent. That he had done nothing wrong. That "the bitch in all black had the wrong guy."

"We're going to take a ride anyway," Pryce told him. "Have a chat."

The guy grumbled, but he was smart enough not to resist arrest. He wasn't quiet about it, though, shouting the whole time Pryce walked him out of the alley and into the backseat that he didn't do a thing.

Pryce guided the guy into the car and scanned the crowd. Whenever the cops showed up, the residents came out in force. A few were faces Pryce knew, people he'd be able to speak to another time. He nodded at Mr. Pickens, who owned the corner store. No doubt the sirens woke him up. Then there was Ms. Moore, who was definitely not sleeping and absolutely still working. Pryce didn't bother her, even though prostitution wasn't legal. As long as that was the worst she did and she answered any questions he asked, she was an ally.

Pryce walked around his cruiser and looked at the rest of the crowd. He was good with faces, but there were definitely new ones. And there were plenty of people in the shadows, hiding from his curiosity as they fueled their own.

Without a reason to ask any of them questions, Pryce got behind the wheel and waited. Another car was on the way to process the scene, and Pryce had to make sure they knew what he knew.

"I didn't do anything," the guy in the back insisted again. "That lady has no idea what she's talking about."

"What does she think you did?"

"Sold drugs to that kid who died. But I don't do that shit. She's got it all wrong."

Pryce nodded, playing along like he agreed with the guy. "Mistaken identity."

"Yeah, man. Exactly. She don't know me. Never seen her before."

"And you were never around that kid, either. No reason to suspect you."

"Right. I don't know her."

"Sara hung out with a rough crowd. She probably got something from a friend."

"Tara," the guy in the back said.

Pryce met his gaze in the rearview mirror and nodded. "Right. My bad. I didn't know her either."

The guy sputtered his excuses as the other car pulled up. Pryce ignored him and got out.

"What do we got?" Officer Maxwell asked as he met Pryce on the sidewalk.

"Another gift. Guy insists he's innocent."

"Don't they all?" Maxwell chuckled. He was a decent cop, but a bit of a jackass, in Pryce's opinion. Not that he disagreed with what Maxwell said.

Pryce nodded. "Yep. Even knew her name was Tara and not Sara."

Maxwell snorted. "Dumbass. What's the scene look like?"

"Couldn't see much. Dark alley, zip-tied to a pole. Can smell the cigarette on his breath, so likely a stub down there somewhere, but could be thousands of them."

"Did you get the zip-tie?" Maxwell's partner, Dempsey, was quiet until then, but he looked over Pryce like he could see the zip-tie.

Pryce nodded. "In a bag. I was ready for it."

"Gotta love our friendly neighborhood vigilante. Tying up the bad guys and letting us know where to pick them up." Dempsey rolled his eyes. None of them were fans of the vigilante.

"Yep. Gave this one a shot to the nuts, though, so assault isn't out of the question," Pryce told them.

Maxwell winced. "Damn. I'm rooting for her."

"Not me," Pryce growled. "She's outside the lines. She's going to be the one we have to rescue one of these days."

"Nah, she's good. I'm starting to have fun on nights again. After all that shit with Damon Street, things were tense. It's time to put the bad guys away and know we're making the city better. She's doing the same."

"Yeah, well, I'm not so sure about that."

Maxwell rolled his eyes and backhanded Dempsey's chest. "Well, we'll go check out the alley. Enjoy your night, Murphy."

"You, too." Pryce shook his head. He wasn't popular. That was what happened when you were a suspect as a rookie cop. It didn't matter that he'd been exonerated. He still had a stain and had to stick far from the line. One toe out of place and he'd be on the other side of the line for good.

And Pryce did not want that to happen.

The guy in the back grumbled the entire way to the station. When Pryce booked him and put him in a cell, he asked when he'd get his phone call. Pryce assured him someone would be in soon.

"Your partner strikes again, Murphy?" Foster called out.

Detective Drake Foster was a thorn in Pryce's side. He'd gone from beat cop like Pryce to detective in record time and had never forgotten bringing in Pryce for questioning. Or let him forget it.

"She's not my partner," Pryce growled.

Foster chuckled. He looked around the station, ensuring he had the attention of everyone there.

He did.

"Well, it's funny how you're always first on the scene. You're always the one to collar the guys she picks up. And you never seem to know anything about what's going on."

"Aren't you the detective? Shouldn't you be the one figuring it all out? Or did I forget that was part of my job now?"

Foster scowled at Pryce, the blow landing exactly as planned. Foster pushed off the edge of the desk and leaned back. He crossed his arms and glared at Pryce. "It's hard to do my job when one of my own is hiding things. You know how the system works and you're keeping her just outside it."

"Bullshit," Pryce snapped. "I'm not doing a thing to help her. I don't know anymore about her than you do."

"Bullshit," Foster parroted, a smirk lifting the edge of his lips.

Pryce shook his head and turned toward the hallway leading back outside. "I'm on duty. And some of us have to actually work for a living."

Foster called out, "I hope your partner doesn't get picked up before you can warn her we're onto her."

Pryce ignored the dig and kept going. He deserved that one, maybe, but it didn't make it easier to swallow.

Pryce got back into his car and returned to where he picked up the guy. The other cop car was gone and nothing was out to prevent someone from going down the alley. Pryce parked at the front of it, mostly blocking the entrance, and got out of his car.

He shined his flashlight around the small space as he walked. He wasn't sure if he'd find anything else, but he wanted to get a look at the scene before too much time had passed.

The pipe was rubbed clean where the zip-tie had been wrapped around it. The heels of the guy's boots dug up the gravel, leaving grooves behind. Nothing else seemed to have been touched. But the woman had to have been back there, waiting for the guy.

Pryce moved deeper into the alley, looking for places to hide. A dumpster was the perfect cover if you knew the person you were looking for wouldn't come down that far.

Nothing. No footprints, no hair left behind, nothing to tell him that's where she was hiding.

Who the hell was she? And how was she figuring out who all these criminals were?

Pryce didn't have the answers, but he was going to find them. And she was going to go to jail for her crimes.

Edie sipped her coffee and stared into the pie case. Her mouth watered at the options. Chocolate, lemon meringue, apple, cherry, peach. She didn't really need to think about which one she wanted, but she was warring with herself.

"They all look good, don't they?" a voice said from right behind her.

Edie jumped, her coffee spilling over the side of the mug.

"Crap, I'm sorry. I didn't mean to startle you."

Edie set the coffee on the counter and grabbed for napkins.

"Let me help you, please. And let me buy your pie."

Edie forced her lips to lift and glanced back at the man speaking. When she saw him, she froze.

He noticed the reaction and took a step back. "I apologize. I know a lot of people are uncomfortable around police officers. My name is Pryce Murphy. I don't think we've met."

"Hi, Officer," Jenny said. "Here, hun, let me clean that up for you. Did you get it on you, Edie?"

Edie shook her head. "I'm good, Jenny. Thanks."

Jenny worked the night shift at Bob's Diner. Edie went in there the first night she brought someone to justice. Her first was a man involved in moving drugs through the city. Most of them were. Because the drugs were what kept Edie captive. What hurt her the most. If they hadn't filled her with drugs, she would have escaped long before she did.

That first night, Edie felt a new kind of high. A high that said she was finally helping. After months as a prisoner, and more months terrified and nearly catatonic with fear, Edie was helping people. Jenny made her feel like she belonged in that diner. Like she had a safe space to be. Edie wouldn't say they were friends, but she liked Jenny and loved the pie.

"Put her coffee and pie on my bill, Jenny," the officer said. "It was my fault it spilled."

Jenny raised an eyebrow at Edie for confirmation. Edie just shrugged. She wasn't really going to argue about a two-dollar cup of coffee and a four-dollar piece of pie. Especially with the man who helped her bring in so many criminals. Even if he didn't know she was the one who delivered them.

"Sounds good. Anything I can get you, Officer?" Jenny held the coffee-stained towel in her fingertips and smiled at the officer.

"Same as she's having. Coffee and pie."

"What kind can I get you two?"

"Peach," they said at the same time.

Edie gasped and looked up at him. He smiled sheepishly and shrugged.

"It's always been my favorite."

"Mine, too," Edie admitted.

Jenny plated two slices of pie and pushed them across the counter. Edie grabbed hers and her coffee and nodded her thanks to the officer. She headed for the back corner where she could sit alone. Far away from the cop she didn't know.

Edie tucked into her pie and savored the first bite. It was perfect, like it always was. She had no idea where the peaches came from, but she knew the pie was homemade. Jenny confessed once that she was the pie master, and Edie bought a slice every time she went into the diner since.

"Mind if I join you?" Officer Murphy asked.

Edie nodded, chewing her overly large bite slowly.

He still stood there. "Does that mean you do mind or that I'm welcome to join you?"

Edie breathed a laugh around her food and waved her hand at the other side of her booth. She wasn't looking for company, and definitely didn't want it from a cop, but she couldn't deny the man who bought her pie. Or who unknowingly helped her so many times.

Or who was so attractive she wondered if the pie was really what made her mouth water.

Officer Murphy took a bite of the pie and groaned, his hazel eyes falling closed. Dark lashes brushed his cheeks, a sharp contrast to his dark blond hair and pink-tinted skin. His uniform stretched tight over a well-defined chest and bulging biceps.

Edie had never understood the appeal of a man in uniform before. But this man was different. She knew he was on the same side as her. It had taken Edie a while to trust the police again after having disappeared and learning no one bothered to look for her, but the police captain convinced her there were good people on the force.

She couldn't help but wonder if Officer Murphy was one of them.

"This pie is amazing," he said, meeting her gaze in a conspiratorial way. "Why did we only get one slice each?"

Edie chuckled. "Well, unlike you, I'm going home and going to bed after this. Too much sugar and I won't be able to sleep."

"Were you working? Is that why you're up?" The question was casual enough, but Edie knew it was not an innocent question.

Edie shook her head. "I saw you take that man away."

He looked at her more closely, then nodded. "I thought you looked familiar. I did see you there."

"You saw me?" Edie breathed. She did her best to be invisible. Blend in with the crowd. If he noticed her in it, he could figure out she'd been in more of the crowds. All the crowds.

Officer Murphy nodded, stabbing another piece of his pie. "Yeah. We're trying to figure out who's capturing these people."

"Does it matter? She's helping."

The officer grimaced. "She might be helping catch these people, but we don't always have evidence that keeps them behind bars. And if she's hurting them, it's assault, and she should be charged. Plus, some of these people are dangerous. She could get hurt."

Edie wasn't worried about getting hurt. Pain was minor compared to what she'd been through. Getting caught would be a problem, but she was careful. And wasn't catching these people helping? Wasn't it worth a minor crime now and then?

Edie knew it was possible she could get in trouble for what she was doing, but she always assumed the police would be happy she was helping. She hid who she was so she didn't have to answer questions. So she could keep helping.

"Did you see anything tonight?" the officer pushed. "Anything that could help me find the woman who's doing this? I'd really like to have a conversation with her."

Well, shit. He already was. But Edie couldn't admit that. "Uh, no," she lied. "I didn't see anything."

READ FEAR TODAY!

ABOUT THE AUTHOR

USA TODAY Bestselling Author Mary E Thompson spent most of her childhood wishing she had a few less curves. She hid in the pages of books because her favorite characters never cared what size her clothes were. Now, neither does Mary, and she writes stories that celebrate women like her. Real women who have curves, chase dreams, and find love, because we should all be happy, no matter our dress size.

Mary spends her non-writing time with her husband and two kids, watching too much TV, cheering for her hometown football team (Go Bills!), and hiding chocolate from her family.

Visit https://MaryEThompson.com/ to sign up for Mary's newsletter, **Romancing the Curves**. Subscribers get free ebooks and other fun stuff, like exclusive, members only content and giveaways, plus are the first to know about new releases and sales!